Brought up in England, Jason Webster has lived for several years in Valencia, the setting of his Cámara novels. The first of these, *Or the Bull Kills You*, was longlisted for the CWA Specsavers Crime Thriller Awards New Blood Dagger 2011. He has appeared in several British TV documentaries, including *The Islamic History of Europe* presented by Rageh Omaar on BBC Television, and the critically acclaimed *Andalusia: The Legacy of the Moors* for Five.

BLOOD MED

Spain is corrupt and on the brink of collapse. The king is ill, banks are closing, hospitals are in chaos, homes are lost, demonstrators riot and right-wing thugs patrol the streets. The tunnels below are at once a refuge and a source of anger. And as the blood flows, Cámara roars in on his motorbike. He is back in Valencia, with his partner Alicia and his anarchist, marijuana-growing grandfather Hilario. In the old police headquarters, the mood is tense as the chief hunts for cuts — who will go, Cámara or his friend Torres? The two men are flung into action investigating the suicide of an ex-bank clerk and the brutal murder of a young American woman. And as the city erupts around them, their case takes them into the heart of the trouble . . .

Books by Jason Webster
Published by Ulverscroft:

OR THE BULL KILLS YOU
A DEATH IN VALENCIA
THE ANARCHIST DETECTIVE

JASON WEBSTER

---◆---

BLOOD MED

Complete and Unabridged

CHARNWOOD
Leicester

First published in Great Britain in 2014 by
Chatto & Windus
London

First Charnwood Edition
published 2015
by arrangement with
Chatto & Windus
The Random House Group Limited
London

A catalogue record for this book is available
from the British Library.

ISBN 978–1–4448–2388–2

Published by
F. A. Thorpe (Publishing)
Anstey, Leicestershire

Set by Words & Graphics Ltd.
Anstey, Leicestershire
Printed and bound in Great Britain by
T. J. International Ltd., Padstow, Cornwall

A Esther, Sebas y Rafa — amigos y policías.
Pero sobre todo amigos.

Note

There are several police forces in Spain. Chief Inspector Max Cámara works for the *Policía Nacional*, which deals with major crimes in the larger towns and cities. The *Guardia Civil* is a rural police force, or gendarmerie, covering the countryside and smaller towns and villages. Both the *Policía Nacional* and *Guardia Civil* report to the Interior Ministry, although the *Guardia Civil* is paramilitary and has links with the Defence Ministry.

In addition to these national forces, towns and cities tend to have a local police force — the *Policía Local*, also known as the *Policía Municipal*. This deals with smaller crimes, official engagements and traffic duties, and is under the control of each respective Town Hall.

As above, so below.
Hermes Trismegistus

'So that makes three last week alone.'

'They're on the up.'

'Yeah, but did you hear about the last one?'

'No. What happened?'

'Shook them up a bit.'

'Go on.'

'So this guy — he's in his early seventies. But he's fit and well. I mean, he's not ill or anything. But he's divorced and his kids left home years ago, no grandchildren, so he's on his own. And his pension's been cut, what with everything going on. And the bank lost all his money. You know — the Caja Levante business.'

'Yeah, I know someone who got stung by that.'

'Caja Levante are going bust so they convince him — and everyone else — to turn his savings into shares in the bank, then overnight the shares lose all their value. So from having about a hundred grand to see him through retirement, suddenly he's got nothing.'

'Wife and kids gone . . . '

'And he's struggling to get by. So he starts thinking, What's the point? Then with everything that happened at the weekend . . . '

'What, the King?'

'Yeah. Seems like it was a last straw for him. So he fasts for twenty-four hours . . . '

'Why?'

'Wanted everything to be clean inside.

1

Thought it would make things easier. That's what he wrote in the note.'

'He explained it all?'

'Yeah, wrote a long note with the whole story. They found it after.'

'So what happened?'

'So he sorts out his paperwork — will, household bills and all that. Even arranged for the electricity and phone people to come round and turn everything off. Then he puts on his best suit, takes a taxi to the hospital, gets out, walks to the front of A&E, makes sure one of the doctors has seen him, then stands to the side — you know, where the ambulances come in and out, on the drive there — pulls out a pistol and shoots himself in the head.'

'Fuck.'

'Drops dead on the spot. They tried to do what they could, but there was no chance. Then one of the nurses found the note on him, saying he didn't want to go on, that he knew the hospitals were suffering with the crisis and that he was donating his body to medicine. Like an act of charity.'

'Jesus. Can they? Use his body for medicine, then?'

'Well, there wasn't much left of his brain. But the rest of him was all right.'

'Fuck.'

1

The story was moving so slowly it made him want to reach for the remote and hit the fast-forward button. But the more trivial details the correspondents gave, the more general anxiety was produced and the more important the man lying in the hospital at the back of the shot was seen to be. This could go on for hours or even days. He should nip out and have a decent lunch; there would still be no developments by the time he got back.

Nonetheless, there was a curious fascination about it — a moment in history. They would all remember this, years later. He could imagine the future conversations now: Do you remember where you were when you heard?

The King was not dead yet — not quite. But the message had been repeated endlessly by the media: he had had a massive heart attack and was undergoing emergency surgery. And while no one was saying it openly, few expected him to be leaving the hospital anything but 'feet first'.

Cámara had been on the beach with Alicia when the news reached him, enjoying one of the premature summer days that early May sometimes brought, seducing people to expose their winter-white skin for a few hours before a cool wind scattered them home in search of warmer clothes.

No te quites el sayo hasta el cuarenta de

mayo, Hilario, his grandfather, had reminded him, trotting out the traditional proverb. Don't cast a clout 'til 40 May. But that was before they heard.

Now the temperature outside barely registered. The King's sudden and life-threatening condition had cast a chill — and semi-paralysis — over the whole country.

Everyone in *Homicidios* was watching the television in the corner of the office as, in faraway Madrid, the authorities struggled with questions of what happened next. The Constitution was clear when it came to a simple death of the monarch. But what did they do if he was left lucid but incapacitated? The doctors might be able to keep him alive, but would he be able to function as head of state? Could the Crown Prince step in? The word 'abdication' had been often repeated in recent years as the King visibly aged, but the idea was viewed as a taboo subject for many: the Spanish monarchy was too fragile an institution to even contemplate such a thing.

Outside, the streets of Valencia were virtually silent, as they were throughout the country. The man who had overseen the building of their nation, who had guided them from dictatorship to democracy, hovered on the edge. And it could not have happened at a worse time. For how much longer could things hold together?

Standing near the back of the office, peering over his colleagues' heads, Cámara watched the pack of journalists gathered at the expensive private clinic in the capital. Occasionally members of the Royal Family — at least those

4

who hadn't been tainted by scandal over the previous years — passed in and out, refusing to comment on developments inside. Through the window of an official car the Queen had been witnessed raising a lace handkerchief to her eye. Was she genuinely upset? No one could say.

The anxious tears among the thousands of Spaniards gathered nearby were more clearly heartfelt. The camera alternated between shots of dignitaries arriving at the hospital, and the worried faces of ordinary people in the street. He was a father figure for them, a central icon around which the country could — albeit tentatively and not without some stress — come together. But Catalonia was already edging towards independence; if the King died it would inevitably fuel the separatist movement there and in other parts of the country — as well as the determination of those bent on keeping Spain united.

Minds were already turning to plans for the funeral. It would be a big and complicated security operation. Police from Valencia and other parts of the country would almost certainly be bussed in to help make up the numbers. Foreign kings, queens, presidents and prime ministers would all attend. The King was a friendly and popular man — the best asset that 'the Spain brand' had, as one television commentator kept repeating. What the State-run media did not mention, however, was the Republican demonstration being held on the other side of Madrid. Cámara had seen references to it on the police intranet. Similar demonstrations were planned for Barcelona and parts of the Basque Country. No one had a clue how many might be showing up. There was talk of tens of thousands.

The door behind them clicked open and someone walked in. Cámara did not need to turn around. Chief Inspector Maldonado, head of the Valencia murder squad, had an unmistakable way of moving that announced his presence, strutting where others walked and pulling on doors as though they were obstacles to his relentless climb where others merely opened and closed them.

'Morning,' he called out, a little too loudly. No one answered, their eyes fixed on the screen.

Cámara could sense it in his blood before he even heard the words.

'Torres and Cámara — I need you in my office now.'

★ ★ ★

They were back in the old police headquarters — the Jefatura building on Gran Via de Fernando el Católico; everyone had seen it coming. The sci-fi fantasy building that had been their home for the past few years was impractical and too expensive to maintain. Valencian architect Jaume Montesa might have won international awards for his spectacular white-concrete designs, but the place had not even survived a decade before serious-looking cracks started appearing up the walls. And every time it rained for more than five minutes the cellars got flooded. Torrential downpours were a common problem in the area, but local-boy appeared to have forgotten that when drawing up his plans. Now, if anyone could find any money, they were going to turn it into an art museum, which was what it had been intended for in the first place — never a police station. No one missed it.

But being back at Fernando el Católico meant they were stuck in their cramped office again: two small adjoining rooms on the ground floor for the entire murder squad. Maldonado had decided it was not enough and had requisitioned another office on the floor above — which he kept for himself.

The three men exchanged no words as they took the lift up. Cámara glanced at their hazy reflection on the scratched steel surface of the doors. Maldonado's jutting jaw and Torres's thick black beard and rounded shoulders were just visible. And himself? He was taller than the other two and looked . . . well, he looked pretty good, he had to say. He was taking care of himself better than he could remember — living with Alicia made certain of that — and it showed.

Along the corridor, Torres edged past and walked into the office directly behind Maldonado. Someone else was there waiting for them.

Maldonado walked to his desk and began shuffling papers with his fingertips, as though moving pawns on a chessboard.

Cámara looked across to the fourth person in the room.

'Oh yes,' Maldonado said as nonchalantly as he could. 'You know Chief Inspector Martín, don't you?'

Torres grunted an acknowledgement. Cámara walked over and shook hands.

'I think I've seen you around.'

'I was on leave for a while,' Cámara said. 'Only been back a few weeks.'

'Interesting time to return.'

'Right, we need to get on,' Maldonado interrupted them. 'Cámara, in case you didn't know, Laura Martín is head of the *unidad de violencia de género*.'

'I *am* the sexual violence squad,' she said. 'It's just me.'

She wore a grey skirt and beige blouse — almost a regulation uniform for a senior female officer — but he noticed multicoloured bracelets hanging loosely on her wrists and a couple of studs in one of her ears. She was two or three years younger than him, he thought, still in her early forties, with hazel green eyes that simultaneously smiled and held back, as though hiding and yet still reflecting some recent horror she had seen. If she had made head of the sexual violence squad — albeit with a team of one — she was ambitious if not necessarily capable; that would become clear later. Her clothes were conventional, but the cut of her red-brown hair and an ironic tone in her voice suggested something more complex.

'OK, listen,' said Maldonado. 'I know it's a difficult day for everyone, but as luck would have it our quiet run has come to an end. Right now.

Four months without a murder in a city this big just isn't natural. Anyway, I didn't want to bother the others. Both cases look straightforward . . . '

'We've got two?' Torres said. 'Four months and then two come in at once?'

'One's a clear murder case. The other's a suicide attempt, but we need to check it out. And as you've so gallantly volunteered it's yours.'

Torres rolled his eyes. No one liked a suicide: they left a nasty taste in the mouth. Especially the jumpers. All those mangled body parts. It never got easier, no matter how many you saw. And besides, there was nothing really to investigate. It was all clearing up.

Maldonado passed him the file from his desk.

'Hang on,' Torres said. 'Suicide attempt? What do you mean?'

'Well, he's not dead yet. Not quite.'

'So why am I looking at it?'

'Look, he's in intensive care, in a coma. But by the time you get your arse in gear he'll probably be dead anyway, right? So we're getting ahead of the game. Just go and check it out. God knows all hell might be breaking loose soon what with the King and everything. Get going now before questions of national security start interfering with ordinary police work.'

Torres shuffled on the spot.

'Why are we involved, then?' he said.

'What?'

'I'm a murder detective. Isn't it clear if it's a suicide attempt?'

'It's in the file. The man's called Diego Oliva.

9

He was broke, about to have his flat repossessed. The usual story. I'm telling you, it's almost certainly suicide . . . '

'An attempt.'

'Whatever. He jumped from a second-storey window — his own. You know what I'm saying. Just go and check it out.'

Torres slipped the file under his arm.

'Well, go on then!' Maldonado barked.

Torres and Cámara exchanged a conspiratorial glance and Torres left the room.

'Right, next case,' Maldonado said as the door closed.

'Cámara, Chief Inspector Martín will be joining you on this.'

Maldonado thrust the file in his direction. Cámara nodded to Laura — they were roughly equals in the police hierarchy, and he was already thinking of her by her first name.

'There's a sexual element to it, then.'

'Looks pretty simple, on the face of things,' Maldonado said. 'Young woman in her home in the Cánovas area. The husband called it in. He's still there.'

He did not need to spell it out; the implication was understood.

'The *científicos* from the forensic medicine department are already there. Go over, get a confession, whatever you have to do, and let's see if we can wrap it up by the end of the day. With a bit of luck you might just do it.'

Laura made to leave.

'One other thing — ' Maldonado sat down in his chair and looked over the papers on his desk.

'The woman's American. Young — only in her twenties. The husband's a local. Probably won't complicate things too much, but it's not normal, obviously. At least not for us. More likely to have been shot had she stayed at home, what with all the guns in America. But there you have it.'

He shrugged. Laura walked to the door; Cámara did not move.

'The chief inspector will be along with you in a moment, Martín,' Maldonado said. 'He and I have something to talk about first.'

2

Something gold flashed from beneath Maldonado's shirt cuffs. Cámara tried to catch a glimpse of it as the head of *Homicidios* waved an arm towards a hard wooden chair on the other side of the desk.

'Have a seat.'

It was a Rolex. Where the hell was Maldonado getting the money from to buy himself a Rolex? Not from a chief inspector's salary, that was for sure. Unless it was a fake, which would not be beyond him. The easy way to tell was by checking the magnification glass over the date: if the numbers were clearly visible it was real; if they were small and hard to read it was phoney. Cámara tried to see, but the watch was either out of sight or moving around too much on Maldonado's wrist.

Maldonado saw that Cámara had noticed his new acquisition and grinned.

'You've been back for how long now?'

He knew the answer but was asking all the same.

'Just over a month,' Cámara said.

'You got quite a lot of time off. Nine months?'

A lot had happened in nine months. His previous boss, Commissioner Pardo, had sent him on extended leave at the end of the Sofía Bodí case. Cámara had been made homeless: his block of flats had collapsed after digging for the

12

new metro line in his street had weakened the foundations. A neighbour and her young son had died when the thing came crashing down.

Maldonado was just one of the others back then, a murder detective, albeit a pain in the arse. Now he was a pain in the arse with power: Pardo had been promoted and in Cámara's absence Maldonado had taken his place.

Cámara had been uncertain about returning to his police job, despite Torres's pleas for him to save them from Maldonado's petty-minded tyranny. Life had been moving in new directions — getting back with Alicia and spending a few months at her place in Madrid — before his grandfather had a stroke and Cámara rushed back to his home town Albacete to look after his ageing — and only remaining — relative. Mercifully the stroke had been mild and Hilario was now almost fully recovered. But events in his home town — the murder of a young woman and the subsequent investigation — sucked Cámara back into work, and fantasies of leaving policing for good were abandoned.

Now he was back in Valencia, in his old job. The country was running out of money and the State could barely afford to pay its civil servants: their salaries had been cut twice already and there were rumours that the measure might be repeated soon. But he knew that if he had not returned when he did there would have been no chance of walking in where he left off. The accountants were looking for any opportunity to reduce costs and a murder detective who had not shown up for months would be an easy

13

target. And then finding some other kind of work would be almost impossible. The fact was that there were virtually no jobs any more. For anyone. Being kicked out of the police would mean a couple of years' dole money and then he would have to live off his wits — like millions of others.

The idea of scavenging in rubbish bins or getting food handouts from the Red Cross did not overly trouble him. The problem was that he had dependants now, people who needed him to earn a wage in order to survive. Hilario had left Albacete and come to live with him. Despite his protestations to the contrary, his grandfather needed someone around, just in case. He had happily accepted the idea of coming to live in Valencia, framing it in his imagination as a new beginning, new horizons. And in his usual way he had been keeping himself very busy since they arrived. But his advanced age — which for so long had appeared not to hinder him — could no longer be ignored. He was in his mid-eighties now, and despite having survived more difficulties than most — the Spanish Civil War as a boy, the Eastern Front as a young man, then the harsh early Franco years back in Spain — he was getting frailer, at least physically. Mentally he was as sharp as ever — perhaps even sharper: *Cambio de pasto engorda a la ternera*, he kept repeating. A change of pasture makes the cow fatter. And pushed back death by at least another ten years.

But it had taken a while to sort things. First cleaning the flat in Albacete and renting it out;

no one was buying any more. Then finding somewhere in Valencia and settling in. They had a place in the Barrio Chino — the old Chinatown, on the edge of the Carmen district in the centre. Hilario had a room at the back with a terrace that he soon filled with pots of bright red geraniums and marijuana plants. And Alicia had joined them shortly afterwards. The newspaper in Madrid had folded and she was out of work; there was no point to her staying in the capital now. Her Valencia flat could provide something of an income, as long as she could find a lodger. But the luxury of her and Cámara having separate lives was not affordable. Besides, now that circumstances had pushed them closer, they found living together more enjoyable than they had expected. Even with Hilario around. Perhaps even because he was around.

In nine months he had moved three times, rekindled an old relationship and solved a murder while supposedly on leave. Much had happened while he was away from the police. Time, he thought, would be better measured by its density than its length.

'I'm sure Personnel can confirm how long it was,' he said now.

The garish watch on Maldonado's hand came briefly into view and Cámara tried to get a glimpse of the second hand, but it quickly disappeared under the shirt cuff again.

'Things have changed,' Maldonado said. 'You know the situation. Things are tight, very tight.'

'I've heard.'

'Now I've been meaning to talk to you since

15

you got back, but have been tied up.'

'Cut the shit, Maldo. There hasn't been a murder since the beginning of the year.'

'Watch your mouth, Cámara.' Maldonado thrust out a threatening finger from his puffy fist. 'We're not just work colleagues any more. I'm your superior now and talk like that will get you into trouble. I'll have you know many here didn't want you back, would have been happy to pay you off and see the back of you. But I was pushing for your return.'

There was something about Maldonado that made him lash out, like a nervous tic. It had got the better of him in the past, and now that he was in the Jefatura again his old patterns of behaviour were falling back into place. Better to hold them in check — or at least to try.

'What's this about?' he said.

'Look, I know we're all upset over what's going on.'

This was a new Maldonado, he thought: a peacemaker, a manager of men. The truth was that the King's illness meant little to him: the man looked closer to the grave each year. So he had not been surprised at the news. What really struck him was the reaction of people around him, as though they could never have foreseen this coming, as though they thought the King would be there for ever. No matter how much politicians insisted that democracy was now deeply rooted in the country, Spain was entering uncharted and potentially very troubled waters.

16

'No one is more worried than I,' Maldonado went on. 'But I have to be frank with you, Cámara, your position is very tenuous right now.'

Cámara pressed his hands together, as though in prayer, and looked straight into Maldonado's eyes.

'Yes, you're back. But for how long? Don't be under the impression that you're safe now you're in again. You're not. All that time off looks bad. They have to make cuts. There's no money. It's a fucking miracle we're still getting paid every month.'

'They want to make cuts?'

'Yes, like I said.'

'Who?'

'The powers that be.'

He waved a hand to the upper floors. On the top floor lived the regional head of the *Policía Nacional*, a political appointee answering directly to the ministry in Madrid. A free and very large flat in the Jefatura building was one of the perks of the job. Some perk, they used to joke.

Cámara tried to get another look at the 'Rolex' as Maldonado's arm moved around. If there was no money, what the hell was he doing wearing such an expensive watch? It had to be a fake. Surely.

'You know who I mean.'

'Be more specific.'

'Look, they want to cut at least one — and perhaps two — members from *Homicidios*. Is that specific enough for you?'

'They can't do that.'

'They can and they bloody well will.'

17

'And I'm the candidate for the chop.'

Maldonado leaned back in his chair.

'You're one of them, certainly. Like I said, I'm trying to be frank with you. I would want to know, if I was in your position.'

'So this case you've just given me . . . '

'The American girl.'

'It's, what, some kind of test? A probation?'

Maldonado tapped a finger on his desk several times before answering.

'Yes.'

'So fill me in. If I don't solve the crime I'm out? Is that it?'

'These things are more complicated, you know that.'

'Fuck that, Maldo. Lay it to me straight. Is that it or not?'

There was a pause as Maldonado milked the drama of his moment.

'That's about the size of it,' he said at last. 'I can't watch your back for ever, Cámara. I need to give them something to prove that you should stay, that you're a good murder detective. But conversely, if you fuck up, there's not much that I can do. The knives are out and they're going to get someone. Do you understand?'

Cámara sniffed.

'Hold on,' he said. 'I'm one of them, you said. There are others you're looking at for the chop.'

'Not me,' Maldonado said defensively. 'It's not my call. It's them.'

'That's why you called Torres in as well.' He gave a hollow laugh. 'Two cases come in at once and who do you pick? Torres and me. We're the

18

ones, aren't we. Torres's neck is on the block as much as mine.'

'Less so, as a matter of fact. Which was why I gave him the suicide and you've got the girl. Yes, you're right, Cámara. It's between you and Torres. But Torres hasn't been on extended leave fucking some journalist while the State paid for the privilege.'

Cámara's legs jerked underneath him as he stood up sharply, his right fist already screwed into a ball to slam against the side of Maldonado's head.

'Punching your superior?' Maldonado grinned. 'Now that really would make my decision much easier.'

Cámara breathed deeply, willing his limbs to relax. Not now, he thought.

'Does Torres know?' he asked at last.

'You're a detective. Find out for yourself. Now fuck off and get going on this American girl.'

Cámara made for the door. Then stopped in his tracks and turned round. Stepping closer to the desk he reached over and pulled on Maldonado's arm. The Rolex swung into view.

'What? What the fuck?' Maldonado spluttered.

He tried to pull his hand away but Cámara held on, his powerful grip tight over Maldonado's forearm. The special glass clearly magnified the digits of the date window to the right of the dial. There was no mistaking it: the watch was genuine.

'Just checking the time,' Cámara said, dropping Maldonado's arm.

'You might want to brace yourself for this one, Cámara,' Maldonado said. 'It won't be pretty.'

He sneered.

'The girl was shot in the head. Several times from point-blank range.'

3

Enough time had been wasted already. The moments immediately after a murder was reported were crucial.

Laura was waiting for him near the entrance to the murder squad offices.

'Torres has taken the car,' she said simply. 'And mine's at the mechanic's.'

There was only one official car for the squad these days — another consequence of the cuts. Detectives usually ended up driving their own vehicles when on police work, or hitching a lift with a squad team.

'I've got the motorbike round the back,' Cámara said. 'We'll take that.'

'Do you have a spare helmet?' she asked. He was already grabbing his keys from his desk.

'You wear mine. I'm sure it'll fit.'

He reached up to the shelf to grab his helmet and was about to pass it to her when he caught the expression on her face.

'Come on. It'll be quicker.'

'I'm not going on a motorbike if one of us doesn't have a helmet,' she said. 'It's illegal.'

Cámara gave an exaggerated shrug. Who cared?

'I've heard about your unorthodox ways,' she said.

'We'll be there in five minutes. No one's going to see. We've lost enough time as it is.'

But he could tell it was pointless.

'I'll talk to the control room,' she said. 'See if there are any squad cars.'

'As you wish.'

The bike was parked on the pavement at the corner by the back entrance. Cámara had bought it soon after returning to Valencia. The city was flat, the weather was good for most of the year, the traffic was terrible and no one bothered where you left a motorbike so long as it did not block anyone's way. The place was made for them.

He had taken his test years before, back in Albacete, where he rode a Bultaco. A licence was a requirement for a police officer and many of his colleagues were bikers — it was something of a cliché. There was even a club for them at the Zapadores barracks, the other police headquarters on the far side of the city. They called themselves 'The Guardian Angels'. Like Hell's Angels only good guys. Supposedly.

Most went for the modern sports bikes these days, the ones that could do almost 300 kph down the motorway but which were mostly made of brightly painted plastic. Cámara preferred an older look, which was why he had picked up a rare second-hand Kawasaki W650, with wire spokes and a naked enginé. It was how motorbikes were supposed to look, he thought. Alejandro, his genius mechanic friend, had done some alterations — putting in a proper, tougher suspension at the back and front, and giving it new, more scrambler-style tyres. It was no crotch rocket, but it was fast enough and could take a beating if necessary. And he liked to think it had a touch of class: at his request Alejandro had repainted it for him in red and black — a tribute to his family's anarchist traditions. And a private joke that no one in the police could know about. Hilario loved it.

The only thing he had not done was change the battery. It was still starting all right, but he would have to get it seen to sooner or later. Today, though, it caused no problem: he pressed the button and it fired into life immediately. Strapping on his helmet, he sped off towards Cánovas.

* * *

The flat was on one of the more fashionable streets — at the quieter end, away from the bars and restaurants that had spread like fungus near the old river bed. At ground level there was a boutique selling hippy-chic clothes, a dry-cleaner's opposite, a gym and what looked to have been a bookshop but was now empty.

Cámara parked his motorbike under an acacia tree, looped the chain through his helmet and locked it to the back wheel. Two policemen stood by the front door of an imposing block of flats with carved art nouveau wooden doors. Stone faces stared through static foliage from the facade, with bulging eyes and bared teeth. The building was solid and exclusive. Prices around here never went down, no matter how deep the recession.

A handful of neighbours were standing around

with anxious looks on their faces. They could sense that something awful had happened: the guards on the door; the vehicles of the *Policía Científica* parked on the pavement nearby; the equipment being rushed in and carried up the marble stairwell in the rattling elevator. But they would not be aware of the full horror that had bloodily burst among them. It was immediate and directly relevant, however, which was why it was enough to distract them — momentarily — from the intense coverage of the King's illness on television.

Cámara identified himself and walked into the spacious entrance hall. At one time all of these buildings would have had caretakers living on the premises — useful witnesses or contacts to fill investigators in on the goings-on inside each flat. Now he doubted if one was still employed. The wood and glass cabin in the corner where the caretaker would have sat, reading the newspaper and sipping hot coffee, had dusty curtains drawn firmly shut.

Waiting for the lift to come down, he heard footsteps descending from above. A young, inquisitive face appeared on the stairs, a man with dark skin and Moroccan features.

'Chief Inspector Cámara, from *Homicidios*,' Cámara explained.

'Yes,' said the man. His accent was southern, from Cádiz. 'You'd better come up. It's only on the second floor. The lift takes ages.'

Cámara followed him.

'I'm Fernández, from the *Científica*.'

They shook hands mid-stairs, neither looking

the other in the eye.

'So what have you found?'

'You should have a look for yourself.'

Cámara recognised the reluctance to talk, the monosyllabic utterances and collapse of protocol. They were less formal in the *Policía Nacional* — saluting and chain-of-command stuff was more the reserve of the *Guardia Civil*. But when truly shocking crimes came along each one of them sucked into a protective space within themselves, doing their job as professionally as ever, but barely speaking. Only later, perhaps even after a few days had passed, sharing a drink at the bar, would anyone talk about what they had seen. And some not even then.

Cámara could smell the blood from outside the flat door — dark and metallic, like earth stuck under your fingernails. Fernández had gone on ahead, donning plastic shoe covers from a box on the floor. Cámara picked up two small bunches of blue plastic, opened them up and wrapped them around his own feet before stepping inside.

The hallway was painted white. A dark wooden table with a light marble top stood to one side. Above it, set into the wall, an ornate clock with gold leaf details ticked in heavy silence. The floor was original, with colourful mosaic tiles creating a geometric pattern in red, black, green and cream. So far, so traditional for a flat of this neighbourhood, he thought. Whoever the dead girl was, she had connections with old Valencia money.

He could see that Fernández had gone off to the left, down a corridor where two or three colleagues were working. The flash from the camera made sharp shadows against the softer light of the sun streaming in through thin curtains beyond. That was where the body obviously lay. He would get to it soon enough. And he gave silent thanks for only having drunk coffee that morning — so far nothing solid had passed his lips.

To his right he wandered into what looked like an extended living room. Here the traditional style of the entrance had been passed over in favour of something younger and more modern. The far wall was painted a thick tangerine colour, while the upper beams had been exposed, with long barrel arches running in parallel between them. A pale and invitingly soft sofa sat at one end, while at the other a large television screen occupied almost the entire wall. Magazines and newspapers were scattered on a glass-topped coffee table, some in Spanish — a copy of yesterday's newspaper — and some in English — *Newsweek, Time* and a copy of the *Financial Times*.

On the sofa, half-covered by a red velvet cushion, was a book. Cámara walked over to take a look. *Blog Your Way to Success*, the title encouraged. *Ninety-nine tips to get you writing — and earning — like the pros.* His English was not fluent, but good enough to get the gist of it. Flicking through the pages he noticed that some had pencil marks on them, while on others the corners had been folded down. He could not make much of the scribbling in the margins. A bookmark fell out and on to the floor. 'Fulcanelli', it said in gold letters. 'New and antiquarian books'. Had that been the name of the closed-down bookshop downstairs? It seemed that whoever was reading had not got to the end. He lifted the bookmark from the floor and slipped it back into the page where it had fallen out. *Chapter Nine*, he read. *On the art of never giving up*.

It was time to take a look at the corpse. He made a cursory inspection of the bedroom as he walked past — unmade bed, more books and a box of tissues on one bedside table; a lamp and an alarm clock on the other — before heading to where the *científicos* were still working. Broken porcelain crunched under his feet and he saw the scattered remains of a blue and white figurine on the floor. A chip of wood was hanging out of a door frame, low down, as though someone had kicked it hard. Beyond it, lying on the floor, he saw the feet of a woman clad in pink house socks with yellow rubber spots on the soles to give better grip on the tiled floor.

He breathed in deeply through his nose, willed his passions to be still, and stepped forward.

Someone had cleaned up as much blood as they could so that he and the others had access to the body, but red stains streaked across the tiles showing how wide the puddle had spread before they got to her. He could see that it had reached most of the walls, covering almost the entire room — a dining room, from the table and chairs pushed to one side — with her head as the epicentre. She was lying on her front. An arm lying flat and stretched out had stemmed the flow in one direction, while her hair had slowed down its progress in another. Yet still it was as if every drop of the three and a half litres that had once flowed under her skin had been pumped free from her body. More bloodstains spattered on the walls and up one of the doors on the other side of the room bore witness to how brutal this killing had been.

Cámara's eyes registered naked, bronzed legs above the pink socks, a blue cotton dress covering the rest of her body almost as far as her knees. A bulge was discernible just below her buttocks where, he felt he could already see, her knickers had bunched after someone had tried but failed to remove them. If he did not know better she might look like someone in the recovery position, waiting for help to arrive after a shock or a fall. But the crushed malformation of her skull, visible beneath the wet matting of her dark brown hair, told a different story.

Fernández stood on the other side of the body.

'Five shots. All to the head.'

The autopsy would confirm the exact number.

'We've found five rounds on the floor.'

He signalled the metal case where the científicos were bagging and collecting evidence.

'It's practically destroyed her.'

What was left of her skull was turned away from him, and for an instant he was struck by a powerful urge to see her.

'Face?' he asked, dreading the answer.

Fernández shook his head.

28

'It's round on this side if you want to . . . '

Cámara shrugged.

'It's all right.'

There was no point looking at something he could already imagine, had seen too often before.

'But if you're wondering,' Fernández continued, 'you might want to look at this.'

He leaned over to the table, picked up a dark blue booklet and passed it over to Cámara.

'Her passport.'

He noticed the Great Seal of the United States on the front and opened it to take a look. Inside was the picture of a young woman with a fresh complexion and bright blue eyes. It was funny how Americans could look good even in passport photos. She had a fringe and a clip at one side of her hair and wore a white blouse just open at the neck.

Beside the photo he read her name: Amy Catherine Donahue. And the date of birth: she was barely twenty-five years old.

The sound of footsteps approaching from the entrance drew his attention for a moment. He looked up and saw Laura Martín entering. She had come straight to the corpse, unlike himself.

Cámara handed her the passport. She looked at it, absorbed the necessary information, and handed it back. Then she stared down at the body, taking in as much detail as she could. She is recording this, Cámara thought to himself, watching as her eyes glanced this way and that, like a multi-directional scanner, catching everything and storing it.

He glanced down at the passport again, looking at the visa pages. There were several stamps for entering and leaving Spain, a French stamp as well as two Arab countries: Egypt and Morocco.

When he looked up, he noticed that Laura had knelt down and was lifting the dress away from Amy's body with a pen to expose her backside. White knickers clung to her skin at an angle halfway down her legs. Dark pubic hair was visible between the tops of her thighs.

She nodded to Cámara. They both knew what it meant; it was the reason why she was there.

'The husband?' she said.

'In the back room,' Fernández said. 'Beyond the kitchen.'

Laura was already on her way.

4

A policeman was standing in the doorway. When he saw the two chief inspectors approach he stood to the side and let them through.

'His name's Alfredo Ruiz Costa,' he said, looking towards the back room.

'Thank you,' Laura said. Cámara nodded to the policeman as he fell into Laura's slipstream.

Amy's husband was sitting on a low sofa in what looked to be a small office space. A computer sat on a desk under a window that looked out on to the street. Hundreds of books were stacked tightly into expensive metal cases along the walls. A rug — probably North African — covered most of the floor. Scattered around the computer and over most of the desk were scraps of paper with black handwriting. Amy's?

Laura took the office chair, spun it around and sat opposite and very close to the husband. The man was in his mid-thirties, Cámara guessed, although his dark brown hair, slicked back over his scalp, was already thinning. Neither of them could see his face — it was still covered by delicate, long-fingered, blood-streaked hands. A platinum wedding band nestled in the hairs covering the back of his ring finger.

He was of slight build and wore a black suit with a white shirt and what looked like a burgundy tie, although from his curled, cramped posture it was difficult to see. Underneath his

31

clothes Cámara discerned the loose-bellied, slouching body of a sedentary man.

Ruiz Costa seemed to be aware that he was no longer alone and slowly pulled his hands away from his face. Dark stubble was already pushing through the pallor of his cheeks, although it was only early afternoon. Cámara glanced down at his feet: the man wore black polished leather shoes. And pink socks. Which was when, he realised later, that he knew.

'My name's Laura Martín,' Laura began. 'I'm a chief inspector with the *Policía Nacional*. And this is my colleague Chief Inspector Max Cámara. We need to ask you some questions.'

The eyes stayed fixed on the floor, broken and unseeing.

'I need you to confirm your name,' Laura continued.

He raised his face very slightly, then coughed, as though trying to bring life back into his mouth and throat.

'Alfredo Ruiz Costa.'

'Thank you,' Laura said. Cámara kept a distance, watching from the side of the room.

'You called this in,' Laura said. 'You called the police.'

Ruiz Costa nodded, burying his face in his hands for a moment before drawing them away again.

'What is your relation to the deceased?'

He tried to breathe in, almost choking.

'She's my . . . I'm . . . We're married.'

'You're married to Amy Donahue. Correct?'

'Amy . . . ' He could barely say her name.

Then the tears came, shuddering, heaving sobs. Laura looked up at Cámara. They both understood. Strictly this was an initial conversation with a witness, a means of quickly gathering basic information about a crime scene. Yet if either of them were honest about it, this should be taking place at the Jefatura, with the man's lawyer present: a formal interrogation of their main suspect. Yet wait that long, change the setting and place a legal representative beside him, and the dynamic would change. There would be time for emotions and nerves to be steadied, for thinking and planned storytelling. They had to speak to him now, had to listen carefully to his first words. But it would be impossible if he broke down.

They waited; Laura did not move. After a few moments, Cámara thrust his hand into his pocket and pulled out a paper handkerchief. Checking it was clean first, he handed it over. Laura took it and offered it to the husband. After a pause, he grabbed it, took a couple of deep, jerky breaths, and then wiped the tears from his eyes and face.

'Take your time,' Laura said. He started moving his head back and forth. Was he nodding or trying to calm himself?

'Yes,' he said. 'Yes.'

'We need to talk to you now,' Laura said. 'These early moments immediately after a tragedy like this are important. You can help us a lot.'

'Yes.' More rocking and nodding. Then he stopped.

'Can you tell us what happened?' Cámara spoke from his position at the side of the room. The sound of his voice, a new voice, changed something. Ruiz Costa looked up, aware of Cámara for the first time.

'I came back for lunch,' he said, glancing back to Laura. 'I came back a bit early for lunch and . . . and . . . just found her.'

More sobbing welled up inside, but he managed to press it down in his chest. Cámara thought he could see beads of sweat forming on the back of his neck. It was not hot.

'Were you at work?' Laura asked. 'Did you come home from work?'

'Yes.' His voice had lowered to barely a whisper.

'What is your work? What do you do?'

From his attire, and the size and postcode of the flat they were in, both of them expected him to say something like 'lawyer' or perhaps some high-up role in a government institution. Even a managerial post in a large company.

'I'm a salesman,' he said. 'For a pharmaceutical company.'

Laura's eyes darted towards Cámara.

'You're the head of sales,' she said, turning back and leaning in slightly.

'No. A salesman. Travelling. I go to doctors, chemists, hospitals.'

Even on a good rate of commission — which was rare these days — he should not have been able to afford such a place.

'Do you always come home for lunch?' Laura asked. Keep it moving.

A long sigh. 'Not always. When I can. If I'm in the city. Like today.'

'So today you came home for lunch.'

'Yes. Yes, I did. I wasn't . . . We hadn't . . . Nothing special. Perhaps just a plate of lentils, or a sandwich. Amy . . . Amy's American, you see. They don't eat much at lunchtime. In America.'

'How long have you been married to Amy?'

He looked up sharply with heavy, deep-set eyes.

'A year. A year last month. She . . . '

He lost concentration, eyes rolling under their lids for a second before he dropped his head again.

'Did anything happen this morning?' Laura asked.

'What do you mean?' he said, returning to them.

'Tell me about this morning, about before you went to work.'

He shrugged.

'Nothing. I mean . . . it was normal, like any morning. I was in a rush, she was in a rush . . . '

'Why were you in a rush?'

'I . . . We woke up a bit late. You know. I had a meeting at work early and then an appointment . . . '

'Did you make it? Did you get there on time?'

'Yes. Yes, I did.'

'What time was that?'

'The meeting? It was at nine.'

'And your appointment?'

'At ten.'

'Where? Who was it with?'

'Dr Olmedo Pérez. He's a plastic surgeon. Has a surgery near the train station. I had some new products to show him.'

'Did you get there on time as well?'

'Yes, almost. I was no more than fifteen minutes late. I thought it might be cancelled, what with the situation. All my other appointments were cancelled today. People are just . . . '

'What time did you finish your appointment with the doctor?'

He frowned.

'I don't know. Maybe eleven-thirty. Or almost twelve. Something like that.'

'And then what did you do?'

Laura was firing the questions like rounds from a gun. Not too hard, Cámara thought to himself. Don't make this feel like an interrogation.

'I . . . I did nothing. I just . . . '

'What? What did you do?'

'My other appointments had been cancelled. I didn't want to go back to the office. So I . . . I just went to the beach. Parked the car and went for a walk.'

'You went for a walk on the beach.'

'Yes.'

'Did anyone see you?'

'I don't know. It was very quiet. Maybe a couple of people were there. I don't know.'

Cámara looked down at the man's polished shoes again. There was no sign of any sand or dust on them.

'Did you walk by the shore?' he asked.

Ruiz Costa looked up.

'Excuse me?'

'When you went to the beach. Did you walk by the sea itself?'

There was a look of puzzlement on Ruiz Costa's face.

'No. I don't think so. Just along the walkway.'

'You said Amy was in a rush as well,' Cámara continued, taking over from Laura for a second. 'Why? What did she do?'

The slip into the past tense. He had not meant to — it could throw things at moments like this to finalise a person, to remove them from the present so suddenly. But Ruiz Costa did not seem to notice.

'She's a journalist,' he said. 'A blogger, I mean. She wants to be a journalist, get a job one day for a newspaper or magazine.'

'In English?'

'Yes.'

'And she had something on this morning?'

'Yes.'

'What?' Laura asked, taking back the questioning.

'I don't know. I don't follow much of it because my English isn't . . . '

'Then after your walk?' Laura began. 'Señor Ruiz,' she said, using his name for the first time. 'We need to know what happened. Did you come straight here?'

'I was walking on the beach,' he said. 'I didn't want anyone to know I wasn't working.' He dropped his head again. 'Sometimes I work six, even seven days a week. It's not often I can just slip away like that. I didn't want anyone . . . not even Amy. I don't know. To have a little bit of time like that. Do nothing.'

'So what time did you come home?'

The husband linked his fingers together, the skin sticky with blood. His hands were trembling.

'I could have come home sooner . . . ' he said.

'What time did you come home?'

He closed his eyes.

'Just before lunch.'

'So, what? Two o'clock?'

Cámara glanced down at the screen on his phone. It was gone half-past three.

'Yes, about then. Perhaps a little bit before.'

'Amy,' Laura said. 'Where was Amy when you got in? Was she here?'

Ruiz Costa looked her in the eye.

'Yes, she was here.'

'Where was she? Where was Amy?'

His jaw began to quiver, teeth clenched as a shudder seemed to grip his body. Then with a sudden, jerky motion, he lifted his arm and pointed to the dining room.

'There,' he said forcefully. A white line of drying spittle was lining his lower lip.

'There.'

For a moment Laura appeared to have lost momentum, caught between helping a grieving man and interrogating her prime suspect for a fresh and violent killing.

'Did you touch the body?' Cámara asked. No more 'Amy'. No more present tense. No more pretending.

The husband looked down at his dark, painted fingers. The blood had dried. No longer crimson but already browning and flaking off in places where he had touched his face or rubbed himself dry. He had not thought to wash his hands, to clean away the stains.

He looked up at them, wordless.

The smell would stay with him for ever.

5

'I was in Malaga, at the murder squad. It was one of the first cases after I arrived. The guy was a truck driver. A Gypsy. He used to leave early every morning and do deliveries around the city and then come home. Sometimes for lunch, sometimes not, but he was always back home by about eight in the evening. So one night he has a row with his wife, she says she's going to leave him. I mean, you know what I'm saying — it must be very serious to make a Gypsy woman threaten to leave her husband. They don't do that. Later we found out he'd been beating her something rotten. Anyway, she threatens to leave, he bangs her around, same as usual. Then the next day he sets off for work as though nothing had happened, doing his rounds. But around mid-morning he comes back home, parks the truck a few blocks away so no one would see it, strolls back home and murders the wife. Viciously, I mean, with a knife. Slashes her face, her hands, her genitals . . . It was horrific, like an abattoir or something. Then he has a shower, washes himself off, puts on a clean shirt and goes back to the truck and carries on with the deliveries, dumping the knife and bloodstained clothes in a rubbish container on the other side of the city. At midday he has lunch with his mates, absolutely fine. And meanwhile his wife is lying dead back on the living-room floor. Then at eight o'clock he goes back home, like normal, and 'discovers' his wife's murder. We get called in and he's sitting there wailing, shocked, bewildered. The whole thing. Some were convinced, but I just knew. He comes up with some story about finding her there, he's distraught, screams for help, calls the police. Him, mind, not a neighbour or anyone. He had the presence of mind to make the call himself. And he tells us some story about a cousin in Colombia who he owed money to and how he'd threatened to hurt his family . . . We took him in, and he carried on with it. There wasn't much we could do. If anyone had seen him coming back home earlier in the day, no one was saying. I mean, no Gypsy's going to come running to us. But, you know how it is, sometimes you get lucky. One of the rubbish collectors heard something rattling in one of the containers that night. Sounded strange, so he pokes around and finds the knife, and then the guy's bloody clothes. Fishes them out and they're on our desk the next day. The *científicos* run them through the DNA testing and it's all his and his wife's, the blood. Straightforward after that. He got sent down. Protesting his innocence all the way, of course. And none of the neighbours or anyone ever came forward, even when it was clear it was him. It was the DNA alone. But, you know? They teach us these things — that the person who calls in a murder is often the murderer; that when a woman is killed, nine times out of ten it's her husband, or boyfriend, or ex-boyfriend or whatever. And we like to think that it can't be

41

straightforward, that it's got to be more complicated. But the statistics don't lie. You know I'm right. I've seen it a hundred times and so have you. We'll haul him in and he'll be singing like a canary before the end of the day. You know the type — wealthy guy, steady job, nice flat. Give him five minutes in the cells and he'll be screaming to make a confession.'

They were standing on the pavement outside the flat. A couple of members of the *Policía Local* had turned up and were maintaining a cordon, keeping people away as the ambulance backed up towards the entrance. The men from *La Pepa* — whose job it was to take corpses away — were about to drive Amy's body to the forensic medicine department at the law courts. The ritual of the duty judge and court officials arriving to approve the procedure was complete and they could start thinking about the next steps. A few metres away a squad car was waiting. Laura would be taking Ruiz Costa to the Jefatura in it. Cámara was already unlocking his helmet.

'Do you bet?' Laura asked him as he straddled the motorbike.

Her timing was crass, if not uncommon. Dark humour, silly competitive games — these were the methods that some used to combat the stress.

'Go on,' he said.

'You're not convinced.'

'I keep an open mind.'

'You don't think a nice man like him could do something so horrible.'

42

He pulled on his helmet and strapped it tight under his chin, firing the bike into life.

'Have it your way,' Laura said. 'But I'm telling you now, I'll have a confession before the Old Man finally pegs it.'

Ah yes, he thought as he sped back up the Gran Vía. The King. For a moment he had almost forgotten about it all.

★ ★ ★

While Laura Martín focused on her 'one shot' approach to the case, Cámara decided to do some background work. It was something he normally did with Torres — his colleague was faster on the keyboard than he was and they could bounce ideas off each other as they delved into the information available to them on Webpol, the police intranet. Now, though, he would have to do it on his own.

Some of his colleagues had already finished for the day. Hangers-on were still glued to the screen. The reporters had changed but after pausing to watch for a second he saw that the situation was the same as before. He was craving a drink, and with an instinctive motion his right hand dropped to open a drawer in his desk where he and Torres sometimes kept their secret supply. But instead of a bottle of brandy, all he found was a forgotten apple from some hurried snack.

Taking a bite, he walked over to the television and switched it off, to the sound of disappointed groans.

'I need your attention,' he said, swallowing.

He only required a few minutes. Albelda was the oldest and had been there for so long he was almost a mascot figure for the squad. With high blood pressure, thick grey hair and a full, almost Gallic moustache, he had made it to fifty-five without rising higher than inspector, but his alcoholism never affected his ability to respond well in an emergency. Cámara told him to find as many officers as he needed and to talk to anyone they could find in the area around Amy's flat — neighbours, passers-by, whoever. They should start with the block of flats itself, then widen out to the rest of the street, both sides.

'Done,' Albelda grunted.

'We need to know what time the husband came home,' Cámara said. 'Eyewitnesses. Positive ID. And get in touch with a plastic surgeon called Dr Olmedo Pérez. His office is somewhere near the station. Can he confirm that Ruiz Costa visited him this morning?'

The other two, Castro and Lozano, were younger, but keen. Tall, with short black hair, Lozano had a permanent recently shaved look underlined by using too much cologne. He was ambitious and struggled to impress. Castro had recently arrived, having finished officer training only six months earlier. She was short and muscular, wore a stud in her nose and tied her brown hair in a ponytail, stretching it tight over her scalp. There was a goodness in her expression, but any innocence still remaining when she arrived had now been shocked out of her. He had heard rumours that she and Lozano

44

were sleeping together. No point splitting them up, Cámara thought. At least not yet.

'Coordinate with Albelda,' he told them. 'Go back to the flat and search it thoroughly. The *científicos* will be close to finishing. We need the weapon. If they haven't found it, you will. Got it? Tear the place apart if you have to, search the surrounding areas. If the guy's a travelling salesman he must have a car. Talk to Chief Inspector Martín. She'll be here soon. If so, get the keys and check it out. And make sure you tell the *científicos* as well — they'll need to take a look.'

He clapped his hands — time to start moving. Seconds later he was alone in the office.

The gun. It had been troubling him.

'We just haven't found it yet,' Laura had said. Perhaps. But how could you fire five shots into the back of a person's head without arousing suspicions? Normally half the neighbourhood would have heard. There would have been at least one call through to the incident room about the strange noise. Even in Valencia, where firecrackers were so common it often sounded as if a gunfight was taking place in the next street. But inside someone's flat? So why no calls? Albelda might be able to dig up something, but why had none of the neighbours come forward while he and Laura were still there?

Unless . . . Surely not. It made no sense.

★   ★   ★

45

Laura did not make an appearance until early evening.

'He's downstairs,' she said. 'In the cells.'

'Has he confessed yet?' Cámara asked.

'He will.'

She walked over to the television and switched it on, as though needing a moment's distraction from the investigation. A nun from Madrid was outlining details of the special vigil she and her sisters were holding as they prayed for divine intervention, calling on everyone in the country to join them in prayer. As she spoke, images of thousands of reporters and well-wishers near the hospital entrance filled the screen, cutting with scenes from the King's life: his early years in exile; arriving in Spain to be mentored by Franco; his coronation in 1975 and his famous television appearance during the coup attempt in 1981.

Laura sat down, her back straight.

'He's not dead yet,' Cámara said. 'Your bet's still valid.'

'Funny,' she said. 'It feels so important and yet at the same time . . . '

'You might be interested to hear what I've found.'

She turned.

'What?'

'It's what I haven't found, rather,' Cámara corrected himself. He tossed over a couple of printouts to her.

'No criminal record. No history of abuse. No court orders to keep Ruiz Costa away from Amy, or anyone else in the past.'

46

'Right.'

'Which doesn't prove anything, as we know. But — '

'Yes, I hear you,' Laura interrupted. 'But . . . thanks. That was probably more my side of things.'

'This is interesting, though.'

She raised an eyebrow.

'He's registered as having lived at the flat since he was a child.'

She leaned in.

'Both his parents are dead,' Cámara continued. 'Father — also called Alfredo — when he was twenty-three. His mother, Clementina, only last December.'

'The flat,' Laura said.

'Inherited. The family home. He stayed put and took it over when his parents died.'

'Explains how he could afford such a big place.' She paused. 'So he married Amy a year ago and then a few months later the mother dies.'

'You think it's relevant?'

Laura wrinkled her nose.

'Mummy's boy, inherited wealth. New foreign wife on the scene. They were probably having problems, Amy and Alfredo. Stopped sleeping together, rows. Perhaps he was seeing someone else. Perhaps she was.'

'That's a rapid collapse in the marriage — just over a year.'

'She was shot five times — at least five times — in the back of the head,' Laura said. 'That's not . . . You don't do that if you just want to kill

47

someone. One shot or two. Perhaps to the back of the head if you're a professional. But five? And the sexual element? Her underwear pulled down like that?'

She got up and walked to the window.

'I'm telling you it's Malaga all over again.'

She dropped her head and sighed.

'It's always Malaga.'

6

The bar where they usually met had closed a couple of weeks before, its metal shutters firmly and definitively shut, like the eyes of a dead man. Now it was another reminder of happier, more prosperous times, an additional scar on the streetscape of a wounded, flailing city.

Instead of finding an alternative near the Jefatura itself, however, they decided to frequent somewhere further away: a small, hole-in-the-wall pub in the Carmen district. There was less chance of bumping into other police there.

They had no set agreement, simply an understanding that come the evening, and the end of their working day — assuming they were on normal shifts — they would each make their independent way there and wait to see if the other could come round and have a drink.

Torres was first that day. Cámara found him sitting at a small table outside, with a half-drunk bottle of red wine in front of him and a small pile of cigarette butts growing underneath his chair. Cámara patted him on the shoulder, ordered a bottle of Mahou beer for himself, and sat down.

'Bad one?'

Torres grunted by way of affirmation.

The eerie silence of earlier in the day had given way to a different mood. In the absence of an official communiqué from Madrid rumours were beginning to fly. Many were assuming the King was already dead and that the announcement was being delayed out of fears for national security. The streets had been practically deserted but now people were coming out of their homes and circling the city centre to give expression to their emotion. Anger, fear, a sense of impending loss, elation in some cases — all these feelings were palpable as a crowd began to gather in the Plaza de la Reina not a hundred metres from where they were sitting.

'Like a swarm of bees that's about to lose its queen,' Cámara said. 'People don't know who they are any more.'

Torres took a gulp of wine.

'They're just bored.'

Cámara took out his packet of Ducados, lit one and then poured his beer into the glass as the smoke rose and danced in the orange-pink street lights above. Torres must know, he thought. Maldonado would have informed him of the situation as well.

'I can see placards,' he said. 'It must be some kind of organised demonstration. Did you catch a glimpse of it?'

Torres shrugged.

'I heard it was something to do with the cuts in healthcare,' he said. 'Arranged it a few days ago. Before all this started.'

He scratched his beard, pushing his chin out.

'They must have decided to carry on regardless.'

'I'm surprised . . . ' Cámara began. But Torres did not seem interested. Silently, Cámara

50

wondered to himself about what the policing arrangements were for the demonstration. A rally like this, on such a night, could turn into something much bigger and very different from how it was originally envisaged. Were the riot teams on alert? He found himself secretly hoping that they were not.

'So this murder case of yours,' Torres said.

'Seems fairly straightforward,' said Cámara. 'On paper.'

Torres chuckled quietly.

'What about the suicide?' Cámara asked.

'Oh,' Torres said with some exaggeration. 'The suicide. Well . . . ' He pulled a face. 'Guy called Diego Oliva. Unemployed for the past four years, can't pay the mortgage, about to get his flat repossessed, so he goes for a dive off the balcony.'

'Is he dead?'

'No. Not yet, anyway.'

'Did you go and see him? Where is he?'

'They've got him at the New La Fe hospital. Intensive care. Wouldn't let me in, obviously, but I caught a glimpse of him through the window.'

'And?'

'Guy lying in bed with a bunch of tubes sticking out of him.'

Cámara sniffed.

'All right. But what are they saying?'

'No one wants to commit. They're certainly not very hopeful, but they reckon there might be a chance. If only a slim one.'

Cámara took a long swig of his beer. Down in the square someone was blowing a piercing whistle, raising the volume of the swirling crowd.

'So what do you think?'

Torres did not react for a moment, his eyes dark under the shadow of his black eyebrows.

'His mortgage is with Caja Levante,' he said.

Cámara sighed.

'Well, he wouldn't be the first.'

The local savings bank had been one of the keenest lenders during the building boom a few years before. Now that the crash had hit hard, it had only been saved from annihilation by direct intervention — and millions of public money — from Madrid. But the price of staying afloat was to take a zero-tolerance approach to mortgage defaulters. Thousands of flats in the city now lay empty after people who had lost their jobs in the recession found they could not keep up with the repayments. Not a few of them had decided to end it all when faced with the loss of their home. Graffiti had started appearing on walls renaming the bank 'Caja Sangre' — the bank of blood.

Torres lifted his eyes and looked down the street towards the demonstration.

'They take his taxes and use them to prop up a failing bank that then takes his home away when he falls on hard times.'

'I don't understand it either,' Cámara said.

'Yeah, but get this.' Torres pulled out another cigarette, lit it and then leaned in towards Cámara.

'The guy's in his late thirties, right? Divorced for a couple of years, no kids. And until three or four years ago he'd been working his entire adult life. Always had a job. Same company. But he was on some rolling temporary contract system. You get paid a bit more in exchange for not getting any job security or labour rights. That kind of thing. But it seems he was pretty well set up. Clever guy. Had a degree in economics, steady job, as I say. Buys himself a nice flat, near the river. Everything's looking OK. Then suddenly, one day, no more contract, no more job. They pull the plug on him. No warning either, by the looks of it.'

Cámara nodded. Who was Torres really talking about? Diego Oliva? Or a future vision of himself?

'But guess who he was working for all that time.'

Cámara recognised the glint of dark irony in his colleague's eye.

'No. It can't be.'

'Got it in one.'

'You mean . . . ?'

'The very same people who are kicking him out of his flat are also the same people who gave him a job for all those years and who then dumped him.'

'He was at Caja Levante?'

'The very same.'

'It's unbelievable. You'd think . . . '

'You'd think they'd look after their own,' Torres said. 'Even if they had sacked him a few years before. But that's how bad things are these days. No one is safe. Not even the guys pulling the purse strings.'

Torres poured himself the last of the bottle of wine.

'And now he's skydiving from the second floor.'

'Second floor?' Cámara asked.

'That's where his flat is. The one he was about to lose. Second-floor flat.'

Cámara frowned.

'What?'

'Not very high,' he said.

'Depends how you fall.'

'I know. But if he wanted to be sure. How did he fall?'

'There's a nasty fracture at the front of his skull,' Torres said.

'But he clearly didn't fall head first. Otherwise he certainly would be dead, even from only a second floor.'

'His arms and legs are a real mess. Bones smashed to pieces.'

There was a pause. Both knew the implications of what he had said.

The bar owner came out to see if they wanted anything else. Cámara asked for another beer and some ham and bread. Torres ordered another bottle of wine for himself.

'I can hang that up inside if you want,' the bar owner said, pointing at Cámara's helmet.

'It's fine, thanks,' Cámara said. 'We might have to come inside in a minute anyway.' He nodded in the direction of the demonstration, where a couple of drums were beating a slow, threatening rhythm to accompany the piercing whistles.

'We could be in for a long night,' the bar

owner said. 'I thought about not opening. But I'm a Republican, so I thought, Damn it. But we'll be closing early if this looks like getting out of hand.'

'We'll keep you posted,' Cámara said. From the corner of his eye he thought he could make out a couple of police riot vans moving down alleyways to the side of them, finding back routes to get to the rally. They sat in silence for a few moments, gauging the mood. Their view was partial as the narrow street only gave them a small window on what was going on in the square.

'Might have to make a run for it,' Torres said, only half-joking.

'And which way would you go?' Cámara asked. 'Towards them, or away from them?'

Torres nodded.

'Well, that's just the problem, isn't it. But you look at any revolution or social unrest, and it's the role of the police that's key. Not the army. The military can intervene one way or another. But the ones who really tip the balance of power are the police. Always.'

'You know,' Cámara said, 'Franco refused to join the rebellion against the Republic until he felt certain that the *Guardia Civil* would be on side. Hilario told me once. And where the *Guardia Civil* did support the military uprising, the area quickly fell into their hands. And where they didn't . . . '

'Like here and Barcelona,' Torres said.

'Exactly. Stayed in government hands.'

'Proves my point.'

'So who's your money on now?' Cámara asked. 'Assuming this does get nasty.'

'If it was just me and you in the police,' Torres said, 'I'd say the government should be boarding their escape helicopters right now. And of course, if everyone in uniform was like you we wouldn't even be having this conversation because the whole country would be some communal paradise with everyone dancing naked through the fields.'

'If only *I* were king,' Cámara sighed.

'But they're not. Too many Maldonados among our colleagues, as you know. So what do we get? A police force that's almost as divided as the country. Which makes me even more worried.'

'Not like you to brood.'

'Fuck off.'

More police vans were appearing. Two of them were trying to squeeze up the narrow street where they were sitting. In a minute they would be forced to pull up their table and chairs to let them get through.

'You're either dealing with one very confused guy who's not sure if he really wants to kill himself . . . ' Cámara began.

'Yeah,' Torres said, pouring himself another glass of wine and ignoring the riot squad members closing in on them. 'Yeah, I know. I'll get one of the *científicos* to check the place out tomorrow.'

He should do more, Cámara thought. He should take a look at the man himself, check for any bruising, take a tissue sample from under his

56

nails — the usual steps to determine if there had been a struggle before he died. Oliva himself might give them some important clues, despite being unconscious.

He was about to say it, but something held him back. Torres knew the procedure, and would certainly be carrying it out himself. Perhaps he already had. But he was hiding something.

The poison — Maldonado's brew — was already seeping in.

A riot squad man jogged up and asked them to move their table so they could get the van past. From the square they could hear the sound of shouting and women screaming. Better to leave now than be forced home with streaming eyes and a burning throat from the tear gas. But Torres took his time, getting up as slowly as he could, acting as though the riot squad were not there.

'Of course,' he said as the van finally rumbled past them, its tyres squealing on the cobblestones, 'if Oliva ever wakes up I'm sure he can tell us what happened.'

7

The entrance was in the back patio behind a small restaurant in the Barrio Chino, not far from his flat. The owner was in on the secret and let people get through to the exit beyond the toilets where there was a hatchway with a metal ladder leading underground. It was originally meant as an air vent and service access point. Now it was the only way to get inside the brand new but abandoned metro line.

Valencia already had a functioning metro system. It worked relatively well, bringing people from the outlying towns and villages into the centre, or shipping students across to the university faculties; it was less a way of getting around inside the city itself. But during the boom years, with so much money seeming to pour in from some benevolent god in the sky, the authorities had decided to build a new line to add to the existing four. This one would go underneath the old part of the city, finally turning the network into a proper urban underground railway. When work on it had begun, the city's mayoress had effusively compared it with the circulatory system: the new tunnels, she said, would be like veins under the skin bringing much-needed blood to the centre.

Cámara had direct and bitter experience of the building of the new line. To date, no official or building contractor or politician had even apologised for the loss of his block of flats. Not even for the deaths of Susana and little Tomás. A neighbourhood pressure group was still clamouring for someone to stand trial and be punished.

Cámara had left Valencia shortly afterwards, and on his return had assumed that the metro line would be complete and running. But because of the economic crash the entire project — which had already cost almost half a billion euros — had been mothballed. The new line only had months to go before it was meant to see its first trains in operation, but now lay silent and abandoned beneath the city streets.

Forgotten. At least by most Valencians.

The restaurant owner nodded to him as he walked through. It was relaxed and relatively cheap, one of the more *alternativo* places. Regular diners might guess what was going on round the back, but would not tell.

There was usually someone sitting out on the patio, a kind of guard to warn those underground in case the wrong sorts were trying to get in.

'Evening, Max.'

Tonight it was Dídac, Daniel's son. He was in his late teens and strong, with dark blond dreadlocks and biceps that seemed to shine in the dark. He took a long drag on the joint drooping between his lips.

'Want some?' he said, offering it to Cámara.

'I'm fine. Thanks.'

Cámara left his helmet beside a pile of coats folded neatly on a stone bench next to Dídac. It could get warm and clammy down in the tunnels and the patio acted as a kind of cloakroom where people could drop off whatever they did not need for the night before picking it up again on their way out in the morning.

'Everyone in?' Cámara asked.

'Yeah,' Dídac said. 'Mostly. Danny's just popped out. He'll be back soon.'

Cámara smiled to himself at Dídac calling his father 'Danny'. When it came to some things he was a traditionalist at heart.

The ladder descended to a small platform, then a staircase took him down even further. A few light bulbs had been strung along to illuminate the way. Some electrician who was helping them out occasionally had found a cable that he could connect the wiring to. The result was that they now had a primitive form of electricity at no cost, although some people still preferred to light candles and brighten up their little corner that way.

The staircase came to an end inside one of the tunnels. A doorway led out on to where the tracks were supposed to have been laid and then it was a short walk to the 'station', where people tended to congregate. He had to be careful as he stepped along in the half-light. The earth beneath Valencia was notoriously wet and soft — ancient Moorish irrigation waterways still coursed beneath the tarmac and concrete — and large puddles could develop spontaneously. There was even a danger of flooding, but luckily it had been a dry spring. The advantage was that it was relatively easy to get hold of water for cleaning. One of the first things that Hilario had done when they arrived was to oversee the digging of a well. He was almost going to do it himself before Cámara and Daniel had stopped him.

'We need your brains and experience,' Daniel had said. 'There's plenty of muscle to spare.'

Helping out every night had given Cámara's grandfather a boost after their arrival in Valencia. Despite his advanced years, it had intensified the sparkle in his eyes.

Cámara mounted the ramp that led up to the platform. Some bodies at the far end were already bedding down for the night, rolling out camping mattresses and sleeping bags. Despite their best efforts to keep the place hygienic — a regular cleaning rota, rules about washing and food, even a smoking ban, which people only followed for the children's sake — the smell of so many bodies living and sleeping in the same place could never really be disguised. Some tried with joss sticks, but to Cámara's mind they only made things worse.

He found Alicia standing at the edge of a group of half a dozen children sitting in a circle. A clown with a red bowler hat and a painted face was telling them a bedtime story.

'Some are even switching off their computer games to listen,' Alicia said. She watched for another moment and he leaned over to kiss her on the temple, gazing at the long, sharp profile of her nose, the dimple on her cheek where she smiled, and the light reflecting from her large brown eyes. Her hair was longer and looser these days, falling to her shoulders and curling in

61

slightly beneath her chin; sometimes she hooked it behind her ears, revealing the gold hoop earrings that she usually wore.

'How many are there tonight?' Cámara asked as they stepped away. He could see that the clearing up had already begun in the 'kitchen'.

'About sixty, we reckon,' she said. 'A Peruvian couple came in about an hour ago. She's heavily pregnant. We're not sure if it's going to happen tonight. They say they can't go to the hospital because their papers aren't in order and they're frightened of being turned away. Hilario's with her. Has he trained as a midwife, do you know?'

Cámara shrugged.

'The thing with him is you never can tell,' he said.

'Even if he hasn't he'd probably give it a go.'

'Yes, but even so . . . '

'Daniel's gone,' she said. 'To see if he can find someone who knows what they're doing.'

She slipped her arm into his. He turned and they kissed.

'You smell good,' she said.

'I wish I could say the same about you.'

She laughed. 'I've been here since six. What time is it now?'

'Past eleven, I should say.'

'Have you had anything to eat?'

'Just a nibble. I could do with something more. Is there anything left?'

She led him over to the kitchen. A team of helpers — Cámara counted three women and a young man — was folding away trestle tables and plastic chairs. On a side counter — what had

originally been designed as the ticket office
— were a couple of trays with leftover tapas.
Cámara helped himself to two slices of toast with
cream cheese, smoked salmon and caviar before
moving on to the *jamón ibérico* and chorizo
sausage dipped in romesco sauce. He wiped up
the remains with a slice of onion-and-rosemary
bread.

'There's some wine left as well,' Alicia said,
passing him a half-finished bottle of Rioja
Reserva.

Cámara chuckled.

'The standard seems to be rising,' he said.
'Not bad for an underground anarchist collective.'

'It's the restaurants round here,' Alicia said,
pushing past him to help clear away some of the
plastic plates. 'Word is spreading. No one wants
to be known as the place where they throw their
leftovers away. Not these days. And it looks
good, being part of this.'

'That could be dangerous.'

'Perhaps. But in the meantime we've fed sixty
people who would have gone hungry otherwise.
It's Hilario who does it. You know how he is. He
charms them — they're almost begging to give
him stuff.'

'I should go and see how he is,' he said.

'Good day?' Alicia asked. She wanted to hold
on to him for a few minutes longer. The irony
was that now they were living together, back in
Valencia, it felt as though they saw less of each
other than before. His police work, her freelance
journalism — no newspaper was offering

contracts any more. And then there was this — trying to give homeless people shelter and food for a night or two while they sorted themselves out. Daniel had started it earlier in the year when he found the secret entrance down into the unused metro line. Millions had been spent building the thing only for it to be abandoned. And with so many people losing their jobs and being thrown out of their homes, what better way was there to help them than by setting up a hostel in the very facility they had paid for with their taxes? There was no more time for theorising, Hilario had said. The situation demanded direct action. There was still a chance, he insisted, that the soul of the country might be saved.

'I'll tell you about it,' Cámara said. 'In fact, I need to tell you about it. It's not nice. But you'll find it interesting.'

Alicia looked at him expectantly.

'But first I need a pee.'

He crossed to the other side of the ticket hall. A man in his fifties who had once been an accountant at a construction firm was sitting with a group of friends playing the guitar and singing protest songs from the 1970s. They did not have to worry too much about making a noise: the stairway of the planned station came out on one of the busier streets in the centre. The traffic would drown out any sounds from underground.

Gingerly, Cámara stepped into the toilet area. One advantage they enjoyed was that the washrooms had been completed before the project was cancelled. There was no running water, but the toilets were plumbed in, so all they had to do was pour water from buckets drawn from the well in order to flush. It was a good plan, and it worked most of the time, but with so many people coming and going — many only stayed for a couple of nights or so until they could find themselves a more permanent place — the system sometimes broke down. Tonight the light bulb had mysteriously vanished, and Cámara fumbled his way towards a cubicle. Kicking the door open, he stepped in something soft and slippery, almost losing his balance as he fell backwards.

'What the fuck?'

He pissed into the bowl, aiming as best he could in the dark, then walked over to the sink. His left foot made a sticky sound as he trod. He pulled his shoe off and strained in the half-glow from the ticket hall to see what it was, but the smell told him instantly. Fighting an urge to throw up, he pulled out some paper towels from the machine on the wall and wiped the turd off with some water. Next time he would bring a torch.

He found Daniel when he stepped back out.

'Alicia told you about the pregnant woman?' he said.

'You found someone?'

'A nurse. She's with them now.'

They were a similar age, but very different. Daniel was one of those men in their mid-forties who still kept the waistline of a twenty-year-old. He wore one large, red-feather earring and often

65

sported a black vest, his fat-less, leathery skin rippling over taut muscles. Cámara could never understand why a man bent on working against the system would spend so long trimming his beard: the goatee that framed Daniel's thin lips was manicured to an almost absurd degree. Who had time in the morning to shave only the top half of their bottom lip? The rest of his time and energy was focused on running the shelter.

'Let's hope they can sort it out,' Cámara said. 'If it's looking like it's going to happen we'll have to get her to a hospital. We can't be delivering babies down here. It's not clean. You won't believe what I've just stepped in.'

Daniel was about to ask when Alicia came running over to them.

'What's the matter? Is she all right?'

'She's fine,' she said. 'No, it looks like a false alarm. But it's Hilario I'm worried about. He's dizzy, has a bad headache. Couldn't stand up. He's mumbling his words. Said something about his blood-pressure pills.'

'Idiot must have forgotten to take them again,' Cámara said. 'Where is he?'

'On the platform.'

They ran over together, Daniel tagging behind. Hilario was lying on the floor, his eyes open but looking pale. A heavily pregnant Peruvian woman was stroking his hair, trying to soothe him. Cámara knelt down.

'I don't know what happened,' the woman said.

'It's the pills,' said Cámara. 'He needs his ACE inhibitors.'

66

He put a hand out to touch his grandfather's face.

'I've run out,' Hilario said. His voice sounded broken and heavy. 'None left. Meant to get some this morning . . .'

Cámara stood up and looked at Alicia.

'We've got to find some. Fast.'

'At this time?' She looked concerned.

'I'll find a twenty-four-hour chemist.'

'Let's just hope they've got some medicines left when you get there,' said Daniel. 'They're running out of basics these days.'

But Cámara was already on his way.

'Take him home,' he called out as he ran back down the platform towards the exit. 'I'll see you back at the flat.'

8

Two chemists in the city centre stayed open all night. After queuing outside both only to be told that they had run out of the medicine he needed, Cámara jumped on to the motorbike and sped off into the suburbs.

It was gone midnight and the streets were mostly deserted. He scooted through the alleyways of the Carmen district, wending his way quickly through the pedestrian streets of the old city before he could find a proper road heading north. As he rounded a corner he caught a glimpse, down at the far end of Calle Caballeros, of the Plaza de la Virgen. Large numbers of policemen wearing helmets and carrying truncheons were blocking the view, but the demonstration that Torres and he had seen earlier in the evening appeared to have turned into a full-scale riot. A tickling, burning sensation in his throat told him that tear gas had already been used. He opened the throttle and rode away in the opposite direction.

The situation in Madrid was still uncertain: he would have heard otherwise. But things were potentially explosive. The country the King had done so much to shape, guiding it along as it shook off the past and took steps — tentative ones at first but then ever more confident — towards a freer and more prosperous future, appeared close to collapse.

Cámara was not a monarchist. But he believed in being grateful. Recent years had not been the best of the King's reign — the scandals, the illnesses, the indiscretions. There was an element of legend or folk tale about his story: as his health and prestige declined, so did that of the country as a whole. Almost like a tale from the Bible. All they needed now was a sign — a plague of venomous toads falling from the sky, or something — and then they would really know that they were fucked.

The road took him to the Torres de Quart city gates, where he turned right and headed up Guillén de Castro, running the red lights as he sped along. Chemists with no basic medicines. He had heard about it, but these things only meant something when they affected you directly. Thanks to another hole in the city's finances there was no public money left to pay pharmacists to keep a full stock. The place felt like a ship springing leaks, taking on ever more water.

He crossed the river and shot up Avenida de la Constitución, away from the city centre. There was one place he knew, a big twenty-four-hour chemist in an immigrant neighbourhood, where he might have better luck.

Here in the suburbs the streets were deathly quiet. No police, no rioters. Just closed shops and offices and ordinary people getting some sleep before facing another day: those without work looking for a job or a way to feed themselves; those with work hoping to hang on to what they had. Not everyone had the luxury

69

of being able to care too much about the news. Getting by, day by day, took up too much time and energy. He counted six, seven, eight people sleeping rough as he rode along — on benches, under palm trees or huddled in the entrances of high-street banks.

He turned and headed up Juan XXIII Avenue. A queue of people ahead told him that the chemist was open. He parked the bike on the zebra crossing and wandered over. His phone vibrated and he saw a message from Alicia: she had got Hilario home safely, but was worried about him. If Cámara did not get back soon she was going to take him to the hospital.

Cámara glanced down the line. There were five people ahead of him: a black man, two Ecuadorean women, and a Spanish-looking woman. At the counter, slurring his words and starting to get irate with the chemist, was a junkie. It seemed that his papers were not in order for the fix he was trying to get. The black man looked back at Cámara and rolled his eyes.

'It's been like this for five minutes already,' he said. 'My little boy is at home being sick. I need to get him some medicine. But . . . '

He tutted loudly.

The others started joining in, telling each other why they were there, what they needed to get hold of — urgently in each case. Cámara put his hand to his forehead. Should he try somewhere else? He was not sure if moving Hilario again and making him wait for hours in the emergency ward was the best option. If only he could get the pills and shoot back. He could be there in less than ten minutes.

The junkie was starting to shout, banging the glass as he demanded his drugs. He was skinny. Physically he would not pose a problem, but Cámara knew from experience that junkies could lash out unexpectedly. And their pathetic appearance could often disguise an unusual strength. Intervene or wait for the situation to resolve itself? If he stepped in, he knew that there would be little chance of getting home before dawn. The bureaucratic machinery of police work would suck him in for the next couple of hours at least.

Two more people — two young Chinese men — had joined the queue. It had never been orderly in the first place and was now more of a mingling small crowd than a recognisable line. But the junkie continued with his rant. Finally, as though aware that things were close to getting out of hand, the chemist relented and handed over a white box, slipping it under the thick partition. The man grunted and slunk off, disappearing into the shadows of a side street.

There was a collective sigh of relief. The next in the queue, the Spanish woman, sidled up, and pushed over a piece of paper. Cámara checked the time on one of the street displays. He could still make it. Once he got hold of the medicine he would text Alicia that he was on his way.

Assuming that they had what he needed.

Something about the sound of the car's engine made him prick up his ears and turn to look. It sounded angry and incongruous. The vehicle was not travelling fast, but it was coming towards them from the top of the avenue and some instinct told him that the occupants had clocked on to this small group of people and were watching them.

The man in front of him sensed it as well, and turned as the car reached the traffic lights near where they stood, made a wide arc and swung round to drive straight towards them, mounting the pavement with a thud before braking just metres away.

Cámara's police mind automatically clicked into action: a dark red, five-door Opel Astra. Four people inside, all male and between the ages of twenty and thirty-five. All were white, clean-shaven, had shortly clipped hair and were wearing light summer jackets.

The information was registered in the second between the car coming to a halt and the doors opening. The men inside were only partially visible, lit by the street lamps above. Friends having a bit of fun, driving up on to the pavement like that for a lark? Or with something more sinister in mind?

Then all four of them got out of the car.

The two Chinese men took one look at the newcomers and ran as fast as they could, quickly vanishing across the road. One of the four men — a younger-looking lad who had been in the back seat — laughed as he watched them go.

Cámara glanced down at the car registration plate, trying to see, but the legs of one of the men were in the way. What was visible, however, was a sticker on the bonnet of the Spanish flag with the black eagle of the Francoist coat of arms in the centre. Instinctively, Cámara lowered his weight and steadied his breathing.

The Spanish woman had got what she came for but was standing still at the counter, paralysed by this new and unexpected turn of events. The Latino women behind her turned to look, then recoiled, shuffling backwards, unsure as to what to do. From inside the chemist's shop, the pharmacist was unaware of what was happening and called out impatiently for the next customer, his voice muffled by the glass.

The four men stepped closer, the three younger ones following the lead of an older member. All of them worked out — it was clear from the bulging shoulders and thick, squat necks. They had the air of a pack of dogs, a curious animal telepathy that forged them into a unit. And their lazy, arrogant and dark expressions implied a capacity for random and acute violence.

It was not clear what they were here for or what their intentions were, but Cámara's hand moved to his back pocket, fumbling for his police ID card. The leader was swinging a large bunch of keys from the end of a thick cord. Cámara noticed his balding, narrow head and a large tattoo on his right forearm of a shield painted in the Spanish colours of red and yellow, with a double-headed axe emblazoned at the front.

There was a movement from behind. The black man pushed past Cámara and stood to confront the group.

'Go away!' he called in a strained, angry voice. 'Go away! We have had enough of this.'

The leader swung his keys in a wider circle. One of the Latino women began to whimper.

'Come on,' the Spanish woman said to them, pulling one of them by the arm. 'You don't want to be here.'

'But I need my pills.'

'Come on, come on.'

And they shuffled away. Cámara and the black man were on their own.

'Enough!' the black man called again. 'Leave us alone.'

'*You* have had enough?' the leader suddenly spat out. '*You* have had enough? What about us? What about the Spanish people?'

He took a step forward, pulling the keys into his fist with a jerk. Behind him, the other three followed in unison.

The black man was scared. The leader bared his teeth.

'Stop!'

He had to move — now before it was too late. Cámara pushed past and held up his police ID card.

'Stand back,' he said. 'Stand back, all of you. Back towards the car. Now!'

The leader looked at him and smiled.

'A direct order from a representative of the Spanish State,' he said calmly. 'And we must obey. Right, lads?'

The others mumbled their assent.

'Yeah.'

'All right, then.'

Without taking his eyes off Cámara, the leader took two large paces backwards. For a moment

Cámara thought he was winking at him.

'That far enough?'

The leader was not scared — not in the slightest. This was part of some game for him, where he knew his role, the others theirs, and in some warped way Cámara realised that he too was one of the players, acting out a part that had been scripted before. Or so he felt. They were obeying him, stepping back and away. But he did not have a feeling of control. The tension, if anything, was worse.

'In the car. All of you,' Cámara said.

'This is the bit where we drive peacefully away, correct?' the leader said. 'Situation resolved. No incident to report. I understand.'

That smile again, joyless and calculating.

'It's been a long day. For everyone. I'm sure this is the right decision.'

At his command, the others climbed back into the car. The leader took one more look at the black man, then again at Cámara. Then he got into the car himself. The vehicle backed off the pavement on to the road again with a loud, exaggerated roar.

The window came down and the leader leaned out.

'There will be other opportunities,' he said. 'Nice to have met you.'

And they were gone.

Cámara stood for a few moments, watching them disappear at the end of the avenue and listening out for the sound of the car above the silence of the sleeping suburbs. Would they turn around and come back? Or had they really gone?

Only when he could no longer hear the engine did he turn round, back towards the chemist's.

The black man had gone.

The pharmacist looked stressed.

'Yes, I've got one more box,' he said when Cámara asked him for Hilario's pills. He opened a drawer, pulled it out and slipped it across.

'That's the third time those pricks have been round here in as many nights,' he said. 'Harassing people, threatening to beat them up. They call the immigrants 'invaders'. Fucking idiots.'

He sighed and passed Cámara his change.

'I need a fucking holiday.'

9

Dear God, he thought, let me never end up like this.

Amy's corpse lay on the cold aluminium table with a plughole between her feet for the leaking fluids to drain away. She lay face up, but her face was so destroyed that the phrase was almost meaningless. The rest of her body, despite having the yellow-purple colour of the recently dead, was young and fresh and beautiful. He would try to remember that, he thought. That and the smiling photo in her passport. Not the mangled mass of bone, hair and flesh that was now her head.

Darío Quintero was carrying out the autopsy. Cámara liked him. They had worked together in the past, and the elderly man with his full grey beard and thin white hands had a way of going about his work that ensured a calm dignity at such horrific and gruesome moments. Cámara had seen him operate many times before. It was not always necessary, but it formed a part of his job. This time he felt that he should be present. But seeing the young woman lying there, something rebelled in his insides. Some people, he thought, could never get used to this, no matter how many times they witnessed it. And he was one of them. On occasion he could stand it better, but it never left him unmoved.

Quintero spoke slowly in a gentle tone as he

walked around the body, his giant-like assistant taking measurements, cleaning up splashes of blood. It was almost like a form of theatre, a soliloquy in honour of the deceased as her mortal remains were examined, prodded and cut apart. She measured 1.57 metres, he was saying, had thick chestnut hair and weighed approximately 65 kilos. Her eye colour was unknown as there were no eyes to speak of left in her skull.

The body was turned over and the assistant began shaving off her hair, collecting it from the floor with a dustpan and brush. The kind you could buy from the supermarket for three euros. Quintero was looking closely at the bullet entry points at the back of her head. Something about the muzzle burns had caught his attention. The assistant stood to the side with the saw in his hand, waiting to cut the top of the head off.

'I'm . . . I'm going outside,' Cámara said.

'I'll fill you in when we finish.' Laura was at his side. She spoke without reproach.

The swing doors gave a satisfactory slap behind him as he walked out, symbolically reassuring him that he had left the autopsy behind. But his stomach and shoulders felt knotted and he rubbed his hands hard over his face as though trying to clean away a stain. Stepping over to a water dispenser, he drank hard and quickly, then belched and gave out a long sigh.

Thoughts of giving up police work, like those that had dogged him in the past, no longer featured in his mind. But there were moments like this when he remembered why, at times, it had been so easy to contemplate, and then so easy to dismiss. The horror and disgust were an essential part of his being a detective. The day you stopped feeling angry was the day you really had to consider carrying on or not. And there were still so many reasons for his blood to boil. Today, that reason was Amy Donahue.

He walked outside and reached for his cigarettes. The forensic medicine department was at the law courts, and as usual there were several dozen people mingling outside: lawyers and judges nipping out for a break, like himself; people with folders full of paperwork, shuffling and organising them before heading inside to the lobby; parents holding babies, come to register new births. This was the official, legal centre of the city and province, where the business of living, dying and breeding was played out.

Further on, in front of an annexe, wedding parties waited their turn to go in and take part in the quick-fire civil ceremony, some in formal suits and dresses, others in more everyday, if colourful, clothes. Would he ever be there himself one day, he wondered? As if unbidden, he knew in that instant who he would be standing next to: there could be no one else. And the thought brought a smile to his face. But would they ever come this far?

His thoughts were interrupted by the sound of shouting and whistles being blown. Another demonstration was getting under way. A banner was unfolded beneath a group of around twenty people. Cámara turned away, but not before registering the words 'corruption' and 'politicians' painted in red on the white cloth. More upset citizens, complaining about the low standards of their supposed representatives. They should take matters into their own hands and stop expecting others to rule on their behalf. More and more, he thought, it was the only way.

He finished his cigarette and hovered at the door for a moment, his mind filled with dread at the thought of what was inside. Finally, after taking a deep breath, he pushed on the door and walked in.

Laura was standing in the entrance. She looked pale.

'Finished already?' Cámara asked.

'We've got what we need,' she said. 'Quintero is continuing, but . . . he'll get in touch if he thinks there's anything more we ought to know.'

She did not look him in the eye.

'I find a drink can help at moments like this,' Cámara said. 'A quick brandy. For the nerves. There's a place round the — '

'No, I'm fine.' She pursed her lips. He felt pleased, somehow, that this affected her as well. She was like him, not one of the others with steel blood running through their veins. Quintero was different: it was his profession. But there were some in *Homicidios* who, he knew, could sit through autopsies an entire day and not be moved by them, as though watching procedures in an abattoir. That was not normal — at least not in his world.

'Shall we head back to the Jefatura?'

'Yes. Let's.'

They had come together by car this time: the murder squad vehicle had been free. Laura drove, and for a few minutes Cámara watched the city speeding by — tower blocks, jacaranda trees with intense purple-blue blossom, small white clouds bubbling out over the sea. May was a good month to be in Valencia, before the thick heat of high summer arrived.

His mind drifted back home, to Hilario. Despite the scare of the evening before, he appeared to be settling well here. The blood-thinning pills had done the trick. Or so Cámara assumed. Alicia wondered afterwards whether it was merely tiredness that had caused Hilario to collapse. He had been working hard all day, and it could get hot down in the tunnel. She should make sure he drank enough water, she said.

The car got caught in traffic as they reached the centre again. Laura beat the steering wheel with the palms of her hands.

'Fuck.'

She was not the swearing kind. He looked at her: her eyes seemed small, the centre of her forehead tight.

She caught the question in his gaze.

'It was as we thought,' she said. 'Shot five times in the back of the head. And she'd been molested. There were abrasions on her vagina.'

'Semen?' Cámara asked. There was an edge to his voice. Semen could give them a very good DNA reading, which could — if they were lucky — lead them almost straight to the killer.

'No,' Laura said. 'Nothing.'

'So . . . ?'

'So I don't know. Rapists don't use condoms — not the ones I've come across. He must have fingered her or molested her in some way. Whatever he did, it shows.'

'All right,' said Cámara. 'Do we have a time of death?'

'It's looking around eleven in the morning.'

'Tallies with Ruiz Costa's story.'

'The gunshot wounds,' Laura said. 'Quintero was very interested in them. By the looks of it, our man used a silencer.'

'Quintero can tell that?'

'Leaves different patterns of muzzle burns on the skin. It's complicated by her hair being in the way. But he wants the *científicos* to have a look at the bullets as well.'

'A silencer,' Cámara repeated. 'They don't muffle a gunshot completely, but it would explain why no one else in the building heard anything.'

'At least as far as we know. We need those reports.'

'Castro and Lozano are on it,' he said.

Castro. In contrast to Laura he thought of her by her surname — she was one of the team, one of the men.

'Well, as long as they are on it, and not on top of each other . . . ' said Laura.

Cámara chuckled. Laura smiled.

'I'm serious,' she said, trying to look as though she were.

'Anything else?' Cámara asked.

'Her fingers,' Laura said, a more solemn expression returning to her face.

'I didn't notice anything.'

'They'd been smashed, broken.'

'What?'

'Almost every single finger had been broken by something blunt and hard.'

Cámara sat back and stared out of the window. They were creeping along the street, but had been held up by a traffic light.

'Before or after?'

'Hard to say. Quintero said he thought it was either simultaneous with death or perhaps just after. The bruising was marginally lighter than if it had happened before she was killed.'

'Her fingers?' Cámara asked, perplexed.

The lights changed and they pulled away.

'Quintero wondered if they had been stamped on. Said he found traces of what looked like black rubber on the skin. Perhaps from the heel of a shoe or boot. He was having it tested.'

'You think it will fit?'

'With the husband?' Laura asked. 'We'll have to check his shoes and find out.'

'You still think it's him?'

'You still think it isn't?'

'I don't think anything. It's too soon.'

They pulled out from behind a bus and sped through a tunnel and past more lights before turning in behind the Jefatura and squeezing into a tight parking spot. Laura switched off the ignition and turned to look at him. As she spoke she pulled out the fingers of her left hand one by one.

'He's her husband. One.

'He called it in. Two.

'No one can prove that he wasn't at home at the time of the murder. Three.

'There was sexual molestation. Four.

'She was shot five times in the back of the head. Five times. Not once or twice. That's five.'

'You're going to run out of fingers,' Cámara said.

She frowned.

'The silencer,' he said.

'He didn't want anyone to hear.'

'What about her hands?'

'So he was angry about something she did. Perhaps he hated this blogging of hers. Or was jealous, or something. I'm sure there's a connection with his dead mother.'

She opened the car door and stepped out.

'Where are you going?' Cámara asked.

She looked towards the Jefatura, and the section of the building where the cells were housed.

'I'm going,' she said, 'to find out.'

10

'Wait!'

He pulled Laura by the arm.

'Let's stop and think before you go charging in.'

'I'm going to arrange a formal interview,' she said. 'Sort out legal representation and get him in for proper questioning.'

Her eyes were hard and tight like black pebbles, her breathing quick and shallow.

'Fine,' Cámara said. 'But you're angry. Calm down first. Let's see what we've got before we start. If it's about the bet . . . '

'To hell with the bet.'

'OK. But there's no rush.'

'We've had him inside for almost twenty-four hours already. If we don't get something by the end of today there will be problems.'

They had a total of seventy-two hours before having to charge him or let him go, which gave them another two days. But Cámara knew as well as Laura that their superiors began to get nervous if a formal indictment was not on the horizon after forty-eight hours. He should have been more anxious himself, given Maldonado's contest between him and Torres. Right now, though, he was more concerned about the head of the sexual violence squad screwing up their investigation.

He put his hand back on her arm, squeezing it

gently at the elbow.

'Come with me,' he said. 'Come to our office. We'll sort things out from there.'

Inside the murder squad rooms, Lozano and Castro were sitting next to each other at a single desk, writing up a report. Lozano looked up as Cámara and Laura entered the room.

'It's just coming,' he said.

'Where's Albelda?' Cámara asked.

Castro jerked her head in the direction of the next room.

'Go and get him,' said Cámara.

Lozano pulled himself away from Castro and slinked over to the connecting doorway between the two offices.

'Castro . . . '

'I'm just finishing now.'

'Leave it. I want to hear it from you in person.'

She stopped typing.

'Sort out an interview with Alfredo Ruiz Costa. He's in the cells. Get him a lawyer. But quickly. Understood?'

Castro nodded, made a note on a piece of paper and picked up the phone.

Lozano came back with Albelda.

'Morning.'

'Right,' said Cámara. 'You all know Chief Inspector Laura Martin from the sexual violence squad. She's on this as well.'

Albelda stepped forward, pulled out a chair and offered it to Laura. She sat down and nodded at him.

'Thank you.'

'OK,' said Cámara. 'I want to hear everything

86

we've got so far. Starting with you.'

He pointed at Albelda.

'Right.' Albelda crossed his arms and began speaking, rocking from foot to foot as he did so.

'The first thing to mention is that Dr Olmedo Pérez has confirmed that Ruiz Costa visited him on the morning of the murder. According to the secretary he arrived shortly before ten-thirty.'

'Right,' said Cámara. 'Just as Ruiz Costa told us. Did anyone see him arriving back at the flat?'

'The short answer is no. There are no confirmed sightings of Ruiz Costa after he left Dr Olmedo's around eleven-thirty. We still don't know what time he got home.'

Castro was murmuring on the phone in the background. She finished talking, replaced the receiver and nodded at Cámara. The interview was set up. In her chair, Laura sat quietly, her eyes fixed on the floor, her hands in her lap, listening intently to what Albelda had to say. Lozano perched himself on the edge of Castro's desk.

'Fill us in,' said Cámara.

'There are eight flats in the building,' Albelda continued. 'Two attic flats at the top and the shops on the ground floor, making a total of twelve properties. Amy Donahue lived on the third floor. Of the attic flats, one is empty — the owners are looking for a new tenant. The other is occupied but the couple living there both work during the day and were out. The first they knew of anything was when we knocked on the door. That high up they probably wouldn't have heard much anyway.'

'How many people were in the building at the time of the killing?' Laura asked, looking up.

'Not counting the shops on the ground floor, and not including Amy and her assailant — or assailants — so far we think there were four. And three of them were in the same flat.'

'Who are they?' asked Cámara.

'On the second floor, diagonally below Amy's,' Albelda said. 'A woman called Ana Navarro has a psychotherapy business. She was there at the time with a client, a man called Enrique Solves Ferrer. And her secretary, Raquel Seguí, was at her desk in the entrance hall.'

'And?'

'And they didn't hear or see anything. According to Raquel Seguí, people come and go quite a bit up and down that staircase. And not just because of their business — the place across the hallway from them is run by a chiropractor.'

'Get your head sorted out in one place and your back in the other,' Lozano grinned.

'Who's that?' Cámara asked.

'A Danish national called Stephan Hansen,' said Albelda.

'Where was he?'

'He had an early appointment at ten which finished at eleven. Then he said he had nothing else on till lunchtime, so he went out to do some shopping.'

'He left at eleven.'

'Says it must have been sometime after.'

'Did he see anything?'

'No one on the stairs. Nothing unusual. The only thing he mentioned was seeing a couple of young men pressing one of the buttons on the intercom phone outside when he stepped into the street. Didn't think anything of it but he thought he heard one of them say *cartero* when it was answered.'

'Postman?' Lozano said. 'Was he sure?'

'Not very,' Albelda said. 'He was already walking away. But he said the postman usually comes round later in the morning, which was why he noticed it.'

'How good is his Spanish?' Cámara asked.

'Good enough. Speaks with an accent. Perhaps not quite fluent.'

'But better than your Danish, eh?' Lozano quipped.

'Two men claiming to be a postman,' Cámara said in a low voice, almost to himself. He looked over to Laura. 'Might explain how someone got into the building.'

Laura shrugged.

'He's foreign. He's not sure what he heard. Did he see Ruiz Costa?' she asked Albelda. Albelda shook his head.

'Did he know Amy and her husband?'

'Said they used to say hello on the stairs,' said Albelda. 'But not much else. He's worried about business. Says people might stop coming to see him now there's been a murder in the flat above.'

'So his place is right below Amy's flat,' Laura said.

'That's correct.'

'God, if he'd been there! He would surely have heard something, silencer or no silencer.'

'What's that?' Albelda asked.

'Autopsy report,' said Cámara. 'Muzzle-burn patterns on the skull. We need to check with the *científicos* and see if the bullets confirm.'

The atmosphere in the room changed. There was something about the use of a silencer that made the killing worse for some reason. There was an intensity and a coolness about it that cut against the brutality of the actual shooting. A question mark hung over all of them. This was different. And strange.

'All right,' Cámara said. 'Albelda, keep going. Who's the fourth person in the building at the time?'

'There's an elderly man on the fourth floor. A widower. Lives on his own. He was at home all morning watching television, he says. Keeps it on all the time to keep him company since his wife died.'

'When was that?'

'About two years ago.'

'Did he know Amy and her husband?'

'He's known Ruiz Costa since he was a boy. The flat belonged to his mother and father. They moved in almost thirty years ago, when he was about three or four. So they've been neighbours from the beginning.'

'And?'

'Well, the parents are both dead. The father was a doctor, which is presumably how he could have afforded such a nice place. The mother was a housewife. Ruiz Costa was their only child. The father wanted him to become a doctor as well, but according to the widower — '

'What's his name?' Costa asked.

90

'Juan Ramón Santiago,' Albelda said. 'According to him, Ruiz Costa never had it in him. Said he hasn't got it up there.' He tapped his forehead.

'What?' Laura said. 'He's saying he's simple?'

'No, not quite that. He didn't want to say. Said he had always thought of him as a nice kid, never really got into trouble or anything. But that he wasn't quite properly balanced. Said the mother's death threw him. Never thought he'd properly recovered. They were very close. Closer than the boy was with his father.'

'And what about Amy?' Cámara asked.

'Very sweet girl, according to Juan Ramón. Always smiling, very cheerful. Spoke excellent Spanish . . . ' He tailed off.

'And?' Cámara prodded.

'Look,' Albelda said. 'It's just neighbours' gossip.'

'What did he say?'

'He wondered what she was doing with Ruiz Costa. Said she was pretty and bubbly, and Ruiz Costa has always been a bit, well, strange. A bit mopey, not too intelligent. He said he didn't think it was the best match in the world.'

'Anything else?'

'No, that was it.'

Cámara felt he could read the thoughts in Laura's mind: a disappointed father, frowning from beyond the grave, resigned to the fact that his son was not up to his own high standards; an imbalanced young man in a close relationship with his mother, recently deceased; a beautiful, foreign wife who, perhaps, could not fill the role

91

that the mother once had . . .

'Outside in the street,' Cámara said. 'What did you get from there?'

'You've got the dry-cleaner's on one side and the clothes shop on the other,' Albelda said. 'People coming and going all day long, as you'd expect. No one in either place was aware of anything happening until police showed up and started cordoning off the area.'

'OK, what about across the road?'

'There's a gym, mostly used by men working out, lifting weights, that kind of thing. No one there saw anything. It's run by a guy called Julio Pont Serra. He says he was out, but someone from the gym was talking to the caretaker from the building next to theirs at the time. A man in his sixties called Antonio Pascual Fuertes.'

'Did you speak to him?'

'Yes. He confirms it. Bit of a handyman, it seems. There's a leaking pipe at the back of the gym, and so he offered to fix it. Bit of money on the side. He was busy with it for an hour or more in the middle of the morning. So again, he wasn't around to see anything.'

Cámara sat back in his chair.

'What about the bookshop on the corner? Fulcanelli's.'

'Been closed for three months,' Albelda said. 'They used to sell healing crystals and tarot cards and that kind of thing. Seeing the future. Went out of business.'

'What, they didn't see it coming?' said Lozano. Castro sniggered. The others were silent.

'So what have you got?' said Cámara after a pause.

Lozano lifted himself off the edge of the desk.

'No gun,' he said. 'Or silencer. We found his car — a white 2005 Seat León. The *científicos* have gone through it thoroughly, but nothing there either. No blood spattering, no weapon of any kind. Just boxes of medicines — the ones he was selling. And corporate gifts for doctors — calendars, notebooks, pens, that kind of thing.'

Laura sighed with frustration.

'But we did get hold of Amy's laptop,' Lozano said.

Cámara nodded for him to continue.

'It wasn't switched off,' Castro said from the back. 'And we thought it might be useful. We could check her email and stuff.'

'OK, good,' said Cámara. 'And have you?'

'No,' said Lozano. 'It's password protected. We can get the tech team to see if they can crack it, though. I was going to call through to them now.'

'Do it.'

Cámara turned to Laura.

'Any questions?' he said.

The phone on Castro's desk rang. She picked it up, spoke a few words, nodded, and then put it down again.

'It's all set up,' she said. 'Ruiz Castro and a lawyer are in the interview room.'

Laura stood up.

'I've got enough,' she said.

11

The room was rectangular, bare and hot.

Ruiz Costa sat at the centre, behind a table, still in the same clothes he had been wearing the day before, although his tie and belt had been removed and his hands were washed clean of blood. Next to him sat a man with long hair wearing a light grey suit with white trainers on his feet. Something in Cámara sank — not for his sake, nor for that of Ruiz Costa, but for the workings of the system. A young woman had been killed and her husband was close to being formally accused of her murder, yet all they could come up with was a young legal aid solicitor dealing with what was almost certanly his first case.

Laura sat down first, opposite Ruiz Costa. Cámara picked up the fourth chair and pulled it back against one of the walls, sitting at right angles to Amy's husband.

'My name's Manuel Badenes,' the lawyer said without standing up. 'I'll be representing — '

'Yes, we know.' Laura cut him off. The lawyer fell silent. Oh God, Cámara thought. This was going to be worse than he feared.

'Señor Ruiz Costa,' Laura began. From his slouched position, hands beneath the table, Amy's husband looked up. His eyes were puffed and red, his complexion pale, with the overhead neon strips giving his skin an almost green hue.

94

Cámara remembered the tones of Amy's dead skin as she lay on the table, waiting for Quintero's knife to cut her open.

'Alfredo,' Laura went on. 'Can I call you Alfredo?'

Ruiz Costa shrugged.

'Have you eaten anything today?' Laura asked. 'Have they fed you?'

Ruiz Costa looked down at his hands.

'Not hungry,' he mumbled.

'I know how you feel,' Laura said. 'Sometimes you just don't have an appetite. I'm the same way today, you know? You see some things, some horrible things, and it just puts you right off your food.'

Ruiz Costa did not move.

'Before we get too far,' Cámara butted in, 'I just wanted to ask — Señor Ruiz Costa, you don't happen to know the password for Amy's email account, do you?'

Ruiz Costa looked up.

'It might prove helpful for the investigation.'

'J A N 12 M I L,' he said blankly. 'It's the date and place of her birth.'

'Thank you.'

Cámara jotted it down on a piece of paper and handed it to the guard with instructions for it to be passed on to Inspector Lozano.

'I've got some very interesting things to tell you,' he heard Laura say as he returned to his seat.

Ruiz Costa's unquestioning cooperation with the password appeared to make little impact on her.

'Is Señor Ruiz Costa — ' Badenes began.

'Your client,' Laura interrupted.

'Yes. Thank you. Is my client being formally charged?'

'Wait and see,' said Laura.

Badenes fell silent again. At the side of the room, Cámara closed his eyes. *Wait and see?* It almost made him want to walk over there and represent Ruiz Costa himself. The lawyer was a waste of space.

Laura turned to Ruiz Costa.

'Talk to me about your mother.'

Amy's husband looked up.

'My . . . ?'

'Yes, your mother. Clementina.'

Ruiz Costa glanced over to Badenes, then to Cámara. Cámara kept his face as expressionless as possible.

'Is this — ?' Ruiz Costa began.

'Relevant?' said Laura. 'I think so. Don't you? She died recently, didn't she? That must have been a huge blow.'

'Yes. I . . . It was just before Christmas.'

'You were close. You and your mother.'

'She was my mother,' he said flatly.

'Of course. How did she and Amy get on?'

'Fine. I think.'

'You think?'

'It was fine.'

He shuffled in his chair.

'No tensions? No arguments? It must have been difficult living together in one flat. A new woman in the home . . . '

'I'm at work much of the day,' he said. 'Amy

96

never said anything.'

Saying her name seemed to cause a twisting spasm in his body. He lifted his hands to his face and sighed deeply, the breath making a whooshing sound as it passed through his fingers.

'Alfredo, Alfredo,' Laura said. 'We're here to help. We're here to sort all this out. And I think you can help us. Anything you tell us now will all help to bring this to a close much quicker. But you just have to tell us, to talk to us. Otherwise the agony could go on for ever.'

She leaned in and placed her elbows on the table.

'It's up to you, Alfredo. Only you can do this.'

Badenes was about to say something, but Laura shot him a look and he fell back into acquiescent silence.

'Tell us about Amy and you,' she said. 'It can't have been easy after your mother's death. You'd lived there with her since you were a small boy. Then suddenly she's gone and it's just you and the new woman. That must have been difficult for you.'

Ruiz Costa's hands were no longer covering his eyes, but they still hovered around his face and nose, as though in silent, secret prayer. He began rocking back and forth, as he had done at the flat.

'Tell us about it,' continued Laura. 'What happened?'

'Amy was wonderful,' he said at last, his words muffled through his hands. 'Wonderful. I can't believe . . . '

'She's dead,' Laura said. 'She is dead, very dead, Alfredo.'

He covered his eyes again, his body shaking with a low, steady sob.

'I've just come back from the forensic medicine department. Amy was there. Do you know why she's there, Alfredo? Do you know why? Can you tell us?'

Badenes butted in.

'Look, this is clearly upsetting for my client. I think — '

'I think he needs to help this police investigation in any way that he can,' Laura finished for him.

She turned back to Ruiz Costa.

'Amy was wonderful, you say. Why would anyone want to hurt her, then?'

Ruiz Costa moved his head from side to side, his words inaudible from behind his hands.

'What's that? We can't hear you.'

He pulled his hands away and looked at her, his face wet with tears.

'I don't know. I don't know,' he cried.

'Did you hurt her, Alfredo? Did you?'

His body stopped still for a moment, as though caught on camera, then his eyes widened before disappearing again behind his fingers, his head falling and almost touching the table.

Laura threw Cámara a glance, angry and determined. He nodded: go on. Continue and let us see where we get. Besides, it was hot in the interview room, and the memory of what he had seen earlier in the morning was finally beginning to fade: it was time to think about lunch.

'Did you hurt Amy, Alfredo?' Laura resumed.

Ruiz Costa's body was curled tight in a ball.

'When did you realise she could never be a substitute for Mamá?'

No response.

'Is that what happened, Alfredo? When did you realise? Is that when you decided to hurt Amy? Because no one could replace — '

The explosion finally came.

'Why are you doing this to me?'

He was trying to shout, to scream at her, but his voice was strangled by the sobbing, and it came out like a broken whine.

'Stop it! Stop it!'

He lifted his head, looking at her through his fingers, trying to fight back and protect himself from her words at the same time.

'I didn't hurt her. I never hurt her.'

'Of course you never hurt Mamá,' said Laura. 'You wouldn't hurt her. You loved her. When she died it destroyed you.'

'What?'

'We're talking about Amy, Alfredo. What did Amy do? Was she not as upset over your mother's death, was that it?'

'I didn't, I didn't, I didn't.'

'Did she not respect your mother's memory? That was when things started to go wrong between you, isn't it?'

'No, no, no.'

'You can tell me, Alfredo. I'm here to help you. Something terrible has happened and I'm here to make it better. But you have to help me help you. You have to tell me everything.'

'I've got nothing to say!'

This time his voice echoed loudly around the room, his red eyes bulging, the veins throbbing in his neck. He stared defiantly at Laura for a second before turning his body to the side and curling into himself again.

A wave of confidence surged through Badenes.

'Are you going to charge my client?' he chirped up. 'If not I suggest we bring this to a close. It is clearly upsetting for him.'

Laura held a finger up to him.

'Alfredo,' she said. No reaction.

'Alfredo.'

She sat back and sighed. Badenes shuffled in his chair, as though about to stand up.

'I've just come from the forensic medicine department,' Laura said. 'You know, Alfredo, where they take dead bodies.'

Badenes was on his feet.

'I think — ' he began.

'Sit down!'

Instinctively the solicitor's knees bent and he returned to his seat.

Laura directed her words to Ruiz Costa again.

'It's where they carry out autopsies,' she said. 'It's a very important job, particularly when we're dealing with a murder case, like with Amy. It can throw up all kinds of useful and interesting facts that help us solve the crime and catch the killer. Do you understand what I'm saying?'

Ruiz Costa was motionless, but his attention was clearly focused on Laura.

'Some of the details are disturbing. Frankly it's

a horrible business, and it's the worst bit of my job, you know? Watching those poor people being cut up and degraded even more. It's necessary, it helps us catch the bad guys. But it's not nice, Alfredo, it's really not nice.'

She leaned in towards the table, linking her fingers together and resting on her forearms.

'And do you know whose autopsy I just saw this morning, before coming here? That's right, Alfredo, it was Amy's. It was Amy's turn on the table this morning. And do you know what they did? They cut her open, all the way open.'

She slid a finger down her chest in imitation of a knife.

'And they even cut the top of her head off. Did you know that?'

From the side of the room, Cámara started chewing on his tongue.

'They do that to take a look at the brain,' Laura said. 'But in Amy's case there was hardly anything left to take out. It had all been blown away by the gunshots.'

A low-pitched squeal was beginning to emanate from Ruiz Costa's body, like the sound of a wounded animal.

'The doctor said the gun had a silencer. Which is why no one in the building heard while Amy was being murdered. That's quite organised, isn't it? To have a silencer. Her murderer must have been prepared, must have thought it through. Clever to think about using that.'

The squealing was getting louder.

'And you know what else we found out from the autopsy? All kinds of things. What Amy had for breakfast — that's because they cut open her stomach. Did I mention that? Lots of fascinating details about her and her life. But there was one more interesting thing. Did you know that when she was killed, someone broke every bone in her fingers? Probably stamped on them. With his heel. We think he was wearing black rubber soles. Is that the colour of your shoes, Alfredo?'

Ruiz Costa pulled himself in tighter and tighter, wrapping his hands over the back of his head to squeeze himself smaller. The sound of his squealing grew louder, as though trying to drown out Laura's words.

Badenes was on his feet again. Laura shouted at Ruiz Costa so that he would hear.

'And she'd been fingered, Alfredo. Her knickers were pulled down and a fist had been pushed into her . . . '

The vomit was white and translucent, thick mucus erupting from the bottom of his stomach. It flew like a bullet straight from Ruiz Costa's mouth across the table. Laura was slow to react, only averting her face when it was already too late. Her hair, hands and shirt were quickly covered in it.

'Ugh,' she said, watching drops of it fall from her fingers on to the floor.

'*Mierda.*'

Badenes was already at the door, calling in a policeman to take his client back to the cells.

Cámara got up, picked out a couple of spare tissues from his pocket, and passed them to Laura.

Any thoughts about lunch were forgotten.

102

12

The Jefatura was a roughly rectangular building occupying a single block along Fernando el Católico. Inside, the central area was a large, open patio that on most days was used as a makeshift car park for those higher up the *Policía Nacional* feeding chain. Shelters were provided along one side to shade the bigger, more expensive cars. Cámara stood under one of them, using a black Audi as a windbreak while he lit his cigarette, then stepped out into a small patch of sunlight. He needed a moment to himself to think. Or rather not to think. There had been too much thinking already in this case, he felt, which was why they were having so many problems. Tackling it head on, going forwards in a supposedly straight line. Laura was going for the big clean catch. It made things so much easier if someone could confess to a killing: hundreds of man-hours were saved — not just in police work, but investigating judges, lawyers, magistrate's clerks — all of them could breathe a sigh of relief when a murderer pointed the finger of blame at himself. You left it at that and moved on to the next one.

But Ruiz Costa was different. And something about this case was different.

Vísteme despacio que tengo prisa. Dress me slowly: I'm in a rush. The proverb summed it up. They were getting tunnel vision, focusing too much on the prize. It was time to go on a different tack, take a sideways look. If he could have his way he would send everyone home for the rest of the day to switch off. Go to the beach, go wherever. And have sex — preferably with another person.

Laura stayed in the Jefatura, using the showers on the premises and changing into a fresh set of clothes that she kept in her office. Once she had cleaned up she would be spending the rest of the day with the *científicos*, she said. Did the markings on Amy's hands match the soles of Ruiz Costa's shoes — either the ones he was wearing now or any other pairs back at the flat? she wanted to know. Had they found anything on her body — fibres, hair, DNA — that matched Ruiz Costa? she wanted to know. The *científicos* hated having officers from other departments breathing down their necks as they worked, but she was not going to give up. The processes could take days in some instances — DNA testing took a week minimum, and usually much longer owing to a backlog of work — but she insisted on being there, on overseeing.

Cámara was not bothered about her disappearing for a few hours. Now, with an empty stomach and no desire to eat, he could get back to his normal way of approaching an investigation — by letting things flow for a while.

Aquí paz y después gloria. Peace and calm for the time being; success and glory would come later.

The cigarette helped settle his stomach and his nerves. They were lucky that the murder squad

104

offices were on the ground floor and he had easy access to this refuge of nicotine. He could come back in half an hour or so and have another. Then perhaps later, if he could manage it, he would get a bite to eat. Or something to drink at least. He could do with a brandy right now.

Something of the mood of the previous day, when they had anxiously huddled around the television set to watch the coverage from Madrid, had carried through. But today, although the news was still switched on in the corner, most were sitting at their desks, their eyes focused on the images on their computer screens, with little of the banter and chat that was normally part of the background noise. At the hospital the surgeons — the best in the country — had completed the operation on the King's heart, but so far there were no further developments, and intense concern over whether he was alive or dead could only be sustained for so long.

'What happened?' Lozano said, walking back into the office after a break. 'Did someone just die?'

It was a standard *Homicidios* joke, and usually raised a smile. But this time it fell flat. Not even Castro reacted. The general glumness was exacerbated by the news that the interview with Ruiz Costa had not produced the result they had hoped for. He had opened up all right, but gastrically rather than verbally.

Cámara sat back in his chair with his feet on the desk, letting his mind wander. Albelda stepped in from the connecting office and

105

walked over with a piece of paper in his hand.

'Maldonado called down earlier,' he said. 'Wants a progress report.'

Without taking his eyes off a distant horizon, Cámara relieved him of the piece of paper, crunched it into a ball and sent it flying in the direction of the wastebasket on the other side of the room, where it landed with a satisfying ker-thunk.

'Nice one,' said Albelda. 'You been practising?'

'Castro,' Cámara called out, his eyes still gazing at nothing.

'Yes?' Castro looked up from her computer screen.

'You're checking stuff on Amy on the Internet, aren't you? Let me guess, her Facebook page?'

'Er, yes,' Castro said, a little startled. 'How did you — '

'And Lozano,' Cámara said.

Lozano glanced over from his desk.

'That's Amy's laptop you've got there, right?'

Lozano nodded silently.

'Checking her emails?'

'Trying to,' Lozano said. 'The password is correct. I can see them but they're mostly in English.'

'Good,' Cámara said. 'Albelda, would you mind taking a seat? I'd like you in on this.'

The elder inspector sat down in a spare chair.

'Castro first,' Cámara said. 'Tell me what you've found out so far.'

'There's a lot,' she said.

'You've got English, right?' Cámara said. She was of the younger generation. The only foreign language Cámara had been taught at school was French and his intermediate English had been picked up subsequently, largely through his own efforts. People in their twenties and thirties, however, had been given obligatory English classes. Castro should be able to make something out of it.

'It looks like Amy had a blog,' Castro said. 'Wrote a lot about Spain, living here, the food and customs and that kind of thing.'

'Did she have any friends?'

'Facebook friends? She's got over a thousand here. But I can't see if they're close friends or just, you know, Facebook friends. There's a difference.'

'What are they saying about her?'

'A couple of people are asking how she is, say they haven't heard from her, is everything OK.'

'So no one on Facebook knows that she's dead yet?'

'Not by the looks of it.'

'OK,' said Cámara. He closed his eyes as he spoke. 'So the blog, travel stuff. Anything else?'

'There's a long article she wrote about meeting Ruiz Costa. How she came over here and they fell in love and got married. Living in Valencia and her amazing life. Almost like a romantic novel.'

'Where in the US is she from?'

'Milwaukee, as far as I can tell.'

Of course, hence 'M I L' in her password. It was also the home of Harley-Davidson, Cámara thought to himself, momentarily distracted.

'Have you read the article?' Albelda called

107

over. 'About meeting Ruiz Costa and her romantic Spanish love story?'

'As much as I can,' said Castro. 'I'm not sure if there's anything there. Seems they were very happy, according to this.'

'Move on,' said Cámara. 'What else are you seeing there?'

'There's a lot more political stuff here in the past few months,' Castro said. 'She's posting up articles from newspapers and magazines about the situation in Spain, about Valencia. And, well, I think she's putting up some material of her own, kind of doing less of the travel blog stuff and more on the crisis.'

'Such as?'

'Well, there's a piece here about a food bank in the Benicalap district. It's got her name on it so I'm assuming she wrote it. Stuff about the new poor in Valencia and how people who used to run their own businesses are now having to live off food handouts.'

'OK,' Cámara said.

'Then there's another piece about corruption. All that money that was siphoned off from the charity fund.'

'Remind me.'

'Last year. A group of officials in local government set up a charity to help starving kids in Africa, then took all the money for themselves. Spent it on cocaine and hookers.'

'Lucky bastards,' Albelda growled.

'What does she say about it?' asked Cámara.

'Just reporting the story as far as I can see. But there's also an interview with one of the lawyers

108

involved in the case. She did that herself.'

'So she's trying to turn herself into a news reporter of sorts.'

'Something like that.'

But still an amateur, Cámara thought to himself.

'She did something on the opening of that new private clinic near Burjassot last month,' Castro said, still reading from the screen.

'I remember that,' Albelda said. 'It cost seventy-five million euros to build that place. No expense spared when it's private.'

'Anything interesting there?' Cámara asked.

'It was opened by a town councillor,' said Castro. 'She's actually quite harsh about it, contrasting the cuts in public health services with this fancy new hospital. And wondering why a representative of the Town Hall was there in the first place. She says he should have been defending ordinary hospitals rather than championing a new private one.'

'Who was the councillor?' asked Cámara.

'Javier Flores,' Castro said. 'He's pretty high up, isn't he?'

'Very close to the mayoress,' said Albelda.

'Well, Amy doesn't have a high opinion of him, from the looks of it. Says his presence there was 'disgusting' and 'an insult to the vast majority of Valencians who can't afford health insurance'.'

'Amen to that.'

'She was getting more political, then,' said Cámara.

'Hard not to be when you've been in this city for a while,' Albelda said.

'What's the last thing on her Facebook page?' Cámara asked.

They waited while Castro scrolled up.

'She posted something in the morning, around half-past nine. Something about going to meet someone who was going to give her a 'scoop'. I'm not sure about that word. It means something like a big news story, right?'

'Hey, listen to this!'

Lozano spun on his chair towards them, his fingers resting on the laptop. Cámara and Albelda both sat up.

'Some ex-boyfriend of Amy's is over from the US.'

'Now?' Cámara asked.

'Right now,' said Lozano. 'Or I think so. Look, there are these emails from him over the past week. Over a dozen of them.'

Cámara stood up and walked over to see. Albelda followed.

'He's in Spain?'

'Yes,' said Lozano.

'An ex-boyfriend from America?'

'Yes. He's called Ryan Cox.'

'What do the emails say?'

'Look, he got in touch just over a week ago.' Lozano clicked open the email.

'Says he's sorry for not being in touch for so many years. But he's coming to Spain — landing in Madrid the next day. And wants to meet.'

'How do you know it's an ex-boyfriend?' Cámara asked.

'Because look. This is Amy's reply. She's says it's all over between them. She's happy he's coming to Spain, but she doesn't think it would be good to meet. She's started a new life, etc. etc.'

'So she's saying no.'

'Kind of. The guy doesn't stop emailing her. He sends another three emails before taking off. Then there's a lull of almost a day. That must have been when he was flying. Then they pick up again. Seven more emails in one day. Once he lands in Madrid, presumably.'

'Seven emails?' Albelda whistled. Cámara could see the dark look developing in his eyes.

'Did Amy always reply?' he asked Lozano.

'Not always. I think that's why he keeps emailing her.'

'What does she say?'

'She's still fond of him, but . . . here it is, that she can't see him and doesn't want him to come to Valencia. It's too soon. That maybe one day they can be friends again, but not right now, not after what happened.'

'What happened?'

'I don't know. I can't find anything.'

'Sounds bad,' Albelda said in a low voice.

Cámara could feel the group adrenalin kicking in. And he could sense . . . something. Was this it?

'How did they leave it?' he asked. 'What do the last emails say?'

'She's saying that she doesn't want to see him, repeats it. And then here, two days ago, he says he's coming anyway. Catching the train and coming to Valencia. She can't stop him. It's fate.'

'He uses those words?'

'Here,' said Lozano, 'see for yourself.'

Cámara leaned down to get a closer look. The sentence was small but clear on the screen.

It's fate.

He stood up straight and turned to Albelda.

'I'll go and get Laura,' Albelda said, walking to the door. 'She needs to see this.'

13

'You heard the latest?'

'What?'

'We're to wear our uniforms at all times when on duty. Direct orders from Maldonado.'

'Fuck off.'

'I'm serious. It's true. Something about respect for the King, honouring the institution of the *Policía Nacional*.'

'Is he dead, then?'

'Still no word.'

'I can't believe it.'

'Well, believe it. It's happening. As of tomorrow. An official memo's gone round. Didn't you see it?'

'I was too busy being a policeman. Trying to solve murders, that kind of thing.'

'Well, it's there. Anyone not complying will be disciplined.'

'Hah!' Cámara put down his beer and shut his eyes. Maldonado trying to justify his existence again. Was this another twist in the game he had started? It would make sacking one of them much easier if he had another 'excuse', such as a disciplinary offence. Or a fresh one in Cámara's case. The murder squad were all members of the investigating police; they never wore uniforms except on ceremonial occasions.

'How it's meant to make us better detectives is beyond me,' Torres said.

'I don't even know where my uniform is. Must be in a box somewhere. Or did I leave it in Madrid?'

Cámara had spent much of the previous summer at Alicia's flat in the capital. It was less than a year ago but it felt like an age away.

'Well, you'd better find it quickly, or borrow one. Otherwise . . . '

Torres let the sentence drop.

There was a greater police presence on the streets that evening. Mayoress Emilia Delgado and her right-hand man, Councillor Javier Flores, had called for 'preventative measures' after the disturbances of the previous night, in which eleven people had been arrested. It was more important than ever, they insisted, to maintain order at such a difficult time for the country. 'Respect' — for the King, for the country, for practically anything that symbolised the status quo — had quickly turned into a new way of describing — and disguising — authoritarian control. On the table between them lay a copy of a local newspaper with a picture of the mayoress on the front. Emilia had condemned the demonstrators as 'scum'.

'You know what I heard one guy say today?' Torres finished his beer and ordered another one for himself. 'The second-in-command of the riot squad, what's-his-name . . . '

'Mestre,' said Cámara.

'Right. He's talking to a group of them about last night, and you know what he calls the demonstrators?'

'What?'

'The enemy.'

Cámara shrugged. For some reason it did not surprise him. It was easy to fall into thinking about ordinary people as 'them' — separate, non-police, second-raters. He had seen it creeping its way into his own thoughts at times in the past. 'They' did not see or know what officers did; 'they' did not have the powers that officers had; the bad guys lived among 'them' — that was where they were to be found. And he did his best to watch it, not to allow it to grow. But for some of his colleagues it was ingrained. Some even had it before they joined: it was why they joined in the first place.

'They were just demonstrating,' Torres said. 'If the riot squad hadn't been so fucking heavy-handed none of this would have happened.'

He motioned to the newspaper. Cámara had already seen the image, folded underneath and out of sight. Next to the picture of the mayoress was a photo taken the night before of a girl in her late teens with a bleeding face, the wound inflicted during the demonstration when a police truncheon had connected with her head. Half the city was irate about this act of 'police brutality'; the other half — the governing half — was congratulating the riot squad for doing such a good job maintaining law and order.

'What do you do,' Cámara said, 'when the real bandits are the people in power?'

He could talk like this with Torres. Their politics were not the same — if anywhere, Torres was somewhere on the traditional Left — but instinctively they shared the bond of not being on the Right, which was where, if they thought about it, most of their colleagues probably lay. Some harder than others, some hardened by virtue of being in the police. The King's sudden illness and the new, strained, almost crackling mood that had quickly descended upon the country was bringing political divisions to the fore. Were people on one side or the other? It was not intellectual; it was visceral. Dress, hairstyle, sometimes just the look in someone's eye, said everything.

But tonight, sitting in the security of their bar on the other side of town, Torres did not want to talk politics. There was only one thing on his mind.

'How's the murder case going?'

Cámara brought him up to speed. Maldonado could try to split them apart, to break the partnership between them that had worked so well and for so long that it had become something of an institution in *Homicidios*, but Cámara was not going to play along. And the best way to undermine things was to be open about his own case.

He told Torres about the findings of the autopsy, and how Laura appeared convinced that the husband was guilty. But the interview with him had not gone well — everyone in the Jefatura knew by now about Ruiz Costa vomiting on the chief of the sexual violence squad — and from that afternoon they were looking into a new lead concerning an ex-boyfriend over from the US. A quick search on Webpol confirmed that he was still in the country, but a trawl through the

116

hotels and hostels in Valencia had failed to indicate whether he was in the city. They would have to liaise with the consulate and see if anything came up the next day. Laura had perked up when Cámara showed her the email exchanges between Amy and Ryan Cox. Did they have a new suspect? Or had Ruiz Costa seen his wife's emails and become jealous? By eight o'clock Cámara decided to call it a day and left her in the office still working on it.

Now he was hungry — he had not eaten properly all day — and the gruesome scenes at the forensic medicine department that morning were long enough in the past for him to contemplate eating something. The bar owner brought him a plate of *montaditos* — pieces of toast with dried cod and red pepper — as a starter before walking over with a bowl of garlic soup, thick with paprika and chunks of bread, and an egg floating on top. In a few weeks' time the temperatures would be rising as they moved into high summer, and such heavy, warming food would be off the menu until October at the earliest.

Torres was not hungry — he had had a heavy lunch. On his own, he insisted, as though underlining the fact that normally he and Cámara shared such a meal on a work day. Cámara ate and waited: would his friend tell him about his own investigation eventually?

After smoking two cigarettes in silence while Cámara chewed and slurped his way through dinner, Torres coughed and began.

'Oliva's still alive,' he said. 'Or at least he's not

dead. 'Alive' might not be the best word to describe him right now. I went back to the hospital to check, but . . . ' He shook his head.

'What are the doctors saying?' Cámara asked.

'They seemed more hopeful today than yesterday. You get the impression these things change by the hour, though. They've managed to stem most of the haemorrhaging, but the guy's a mess. Who knows if he'll be able to tell us anything even if he does come round.'

'So what's been going on?'

'There's a housing pressure group that specialises in cases like this — in people being kicked out of their homes because of mortgage defaults. They've picked up Oliva's case, want to turn it into a big deal. They're talking to the media, and they've been on to me trying to pick up new info they can use for the campaign.'

'Have you got any?'

Torres shrugged; it meant yes.

'They're talking about over a dozen other suicides this year. Usually jumpers. It's quite common, it seems, to do it from your own balcony. There's a certain poignancy there, I suppose. They're about to kick you out so you launch into the great unknown from your own home — the home that the banks are about to repossess.'

'Anyone done it any other way?'

'Non-jumpers? Yeah, there was a couple a month back. In their seventies, they've lost everything, so they sit on the sofa together hand in hand and take an overdose. And that's where they found them. Then there was another guy who threw himself in front of a commuter train. But he had a ground-floor flat, so throwing himself out the window wasn't really an option. Well, it was an option, but at best he would have sprained his ankle a bit.'

'So as far as these people are concerned, Oliva is just one more suicide to add to their list.'

Torres nodded.

'They've been kicking up a fuss about it all day. Thought we might see them here tonight, in fact.' He glanced up the street to the square where the demonstration had taken place the previous night. 'But perhaps the massed troops of our colleagues up there have put them off.'

He pulled out another cigarette and lit it as Cámara finished off his dinner.

'It's a fucking scandal, the whole thing. You know that Caja Levante was funding most of the building that was going on in the boom years, right?'

'Probably. I could have guessed.'

'Get this — ninety per cent of all the money for the new museums and opera houses and Formula One and all the pharaonic wet-dream stuff that's been built over the past fifteen, twenty years has come from Caja Levante. Emilia would say, I want a hundred million for whatever — a new football stadium — and they would write out the cheques, no questions asked. So they kept lending all this cash, millions and millions of it, and then when everything fell apart they were left with massive debts and almost went bust. Except that the government stepped in and bailed them out at the last minute. With our money.'

'How did they get away with it?' Cámara asked. 'Banks are supposed to be good with money, right? Anyone tries to get a loan from them and you have to jump through hoops first.'

'And that's just small stuff for these guys. But when it comes to vast amounts for new buildings they couldn't give it away fast enough. It's because Emilia had her cronies running the bank. They weren't going to say no to anything.'

Cámara laughed. 'It's so simple. What a great scheme.'

'You know they used to have board meetings in Bali.'

'What?'

'Fly everyone out, including husbands and wives. Have a week seeing the sights, relaxing on the beach, then a quick hour-long meeting in the hotel and back home.'

'I love it,' Cámara said.

'What this country needs . . . '

' . . . is a fucking revolution.'

They clinked glasses.

'Poor old Oliva,' Cámara said. 'Just another suicide statistic.'

'And he's not even dead.'

'Are you sure it was a suicide attempt?'

Torres took a long time stubbing his cigarette out.

'I went to see the ex-wife today,' he said at last.

'Oliva's?'

'The same. She's absolutely cut up about it.'

'How long have they been divorced?'

'A couple of years. But they stayed in touch.

120

She said he'd been depressed. That was the reason why they split up — she couldn't cope, she said. And he wanted to be alone, like he just disappeared into himself. Said she couldn't get at him any more.'

He stopped for a moment and sniffed.

'Yeah, well, we've all been there to some degree, I suppose. But anyway, they've stayed in touch, and he was really down about money and he was going to lose his flat. But they'd been seeing a bit more of each other recently.'

'What?' Cámara said. 'Like, physically?'

'I don't know. But she said Oliva had asked her if they could get back together.'

'When was this?'

'A few days ago.'

'And what did she say?'

Torres knocked back his glass of wine.

'She said yes.'

14

The one aspect of the case that no one was mentioning, and which was staring them in the face, was the matter of Amy's work, her blogging. Was there a connection with her murder? An under-achieving husband mourning his mother's death, or a jealous ex-lover — or some combination involving the two — was still the obvious line to pursue. But something was niggling him about Amy's online life and the investigations she appeared to have been carrying out in the weeks before she died. That word — 'scoop' — kept floating back into his mind, quietly signalling to him from beyond the noise generated by the suspicions of his colleagues. And he had learned long before that these were precisely the thoughts that needed attending to. It was not a gut feeling — it was too calm for that. It felt more like a lighthouse, its steady flashing faintly visible on the other side of the storm lashing around him. It was time to heed its call.

Alicia would be ideal for the job. After being sacked from the Madrid newspaper, she had been freelancing whenever she could get the work, writing occasional articles for a national magazine that, miraculously, could still afford to pay journalists to carry out proper investigations. Then there had been some media consultation with companies developing brand awareness. But none of it was regular, and she was effectively living off the money she got from renting out her Valencia flat. Buying it outright had been the one good thing that she got from her divorce settlement years back. After she moved in with Cámara, it provided a necessary, if small, amount of cash — rents had gone down sharply across the city as the crisis kicked in, almost dropping by half in some areas.

Now, although she was kept busy helping out in the metro station, she had the time to do some research for him. Her English was better than his, and although not a news blogger herself, she would have a better understanding of what Amy had been up to. More than that — she had a playful, analytical mind: she would undoubtedly see or mention something that could be of use.

The tendency in the police was never to take work home; it had practically been part of the course at the officer academy. And the culture inside the Jefatura enforced it. Police stuff was what you did with your colleagues; it was what bound you together. And also separated you from those outside. And much as you loved them — or not in some cases — family was not police, they should not be involved. Many justified it on the grounds of keeping their own sanity intact. Take it home with you and you would soon crack up: it was necessary to have a division between work and the rest. But some things you took with you anyway, he had found, whether you wanted to or not. And by carrying it around silently, not sharing it with those closest to you, you ended up creating new divisions — emotional ones.

Best to talk about it, otherwise you became a stranger at home.

But there was another reason that many used to justify not speaking to their family about work: keeping them safe. The police acted as a shield, keeping the bad people away from the good, and if the bad ever did get through to cause harm, then the police hunted them down and made sure they never did it again. And in this business of protecting, the police saw horrible things. Should ordinary people — especially the ones they loved most — be exposed to what they knew?

Then there was the ever present threat of revenge. A policeman's weakest point was always his family: criminals sometimes hit back. Which was why almost all officers lived on the outskirts, their addresses known only to a trusted few. Cámara bucked the trend as he always had by staying in the heart of the city, but the danger existed for him as much as for the others.

He remembered the plughole at the bottom of the metal table, drinking up the fluids as they seeped out of Amy's corpse. There was a rare and disturbing violence about her killing. He knew what Alicia's answer would be, but doubts about getting her involved gnawed at him as he rode the short distance home.

'Something is happening, something quite important. It's just not totally visible yet.'

Hilario was in the kitchen, crushing ice with a hammer to make some cocktails. Cámara saw sprigs of mint and a bottle of rum on the counter: mojitos. He had arrived just in time.

124

'Feeling better?' he asked.

'Better than you.'

He kissed his grandfather on the cheeks and looked fondly into his eyes.

'One of those will perk me up.' He motioned towards the line of glasses waiting to be filled.

'One of these babies can wake the dead. If you learn how to mix them right. They know a thing or two, those Cubans. Best health system in the world.'

'They cure everyone with mojitos?'

'They have to. Sugar cane, limes, mint — they don't grow much else there.'

He poured the mixture into each glass and gave one to Cámara. A small amount was left in the jug. He tipped it into the final glass.

'This one's for Alicia,' he said with a smile. 'She needs it more than you.'

They walked through to the living room. The flat was large. Despite the cuts, Cámara's salary was still enough to get them somewhere decent, particularly in a less sought-after part of town. Valencia had changed and become more gentrified over the past couple of decades, but the Barrio Chino retained a rough edge, not least thanks to the Latin American and sub-Saharan prostitutes pacing the streets below. Which meant that good deals on flats could still be had. So used to evicting drug dealers from his property, the landlord had almost cried with joy when Cámara told him — in confidence — where he worked.

They had the entire first floor: what previously had been two separate flats had been knocked into one. The three of them cooked and ate and spent a lot of their time together, but the arrangement meant that Hilario could — if he wanted to — retreat into his own 'quarters' at the back, and a sufficient level of privacy was maintained for Cámara and Alicia to live as a couple.

It had been surprisingly easy. Despite his stubborn refusal to get old, Hilario could not live on his own. The obvious thing was for Cámara to take him to Valencia with him. But at the same time Alicia was being made redundant in Madrid and thinking about what she was going to do, and where she might go.

'Move in with me,' Cámara had blurted out, the words barely formulated in his mind. 'I mean, with us.'

Would she want to live with him if his grandfather was also around? Would it be a good idea if she did? How would it work? Would it damage their relationship? A hundred doubts had skipped their way through his brain in the split second it took her to respond.

'OK.'

And that was it. Four months in and everything going so well, he wondered why he had questioned it in the first place. Alicia and Hilario had met for the first time the previous November. Now they acted as if they had been friends their entire lives, and working together in the metro refuge gave them something in common beyond sharing jokes about Cámara.

Alicia was sitting in an armchair reading *Confessions of a Revolutionary*. Hilario waved

126

the mojito in front of her face. She looked up, smiled and took the drink. Seeing that Cámara was also there, she got to her feet and kissed him affectionately on the mouth.

'Hello.'

And seeing her face — her gazelle-like eyes, her fine nose and the tiny gap between her front teeth — he felt, as he always did, the light expanding within him.

He leaned down to kiss her again.

'He's got you reading Proudhon, then,' he said.

'It's strangely relevant stuff, for something written a hundred and fifty years ago.' She took a swig of the mojito and gave a low grunt of delight.

'Mutualism, a people's bank offering no-interest loans to ordinary people.' Hilario stood by the window, looking down into the street. He was steady on his feet, his back straight, limbs relaxed and strong.

'She's right. More people should be reading him. They might better understand what's going on. It's happening now, right in front of us — small, anarchist societies are being created below the radar. People getting on with life in their own communities, having as little as possible to do with the apparatus of the State.'

Cámara flopped on to the sofa and beckoned Alicia to join him. It was late — past eleven — and he was not sure if he was in the mood for this. When he was younger his grandfather had been the lightning rod for his anger and resentment. Hilario had brought him up, taking on a familial duty that Cámara's parents had given up on after the murder of their daughter, and now he was his only remaining relative. As a young man Cámara had thanked Hilario by rebelling in the most acute way that he could imagine against his anarchist beliefs — by joining the police. But the anger and self-pity had subsided over time and he had come to love his grandfather deeply, to respect and even — this was the most incredible thing — to share some of his ideas.

But despite seeing him in a much more positive light, Cámara recognised that Hilario had one fault: a tendency — on occasion — to preach. And tonight he felt some kind of sermon brewing.

Not for the first time, though, Hilario read his thoughts. He turned, as though to start speaking, then faced the window again and drank from his glass. Alicia snuggled up to Cámara and rested her head on his shoulder.

'Daniel said an interesting thing earlier,' she said.

'What was that?'

'We were talking — him, me and Hilario.'

At the window, Hilario did not move, watching the women shuffling in and out of the shadows on the pavement below.

'We were wondering — well, Hilario said something about setting up more places like the refuge, taking over other stations along the line. You could have a whole underground city there.'

'And what did Daniel say?'

'He said we weren't in the business of building empires.'

Cámara laughed, and Hilario stepped away from the window.

'He's more anarchist than me, that man,' he said with a grin. 'Never thought I'd ever say that of anyone.'

Cámara kept silent; he could tell that there was something his grandfather needed to say.

'Change is coming,' Hilario said at last. 'Change is happening, and more is coming. Things like the refuge. There's more stuff going on around the city. Similar. Someone mentioned they're setting up an alternative currency system in the Ruzafa area. People are bartering more. New ways of doing things are popping up. They might not all survive, but it shows people want something different.'

He sat down in the chair where Alicia had been earlier. The copy of Proudhon was lying open on the armrest.

'Sometimes I think there's a default setting for this country, and that after a brief interlude we're going back to it. Spain is about poverty and struggle . . . ' He paused. 'And brilliance. And I can see all three of them — like laws of nature or ancient gods — playing out their drama once again on our little stage.'

He took another drink.

'And we are not the audience. We're the players.'

'You're talking about the King,' Alicia said. 'You think there's going to be a big change.'

Hilario thought for a minute before answering.

Cámara could not remember him in such a pensive mood.

'It may or it may not take place,' he said eventually. 'I think more and more that these seemingly important events are no more than the outwardly visible side of something much bigger taking place, the small tip of a much larger iceberg under the surface. The King is close to death. He was not a bad man, neither was he all good, but on balance he probably acted more to the better interests of the country than against them. What happens next depends on how people react. But in some ways I think the result was predetermined a long time ago. Or not. The future, like the past, is always in motion.'

He finished his drink and stood up.

'I need to go to bed,' he said. 'And you youngsters need some time on your own. If I keep you up any longer you won't have any energy left for sex.'

Alicia giggled.

'Oh, I'm not sure about that.'

'It's this,' Hilario said, hovering in the doorway as he made to go. 'It's almost like a natural law.'

Alicia fell silent.

'The importance of things — the real importance of things — is in inverse proportion to the amount of attention they demand from us, or the noise they create. Follow the things that don't call out to you, listen to the quieter voices, and you could do far worse in life.'

He looked Cámara in the eye.

'Just keep going straight,' he said. 'That's all you need to do.'

He turned away and left them, his feet padding softly along the corridor.

'Don't make too much noise!' he called out.

Alicia smiled, then looked up at Cámara.

'He seems a bit odd tonight.'

Cámara stood up, pulling her with him out of the sinking contours of the sofa.

'Come on. Finish your drink.'

Inside the bedroom, he pushed her backwards on to the bed and started taking his clothes off. His pistol fell out and he slipped it into a jacket pocket.

'Is this the bit where I make a joke about your big gun?' Alicia said, a grin stretched over her face.

'Shut up and take your clothes off.'

'Ooh,' she said, yanking her shirt over her head. 'You're steaming tonight, baby.'

Naked and erect, Cámara crawled on to the bed, his body over hers.

'I said no more talking.'

★ ★ ★

When they had finished, and lay curled in each other's limbs, he mentioned the case to her, the blogging and the scoop. He could feel her face rubbing against the hairs on his chest as she nodded. Yes, she would do it.

And they fell into blissful sleep.

A full half-hour passed before either of them heard the banging.

15

Later Cámara could not say whether Hilario's arm rhythmically striking his bedroom door like that had been deliberate or fortuitous. The glass panel rattled slightly, which meant that the sound travelled across the flat. But competing against the background hum of the city, the noise of their lovemaking and the weight of their own bodies subsequently demanding sleep, it took Cámara and Alicia longer to hear it than they would have wished.

Hilario had managed to make it out of bed and across the floor, but there the paralysis had stopped him and he was now soiled and dribbling at the mouth. His eyes stared wildly ahead, fixed and desperate. His pyjama top was open, as though he had ripped at it, and the pasty loose skin of his chest seemed to flash in the half-light, contrasting with the deep tan of his face and hands.

I'm losing him, Cámara thought. Not with his mind, but with some lower, gut-like brain. A second later Alicia was by his side.

'Oh my God.'

'Call an ambulance now. I'll clean him up.'

He sprinted to the bathroom, grabbed cloths and towels, and was back with his grandfather as Alicia was dialling 110 from the landline in the hall.

'We'll sort this out,' he said. 'Don't worry.

We'll get you to the hospital. You'll be all right.'

Hilario's body was tense and quivering like a fist. His breathing was short and stuttered, a low grunting sound coming from his throat. The left side of his mouth arched down as though being pulled by a dentist to inspect his gums. Cámara pulled his pyjamas off and quickly rinsed him down. They needed to act as quickly as possible; everything would depend on how soon he could get medical attention.

Alicia appeared in the doorway and Cámara looked up. Her expression worried him.

'What is it?'

'The ambulance people.'

'What?'

'They said they couldn't promise they would get here for at least an hour.'

It took a second for the information to sink in.

'What?'

'The cuts. They're overstretched . . . '

'You told them this was a stroke.'

'Of course I bloody did. But they wanted to know how old he was and — '

'What did you say?'

'Well, I didn't expect the question. I said he's in his eighties, and then — '

Cámara stood up and touched her on the arm.

'Are they putting him low on the list because he's old?' she asked.

'It's not your fault.'

'I can't believe it.'

'We need to get him to a hospital as quickly as possible. Where's your car?'

'I — I parked it about three blocks away.'

'Get dressed, go and bring it here.'

She ran back to the bedroom. Cámara knelt down next to Hilario.

'It's all right,' he said. 'We've got it sorted.'

There was only one flight of stairs to carry him down. Cámara dressed Hilario as best he could, and wrapped a blanket around him. Then as quickly and as smoothly as possible, they carried him down and into the back of the car. The engine was still running. Cámara got into the driving seat.

'Come on,' he cried. They set off before Alicia could close the door.

It was late and the streets were empty. Alicia sat in the back, holding Hilario's hand and murmuring to him gently. Cámara jumped the traffic lights, driving quickly but smoothly — the last thing his grandfather needed was to be thrown around by sharp cornering and heavy braking.

'How's he doing?' he called to Alicia as they hit a patch of straight road.

'The same,' she replied. The tone of her voice said everything.

The street lights flashed overhead in a steady, bloodless pulse.

The new hospital was bigger, cleaner, better equipped and further away than its predecessor. The streets turned into avenues and the avenues into boulevards as they moved away from the centre and progressed outwards to the far edge of the city. Alicia's car was stiff and middle-aged. When, eventually, they arrived, they had to circle around the vast white complex before finding the right bit: some genius had decided to build the emergency ward at the back.

An orderly tried to stop them parking in the covered bay outside.

'Not here. This is only for ambulances.'

'Find a stretcher,' Cámara said, getting out of the car. 'This man is having a stroke.'

The orderly turned on his heel without a word and went inside. If he was not back within half a minute Cámara would commandeer a stretcher from somewhere himself. He peered into the back of the car. Alicia's face was lined and strained. Hilario looked pale, the expression in his eyes becoming gradually more vacant.

Cámara ran inside. Large transparent bags filled with rubbish were lined up against the wall and he almost fell over them as he looked for the orderly. There was no sign of him. The reception area was full: two rows of red plastic seats were crammed; at least four people were lying on the floor, catching some sleep; a couple of babies were screaming in unison in a corner; a large, elderly woman doubled up as she struggled with a relentless hacking cough. A queue of six or seven others was grouped around the reception desk, where a miserable-looking nurse was taking her time dealing with each new patient.

Cámara ran over, jumped to the head of the queue and started speaking over the voices of the others already there.

'My grandfather. Outside. Having a stroke.'

The nurse carried on as though he did not exist, tapping at the computer and glancing up occasionally at the person she was attending to.

135

'Didn't you hear me?' Cámara cried. 'We need a stretcher now. The man's in a serious condition.'

He banged his fist on the counter. She looked at him.

'Do that again and I'll call security.'

He had her attention at last.

'The person outside is very important,' Cámara said. It was a common trick, which usually got sleepy civil servants to click into action for fear of 'consequences' otherwise. The nurse finished dealing with the person at the head of the queue before answering.

'Important? Important?' she said. 'You're trying to tell me he's more important than anyone else here? If he's that special why don't you take him to a private hospital. If not, you can get to the back of the line and wait your turn.'

Cámara's head began to spin.

'He's having a stroke!' he shouted at the top of his voice. The nurse looked at him sourly, her eyelids heavy with fatigue. Then she pressed a button on her desk and indicated for Cámara to stand to one side.

'Next,' she called.

'What's going on?' Cámara asked. The person behind him in the queue barged in front, shouldering him out of the way.

'Someone will be coming,' the nurse said, waving towards a door leading into the hospital. 'Now wait like the rest.'

Cámara pulled himself away. The door she had indicated had a large red-and-white NO ENTRY sign painted on it.

He dashed back outside. Alicia was still in the car, holding Hilario's head against her chest while she smoothed his brow with her free hand. Cámara could see the flashing lights of an ambulance in the distance: they would have to get Hilario out and move the car before it arrived. Beyond a low wall to the side he caught sight of the metal frame and grey wheels of a stretcher. He ran over; it had been stripped of sheets, but would do. Wheeling it across, he pulled up in front of the car.

'We'll have to do this together.'

Alicia did her best to heave Hilario out through the door. Cámara held him by the shoulders and Alicia uncurled herself out of the car and took his legs. After a couple of moments Hilario was lying down on the stretcher.

'Drive,' Cámara said. 'We can't leave the car there. Then come and find me.'

The ambulance was already pulling in, blowing its horn for Alicia's car to be taken out of the way. She jumped into the front and screeched off.

'What? Hey!'

The orderly reappeared.

'You can't take that,' he said. 'We need that stretcher.'

'Find another one.'

Cámara pushed Hilario through into the reception area. It would be pointless staying in there: he could be made to wait for ever. Working his way through the mass of people, he headed towards the forbidden door. With a loud buzz it

137

swung open automatically as he approached it with the stretcher.

The cries of the reception nurse and orderly angrily calling him back were soon muffled as the door closed behind him.

He was in a corridor, with small rooms on either side. Yet inside the hospital proper it was as busy and chaotic as in reception. A sticky brown stain streaked across the floor. An old man, naked but for his underpants, was standing in a doorway with a breathing mask over his face and a drip hanging loosely from his arm.

'Where are they?' he repeated in a hoarse voice. 'Where the fuck are they?'

People shuttled in and out, back and forth. One, wearing a green robe, almost crashed into Hilario. She steadied herself, looked strangely at Cámara, wondering who he was and what he was doing, then dashed off, too busy with other things.

'Excuse me!' Cámara called. There was no response. From somewhere he could hear a horn-like sound, beating with a fixed rhythm. Was that an alarm? Had the nurse in reception called security?

He needed to find a doctor. He could hardly hear his grandfather breathe any more.

The stretcher squealed as he inched it forwards. Each side room was filled with patients, with family members crammed in around the bed. Empty boxes and plastic wrappers lay on tables or on the floor where they had been discarded. Mixed with the stench of bleach was a yeasty, sickly smell — antibiotics, perhaps, or infection.

'What is this? What is this?'

A man with grey stubble stood in front of Cámara, halting the stretcher's progress.

'You can't barge in like this. You have to go back. Can't you see how busy we are? There's enough to deal with without idiots like you wandering around the place.'

'Are you a doctor?'

'You'll have to leave. This way, this way.' The man took the end of the stretcher and tried to swing it round, towards the exit.

Cámara placed his foot in the way. The stretcher halted.

'Are you a doctor?'

'You have to leave. Otherwise we'll call — '

'Look at his face!' Cámara shouted. 'He's having a stroke.'

The man paused for a second to look at Hilario. His face was badly contorted now, his eyes beginning to curl up into their sockets. But Cámara could see the doctor's reaction: old man, probably far gone. It would not be worth the effort with this one.

'I'm sorry. Everyone in here is an emergency case.'

Cámara dropped his hands to his sides. He felt something in his jacket pocket brush against his wrist. The doctor was reaching out to grab the stretcher again. This time he would not be stopped.

The bullet made a neat hole in the ceiling, barely bigger than the 9-millimetre round itself. The sound of the gunfire seemed to echo through every room in the hospital complex.

The doctor's mouth gaped open as he stared at the gun now held next to Cámara's head. In an instant his attitude changed. A nurse had appeared from a side room, attracted by the sound of the explosion. The doctor pulled him by the arm.

'Room twenty-one,' the doctor said. 'It's urgent.'

The nurse did a double take from the doctor to Cámara, who lowered the pistol to the level of his hip.

'Right away,' he said.

The two of them began pulling the stretcher along. Cámara followed them a pace behind, not lowering his hands. Only when Hilario passed through the swing doors at the end of the corridor did he drop his arms completely and put the gun away. Which was when the security guard pounced.

It took some explaining — using a firearm in a hospital, threatening to shoot a doctor dead, and finally bloodying the nose of a security man as he resisted being apprehended. But a *Policía Nacional* badge helped, particularly when backed up with an ID card stating clearly that he was a chief inspector.

Alicia found him alone in a room they had shunted him into — not quite a cell, but it was thought better to keep him on his own, and under some degree of control. For the time being, now that they had taken a proper look at him, they were more interested in Hilario's condition.

Alicia and Cámara sat for hours on hard chairs, barely speaking to each other, Alicia with her back straight and eyes closed, Cámara leaning forward, his elbows on his knees. When the doctor came back, shortly before dawn, Cámara did not bother to look up.

They stood together outside for a moment. The sun was rising and reflecting on the cold hard paint of a thousand cars stretching out across the car park.

Another day. The beginning. And the end.

Alicia pressed a tearful face against his shoulder.

The sky ached so much he felt he would break.

16

He blinked. And blinked again. Scenes flashed before him like photos from a slide show.

A new shift. This doctor seemed to know nothing. He was sympathetic, if rushed. These papers to sign, these decisions to be made. He needed to think about costs, options. There were some good deals worth considering. Difficult, he knew, but necessary. So sorry for their loss.

The fine crescent of the dying moon dipped over the horizon and the sun began its relentless rise, whitening everything in sight. They stepped outside for a smoke. His stores were running low. It would be impossible to buy more here, in the hospital.

Alicia slipped her arm into his. She was with him, close to him, making him know that he was not alone. That she was not about to leave him.

The cigarette burnt his finger as he drew hard. He looked down: the pain called to him from a great distance, a barely audible scream from a ship sinking at sea. He stubbed the cigarette out on the ground, licked his finger, blew on it, and walked back inside. The automatic doors buzzed like a wasp as they swept back to swallow him in.

A paper cup of icy water was thrust into his hand.

'You need to drink something. Here.'

The liquid cut into his teeth.

The body lay on the bed, a sheet covering as far as Hilario's neck. His face still bore the signs of the twisting contortions of its final minutes. Cámara leaned over and tried to mould it back to its proper shape, an expression he could recognise. The skin was cold and oily under his fingertips. And it hardly moved. Best not to see him like that. He did not want to see him like that. He was told to stop, but continued nonetheless. A hand rested on his arm. It was Alicia. Stop. Come away.

His hands ached with exertion. A bead of sweat trickled into the corner of his eye.

'I never thought it would be like this.'

'I always knew it would be like this.'

There was a window of tinted glass at the end of the corridor. He stood by it, looking out over roads and motorways, the new river bed, patches of green, half-built abandoned tower blocks, cars and trucks and cars. And saw nothing.

The ceiling strip lights burnt and glared.

'You're in a state of shock. You should go home. I can take care of this.'

'I'm fine. I can manage. Just a few more things to sort out. Then we'll go.'

A call to Personnel. Family tragedy . . . compassionate leave . . . Have to be cleared. Call in again tomorrow.

'Chief Inspector?'

A man in a grey suit, standing, not sitting. Refusing to sit. He heard the word 'security' and switched off.

The man spoke at length. He nodded when the tone of voice seemed to demand a response. Then the man walked away.

'What did he say?'

She gave a concerned smile.

'It's sorted. They won't be pressing charges, or even making a formal complaint. In light of the circumstances.'

'I should have shot that doctor.'

A new figure, a familiar figure, standing in front of him.

Torres, holding out two packets of Ducados.

'Thanks.'

Alicia stood up and Torres kissed her on both cheeks.

'I'm going to get some coffee.'

And she left them alone.

Torres sat, one seat away. He stretched his arm across and touched his friend's shoulder.

'I'm sorry.'

He nodded thanks, and chewed hard with his front teeth on a piece of food that had dislodged itself from somewhere in his mouth. Last night's dinner? Lunch? What had he last eaten?

'The squad send their condolences. And their best wishes.'

'Thanks.' His voice stuttered. He coughed to dislodge a ball of phlegm that had stuck in his throat, then swallowed. The morsel of food went down with it.

'Thanks,' he said again.

'Laura's running things on the case.'

'Good.'

'Everything's fine. Everything's sorted.'

He knew it was a lie.

'Maldo?'

'Don't worry about it. We've got you covered. All of us. They love you, Max.'

Max. Torres never called him Max.

'You can take a last look, if you like.'

Another new face. Another shift? Outside, the white midday light seemed to have softened. A woman this time. He felt the weight of his pistol in his jacket pocket. It must have been returned to him.

A last look? At what? A dead body? That was not Hilario. But yes, he would like to.

The buzzing again. The wasp had entered his skull.

The flat, their new life in Valencia, Hilario's things.

There will be time for that later.

Alicia poured him a glass. Brandy, sweet, burning fumes. His shoulders gave one violent shudder, and then the tears came.

They wrapped into a ball on the sofa. His head would burst with so much crying.

The dying light of day cast slithering inky shadows over the walls.

'Do you want something to eat?'

'No. Thanks.'

'Another drink?'

'Perhaps.'

'Something else?'

She reached for the old coffee jar on the shelf where Hilario kept his home-grown. Inside, the slim red packet of cigarette papers nestled on the bed of dried green leaves. The smell, sickly and inviting, reached out to stroke his face.

'Not tonight,' he said.

Not tonight.

Above, high above, the black sky winked.

Amor y muerte, nada mas fuerte. Nothing is stronger than love — or death.

17

The funeral was held late the following evening, the last of the day.

After showering and washing himself clean, Cámara had headed to the funeral parlour, where Hilario's corpse, already beginning to rot from the inside, lay on a table in a small beige room. Alicia had offered to go with him, to pass the night with the dead, but he refused.

'One of us, at least, needs to sleep.'

He made sure his gun stayed in the flat.

She prepared a bag of Hilario's clothes to take with him — a brilliant white shirt and a dark pair of trousers. One of the funeral directors used them to dress the dead man's body before wheeling him into the room. There was no tie, and someone had done the shirt buttons all the way up. Once he was left on his own Cámara undid the top two. Less formal, more appropriate. He could not have Hilario choking on a tight collar.

And he smiled to himself — his grandfather would have liked that.

After sitting in silence for a couple of hours he stood up and walked around the body a few times. Someone had managed to do a better job pushing his face into a more normal expression. But his nose was already looking different, his mouth thin and tight.

'Go away,' Hilario would have told him. 'Go

out and live. Or sleep. Or eat something, for God's sake. Don't mope round here. This is not me. I am elsewhere. You already know that.'

But Cámara stayed — sitting, standing, pacing the room a little, glancing at the dead body.

This is important for both of us, he thought. Proper mourning, proper burying of the dead was the only way to make sure they did not haunt you through life.

When he stepped out into the morning light of the following day, he felt changed.

The small cemetery at Benimaclet, in the fields just beyond the ring road, was the only one in the city that could accommodate them. Cámara agreed and signed and paid. The numbers on the bills that slipped in and out of his sight were far too high, but the money would come from somewhere. Even if he was about to lose his job he would find some way of covering the expense. His grandfather might have been an anarchist, a believer in neither Church nor State, yet he would leave them in as proper a fashion as Cámara could allow.

'Burn me and put my ashes under a tree somewhere,' he had once said. The crazy thing was that cremation was the more expensive option.

It was a hot day. He took the motorbike, riding back to the flat in the late morning to eat something at last and catch a couple of hours of sleep. Alicia offered to drive him in her car to the funeral parlour for this last time, but he shook his head. She grabbed her bag and helmet and left the flat with him.

'I'm coming too.'

He was exhausted and his mind was dulled with pain, but riding forced him to concentrate, to sense his body again as he cornered, turned and wove his way through traffic. It was difficult, but it felt the right thing to do.

'Be sad but don't sink into sadness,' Hilario would have said. 'Change, adapt, move forward, live.'

He would have been proud of him.

It was just before five when they reached the funeral parlour. Hilario was still in the small room where he had left him.

'I could have come,' Alicia said, crying. 'I could have been with him while you were resting. He's been here on his own.'

'It's all right,' Cámara said, kissing her head. 'Everything's all right.'

The hearse left the centre at six. Cámara and Alicia followed behind. They rode helmetless, out of respect.

A crowd of around two hundred people was gathered at the cemetery entrance, Cámara's police brain automatically estimating their numbers. The previous burial must have been of a popular person, he thought. Then he caught sight of Daniel, Dídac and several others from the underground, and realised they had come to see Hilario off.

'I had no idea so many people in Valencia knew him.'

Torres was there, along with Albelda, Castro, Lozano and half a dozen others from the murder squad. Each one embraced him. Castro kissed him affectionately.

'I'm so sorry.'

He thanked them all and tried not to cry. It moved him more than he could have imagined to see them there with him.

'I appreciate this.'

Lozano held a large wreath in his hands. On it, printed in gold letters on a dark blue ribbon, he read the words, '*Deepest sympathy and commis-erations from the Spanish National Police murder squad (Valencia)*'.

The old anarchist's death was being mourned by agents of the State. He choked as the tears mixed with laughter.

Daniel and the others from the metro kept to one side, not wishing to get too close to the members of the police who were also present to mourn Hilario's passing. Cámara shared a few more words with his work colleagues before heading over to talk to them. Alicia was already there, along with Enrique, Cámara's flamenco-singer friend from the Cabanyal district.

Daniel embraced Cámara tightly, as though holding his weight in case he might fall.

'I owe your grandfather an enormous debt,' he whispered into his ear. 'He taught me so much, showed me the way. Now I must live by what he said.'

He pressed his face hard against the side of Cámara's head.

'And I must pay the debt through you, his only blood relative.'

He relaxed his grip, but still holding Cámara,

150

he looked him in the eye, with a black, energised expression on his face.

'I will do anything for you. You know that. Absolutely anything.'

He kissed Cámara on the cheeks, embraced him once more and then pulled himself away, tears shining on his face.

'Everyone wanted to come,' he said. 'Once word got round. Look how many have shown up.'

Cámara recognised a handful of the faces there, but mostly they were unknown to him. He saw people of all kinds: middle-aged men wearing suits, like bank clerks; young men and women with tattoos and loose, colourful clothes; a dozen Moroccans — men, women and children — huddled in a small group at the side; Ecuadoreans and Peruvians, shorter than the rest, with broad noses and straight black hair; a group of five black Africans standing at the centre, chatting with some of the metro helpers. Then there were others already walking into the cemetery. So many that he could scarcely believe it.

'They're all here . . . ?' he started.

'Because of Hilario,' Daniel said. 'He helped a lot of people, in a genuinely kind way. That travels, people sense it and respect it. When they heard what had happened they all wanted to come. Even people who only met him once or twice and have moved on. The word spread, as though it had a life of its own. And here we are.'

There were no relatives to inform. Cámara was Hilario's one remaining family member and now he was the only Cámara left. But this was his grandfather's true family, he thought, a random, ill-defined tribe united only by their appreciation of him and his kindness. It was the best send-off he could have hoped for.

A flame appeared, then another and another. Someone had brought some home-made torches — toilet rolls dipped in diesel and stuck on the end of poles. Within a few minutes several dozen were lit, held aloft by the mourners; and the group, as though acting by instinct, moved en masse towards the entrance of the cemetery. The attendant looked shocked when he saw the fire, and was about to say something, but thought better of it faced with so many people; it was the last burial of the day.

Alicia held Cámara's hand as they walked through the gate and into the small enclosure. Niche walls with holes for the dead three high stretched ahead of them in neat rows. The funeral directors carried the coffin on a cart with pneumatic wheels, the group following them. Some of the Moroccan children ran ahead, laughing as they skipped through rose bushes growing in patches of garden. No one tried, or wanted, to silence them.

There was no ceremony, no speeches were made as the coffin was hoisted off the cart. Cámara stood by a pillar of the colonnade, his chest constricted, his throat tight, face muscles aching. The sun was beaming low orange light on to them, sharp and defining, casting slashing black shadows over the bodies of the mourners. The torches burnt slowly, the smoke rising from each one and joining above their heads to form a single grey-and-white chimney shooting high into the windless sky.

From the side, Enrique began to sing:

I throw my voice to the wind
And cry to the highest heavens
Because I have
A living flame
In my breast.

It was a *seguiriya*, the saddest style of song in flamenco.

Cámara took a step forwards as the coffin was placed into the niche and laid his hand on the wooden top. Just a second, a last goodbye to the person he loved most in the world, the man who had done so much to make him who he was. Pulling his hand away, he placed his fingertips to his mouth and kissed them.

Goodbye. My grandfather, my father, my friend.

The cemetery workers pushed the coffin all the way in. A woman gave a high-pitched wail and buried her head in the neck of a friend standing nearby. The collective sound of a mourning, crying, silent and sobbing group of people swept around them like a fog.

'¡Ay, Hilario!'

Hilario. Their Hilario.

The cart was wheeled away. Another man appeared with a small bucket and a pile of bricks and started closing up the niche hole, deftly spreading the mortar over at the finish to seal it

153

up. In less than five minutes he had packed up and was gone.

Slowly the group began to peel away and Cámara remained with Alicia for a moment longer. The plaque would be going up a few days later. They had agreed the wording at the funeral parlour earlier that afternoon.

Hilario had been surrounded by death for much of his life — a father executed by the Francoists; his wife lost to cancer; his son, granddaughter and daughter-in-law all lost in the few short years before he took in Max. Yet Hilario had loved life; he had rarely, if ever, dwelt on the past or the dead themselves. You mourned, you got through it, you digested and understood and learned from the experience, and then you moved on. Visiting cemeteries to remember lost loved ones had never been part of what he did or who he was. And Cámara would try to live by that, by what Hilario had taught him. This niche, he knew, only held his grandfather's physical remains. Yet he would be returning — at least for a while. Perhaps only later, in years to come, would he be able to walk away and leave it behind for good.

Hilario, I am you. I am an anarchist. I am a Cámara.

Alicia stayed close by his side as they paced towards the exit.

Behind them, a group of tiny flies darted around the fresh cement of the niche, like a mist, ready to find a crack or the tiniest of fissures and get inside to begin their work.

18

It was Torres's way of telling Maldonado to fuck off: notes from his case were left in a neat pile on the corner of Cámara's desk with a hip flask of brandy on top as a paperweight. Cámara lifted the flask to his lips, took a long swig and let his body relax into the chair. He was going to need this.

The new law, passed only a month before, reduced the amount of leave given to civil servants after the death of a family member from four to two days. As a chief inspector, Cámara still had some say over his work conditions — although ever fewer. Yet the new law did not say at what time on the third day he had to return to work, and so he had arrived at a quarter to midnight, making sure that the policeman on reception duty made an official note of his time of entry. It was calm that night — the mood in the streets appeared to have quietened as, in Madrid, doctors still struggled to keep the King alive and the novelty of his condition wore off. Hardly anyone was left in the Jefatura, and Cámara and the policeman — a man called Azcárraga — had a smoke together on the central patio for a few minutes.

'My wife's ill,' said Azcárraga, 'and can't look after the kid. I asked for a different shift so I could help out.' He laughed. 'So they gave me the graveyard slot. Bastards.'

Cámara nodded sympathetically.

'Who's in?' he asked.

'Just me and you and the guys in the situation room. Four of them. The rest are out on patrol. Or in bed.'

'You should lock the doors and put your head down for a few minutes. Looks as though you could do with some sleep. If anyone tries to get in they'll rattle the doors so much you'll wake up.'

'Yeah, nice idea. I might try that.'

'I'll cover for you.'

'Thanks. Here, aren't you lot supposed to be in uniform these days? Heard something about it.'

'You going to grass me up?'

'Hah! Don't be daft.'

They headed back inside.

'I'll come and check on you in an hour or two,' Cámara said. 'We may be doing night shifts but I'm sure there's some work directive about mandatory breaks every so often.'

'I'll look it up,' Azcárraga said. 'Nothing better to do. No demos scheduled for tonight.'

'Let's hope it stays quiet.'

The truth was it was worth an excuse to get up and walk around every so often. He did not like the murder squad offices — they were small and dark and grubby. In the previous building — the sci-fi structure designed by local architect Montesa — the lack of common-sense things like enough toilets or storage space had been a nuisance, but at least everything was white and somehow uplifting. This place, however, back in

156

their old home, felt like a pit.

He had slept deeply the previous night. Long after the cemetery closed he had remained with a core group outside the entrance, talking, embracing friends and smiling that so many people had come, that there were so many good memories of his grandfather. At the flat, he had barely enough energy to get undressed before falling into bed as exhaustion gripped him. He had expected to dream of Hilario, to find him and communicate with him in some way, but when finally he awoke, late the following morning, he had no recollection of any of his dreams.

There were bureaucratic matters to start dealing with — banks, government agencies, the funeral parlour. He knew it could take months. Long after a person was physically dead a thousand pieces of paper could still be clinging on to their life, more reluctant than the people who loved them to let them pass away.

And throughout it all Alicia had simply been beside him. She was mourning Hilario as well, but she slipped into the role of carer more easily than he would have imagined, preparing food, helping to arrange the next steps in the cleaning-up process, making a first stab at sorting out Hilario's things — and they were both surprised how few he had: just some clothes and books and personal effects. Cámara had been certain that his grandfather had owned more. Where, for example, was the Luger pistol that he had brought back with him from the Eastern Front? Had he got rid of it during the move from Albacete? He must have thrown away much else besides — papers, furniture, his computer. It was almost as if he had been stripping himself down, doing away with his possessions until he was left with a handful of basic necessities.

It was almost as if he knew that soon he was going to die.

There were other mysteries — a letter from a financial adviser referring cryptically to the 'recent work' he had carried out on Hilario's behalf, for example — but they would deal with each one in time. Right now he had to clear his head enough to get back to the Amy Donahue investigation.

He had dozed again in the evening, then drunk a full pot of coffee before setting off. Alicia had kissed him as he left.

'I think I'll stay up as well,' she said. 'If you're going to make a habit of this, I want our body clocks to be on the same time.'

'It's for the best,' he said. 'It's the only way I'll get anything done. No one to distract me.'

He drew her tightly towards him.

'Thanks.'

Sitting at his office desk he took another swig from the flask of brandy and started going through Torres's notes. His colleague had guessed correctly that Cámara would be popping in some time. And by sharing his findings he was doing his best to undermine Maldonado's attempt to get the two detectives competing. Although much was at stake. For both of them.

The first thing that Cámara read was that

Diego Oliva was still alive and being treated at the hospital. According to the latest prognosis, the doctors were cautiously optimistic that they might be able to lift him out of the coma at some point soon. Although the risk of infection and complications was still high.

The word 'hospital' triggered a flash, and he did his best to push it to one side. Was Oliva's intensive care unit far away from the emergency ward? Thankfully the bullet fired from his gun had caused only superficial damage to the building. Although he had a hazy memory of the security official complaining that it could have cut through wires or piping essential for patient care.

His mind was wandering. Another drink of brandy and back to Torres's notes.

He flicked through them: the rest appeared to be a summing-up of what Torres had already told him. But there was one new piece of information. Before losing his job at the Caja Levante bank, Oliva had worked directly under a woman called Felicidad Galván, the head of the investment department and a senior member of the board. Torres had talked to work colleagues who told him that there had been bad blood between Oliva and 'Feli' when his contract was not renewed. Torres wrote that it might or might not be relevant, but that he was going to look into it further.

Cámara wondered for a moment. It seemed fairly normal that an employee would be upset that his contract was not being renewed. What was meant exactly by 'bad blood'? Whatever it was — and Torres's notes were ambiguous here, if clear elsewhere — it must have been enough for him to warrant making further inquiries.

Unless Torres was hiding something. The thought popped up almost of its own volition and Cámara swept it away. Why leave his notes on Cámara's desk in the first place?

He had no idea how much time had passed, but he fancied another cigarette by this point so he went to look for Azcárraga at reception. He was unable to find him until a rumbling sound came from below the desk. There, lying underneath, with his police cap under his head as a makeshift pillow, Azcárraga was snoring. Cámara went out on to the patio on his own, smoked and stared up at the few stars visible against the street-light fog.

The idea came as he walked back inside. Torres might have left notes on his desk, but the person he had expected to had not done so. In fact Laura Martín had not even sent him an email with developments in the Amy Donahue case. It was probably an oversight — unlike Torres she would not have guessed that he was going to work through the night on his own.

Her office was one flight up. It would almost certainly be locked, but he knew spare keys for all offices were kept at reception. Being careful not to trip over the dormant figure of Azcárraga, he found the right one from the board hanging at the back of the key cupboard, flicked it off its hook and skipped up the stairs to the next level.

Laura's office smelt of air freshener; he walked straight to the window and opened it. The place

160

was little smaller than the murder squad's — not bad for a one-woman team. He noticed a small teddy bear sitting to the side of her desk. They could come in useful if a child needed distracting while a witness was being questioned — not an uncommon situation in her cases, he thought.

Along the shelves were lined academic studies of sexual violence and profiles of the kinds of men who tended to commit it. They were the set texts and he had seen them before. Nothing like them had really existed when he was training to become an officer. Awareness of the problem had only developed recently and there were still people — politicians even — who wanted to play down its importance. Unbelievably, a couple of months back the current health minister had insisted that only women who had been actually hospitalised by their attackers should be added to the sexual violence statistics. A slap or a punch was all right — as long as the husband did not break anything.

Cámara glanced around, interested in what the office told him about Laura. There were very few personal things, he thought. Apart from the teddy bear there was a small photo of Laura with a small bearded man — a wedding shot. Laura younger and heavier — she had lost a lot of weight since then — in a white dress with an oversized veil; the man in a grey suit with a white rose in his buttonhole. He had the air of a university professor. There were no photos of any kids.

On the whole, the place was neat and orderly, much like the impression he had formed of

Laura herself. This was a woman who did things as they were meant to be done — a rare bird in the *Policía Nacional,* where pretty much everyone learned soon after leaving officer training that the only way actually to get things done was to bend the rules and skirt the many bureaucratic obstacles that were put in their way. Cámara had taken to it like a duck to water. Others went so far that they ended up acting in a more criminal manner than the people they were supposed to be catching. A very small minority carried on in the 'legal' fashion, doing everything by the letter. Laura was one of them. Being in her office felt like stumbling upon the lair of an endangered species.

What he knew, though, was that finding her notes on the Amy case would be fairly straightforward. Developments would be on Webpol, for all to see. Yet her thoughts and conjectures would be typed and arranged chronologically and placed in a very logical filing system. Like that cabinet over there.

He walked over to the grey rectangular tower at the side of the office and looked at the tickets on each drawer. They had beginning and end dates on them. The third one down only had a start date and was still being used. Would it be locked? From what he was learning about Laura it seemed more than likely, but he gave it a pull anyway. To his surprise it opened, catching at first but then running smoothly after an encouraging tug. He smiled to himself: perhaps Laura was less predictable than he thought.

The last folder hanging in the drawer was

marked '*Amy Donahue/Alfredo Ruiz Costa*'. Cámara pulled it out and sat in Laura's chair to have a read.

The first page was a report sent in from Madrid on a US citizen. The passport picture showed a young man with curly blond hair and sideburns. After giving his passport and visa numbers, his name appeared underneath — Ryan Cox. It was Amy's ex-boyfriend, who had been planning on coming to see her in Valencia.

Cámara glanced through the text, written in police officialese. '*Sought by the Valencia sexual violence squad . . .* ' Blah blah. So Laura had not put in the request in the name of the murder squad, he noticed. '*The individual was located at the Hostal Los Angeles in Madrid, where he had been resident since his arrival on . . .* ' etc., etc. Cámara skimmed down, looking for the important bit.

'*The individual insisted*' — here it was — '*that he had not left Madrid since his arrival from the USA seven days earlier except for a tourist excursion to the Escorial on the 5th. When questioned, he said that he had not travelled to any other cities in the national territory. Asked if he had any intention of going to Valencia, he said that he had considered going some days prior in order to visit a friend but had changed his mind and decided to stay in the capital. The manager of the Hostal Los Angeles was able to corroborate his story, testifying that the individual had stayed every night at the establishment, and that over the past few nights he had been returning with a Spanish girl. He assumed they were having relations . . . If further corroboration required . . . '*

The position seemed clear: Cox might have been about to come to Valencia, but had changed his mind when he managed to find a girl to sleep with him. Thoughts of Amy must have gone out of the window. He wondered if Cox knew that his old girlfriend was dead.

The report from the Madrid police was two pages long. Clipped to the back of it was a short typed note dated the previous day and signed by Laura. Cámara glanced through it quickly, but could already tell what it would say: her suspicions were still with Alfredo Ruiz Costa, Amy's husband. Her latest supposition was that Ruiz Costa found the emails from Cox and that this had sparked him into a jealous rage.

In the meantime, as their seventy-two-hour limit to hold him had passed, she had recommended he be granted provisional freedom pending further investigations.

Ruiz Costa had been allowed home the previous day, as Cámara had been burying Hilario.

Cámara smiled to himself as he read the last paragraph: Laura was disappointed that Chief Inspector Max Cámara, her colleague on the investigation from the murder squad, did not appear to share her conviction that Ruiz Costa was the perpetrator, but she was confident, given her past experience with similar cases, that a breakthrough — either by way of more evidence or through a confession — would be forthcoming.

Back at reception, Azcárraga was waking.

'Been sneaking about?' he asked as Cámara placed the key to Laura's office back on its hook.

'Secret.'

Azcárraga got to his feet and shook himself down.

'God, I needed that. Nothing happened, has it?'

'Nothing,' Cámara smiled.

'You would tell me, wouldn't you?'

'Don't worry. Go and wash your face and get ready for the early-morning lot coming in. They'll be here soon.'

'Right. Thanks.'

He would be heading off soon himself, he thought. He had not quite done his regulation hours, but he had forgotten to bring something along to eat, and the machines only offered dry, tasteless sandwiches and crisps. Spying in Laura's office had made him hungry.

He stepped into his own office to collect his things. Something about Torres's notes seemed to call out to him and he sat down again, taking a last drink from the flask. The brandy would give him enough energy for the ride home.

He took the small pad and started flicking through again. There was one section that he had meant to look at in more depth — the interviews with Oliva's neighbours.

Wading through the statements he could see that none of them had anything to add — they either had not been there or had seen and heard nothing. Lots of impressions about Oliva himself, however. None of them thought that he would be the suicidal type, despite all that he had been through in recent years.

But there was something there. A switch seemed to click inside his head. Yes, where was it? He sorted through the papers again. Something had caught his eye but only now did he see its significance. Where was it? Was his mind dulled by working through the night, fuelled only by alcohol? Had he made it up, or dreamt it? If it was true, it was huge.

He read and reread the interview statements. There was one word, just one word that he had seen and which had the potential to change everything. Not only Torres's case, but the Amy investigation as well.

Finally, reading the second interview for the third time, he saw it: his eyes must have jumped over it before. But it was there: the neighbour on the first floor.

And the word, that word, the word that had sounded in his head like the screaming whistle of a train.

19

'We'll go in my car.'

Torres was adamant.

'All right.'

They walked through the patio and out to the back street. The paintwork on Torres's Seat Toledo had blistered over the years. Torres squeezed the car out of its tight parking space, barging against the vehicles at either end as he manoeuvred round, and they set off. Cámara wound down the window; there were hardly any electrics in the car, he noticed. Although there was a button for air conditioning. He hoped for Torres's sake that it worked. They did not need it now, but within a month's time it would be indispensable.

He opened a new packet of cigarettes, peeling off the plastic around the top and ripping into the silver paper. The image of a man with an unfeasibly large and festering growth on his neck stared up at him from the packaging. The man also had a long, drooping moustache and looked like a refugee from a 1970s prog-rock band. If the authorities wanted to scare people away from smoking they could at least use ordinary people for the photos. Otherwise the exercise turned into a useless freak show. 'Serves him right,' too many people would think, 'for being a hippy.'

Cámara had already lit the cigarette before Torres asked him to stub it out.

'I've got to keep this car in good nick,' he said unapologetically. 'Might need to sell it some day. If everything goes tits up.'

Cámara did his best to put out the burning end without damaging the rest of the cigarette, and placed it behind his ear for later.

'I still don't think this is a good idea,' Torres said. 'I mean, what good's it going to do?'

It was late in the afternoon. Cámara had gone home and slept shortly before dawn. When he awoke, around lunchtime, he sat up, examined his conclusions of the night before, and finding that they had survived the test of being slept on, decided to act. By the time he got to the Jefatura and located Torres the working day was almost finished.

Cámara was surprised to see Torres in his uniform. He had forgotten about Maldonado's new directive himself, but the fact that his colleagues were following it was unexpected.

'Shut the fuck up,' Torres had said before Cámara could say anything. 'Some of us have responsibilities.'

And this was how they always got you. They promised you regular pay, pensions and perks. And you built something around those promises — a home, a family, children, the rest. Happily you placed the noose around your own neck and stood over the trapdoor. And then one day they threatened to pull the release on you, and only then did you realise how stuck you were, that there was no way out but down. And paralysed by fear and your own stupidity, you did whatever they asked. All it took to bring you into line was to give a little twitch on the lever again.

'What are you doing here anyway?' Torres asked. 'I assumed you would only come in at night.'

'We need to go to the hospital,' Cámara said, 'and see Oliva.'

And after a minor confrontation over their means of transport, they had finally left the Jefatura.

'You shouldn't stick around here anyway,' Torres said. 'Not dressed like that.'

The car moved slowly through heavy evening traffic.

'Take me through this again,' Torres said. 'Why are we going to the hospital?'

Cámara hung his arm out of the open window and drummed his fingers against the outside of the car door, his fingers searching for something to fiddle with.

'Because we have to find out once and for all what caused Oliva to fall. His own will, or the will of others.'

'And you think the hospital will be able to help? We'll get the DNA tests from the material underneath his nails in a few days. That should tell us something.'

'The DNA testing could take weeks,' Cámara said. 'They're backlogged as it is. And you're not going to get this bumped up the queue if everyone thinks it's just another suicide attempt. In the meantime the only person who can really help us might have kicked the bucket.'

'You want to talk to Oliva himself? Good luck. He's in a fucking coma.'

'We need to go round, present ourselves to the doctors and impress on them the importance of doing all they can to get Oliva lucid enough for us to speak to him, even if it's just for a few minutes. You being in uniform will help.'

'Fuck off. What, you think they're not doing everything for him as it is?'

Cámara paused before answering.

'We need to tell them this is now an attempted murder inquiry.'

Torres snorted.

'But it's not an attempted murder inquiry.'

'It is now.'

The car inched forwards before they were stopped at another traffic light.

'You seem to have forgotten,' Torres said in a low voice, 'that we're not on this one together. This is my case. I'm looking into what appears to be an attempted suicide, and the only person who can decide to change it to a murder investigation is — '

'Maldonado?' Cámara could feel a knot forming at the centre of his forehead as he watched Torres slipping away. 'Yes, officially perhaps,' he said. It felt like talking to a child. 'But the doctors don't know that, do they.'

Torres grunted as he shoved the Seat into first gear and they broke away from the traffic with a jerk. The car was not in the best of shape. If Torres ever did decide to sell it he would be lucky to get seven or eight hundred euros for it. Few people had money for anything but the basics these days. Houses, cars — the usual assets that people owned and which might, in an emergency, be sold to raise some cash — were losing value.

If he wanted to, Torres could turn the car around, or simply tell Cámara to get out. For a few blocks Cámara waited for it to happen, for a sudden swerve on the wheel as Torres rebelled against his presence.

'What's the urgency, anyway?' Torres asked as they approached a roundabout. Would he carry on straight towards the hospital or use the junction to do a U-turn? There were four cars ahead of them in the queue waiting to pull out.

'There was something in your notes,' Cámara said. The first car set off and they moved forwards. Only three cars ahead of them now before the roundabout.

'When the American girl, Amy, was murdered, one of the neighbours overheard some men around eleven o'clock ringing the front doorbell.'

'And?'

'They called out that they were postmen.'

The second car pulled out into the flow of traffic. There were only two cars ahead of them now.

'So?'

'So they almost certainly weren't postmen. The witness said that wasn't the normal time for deliveries to be made. That the *cartero* always came later in the morning.'

'Could have been one of the other delivery companies. One of the private ones.'

The traffic lurched forward again. There was now only one vehicle between Torres's car and the roundabout.

171

'Unlikely. They weren't dressed in any uniform.'

'All right. So what the fuck has this got to do with Oliva?'

They were now at the interchange themselves. Torres turned from Cámara to look left, waiting for a gap in the traffic so that he could pull out. The road to the hospital lay ahead; the Jefatura in the other direction.

'In your notes,' Cámara said, 'one of Oliva's neighbours said the same.'

'What?'

Torres was not listening properly, focused more on the traffic flowing heavily from the side.

'One of your witnesses — a man called Hernández — mentioned the same word. *Cartero*. Said he heard it from the intercom. Someone trying to get in from the street.'

A gap emerged in the traffic.

'It was just before eleven o'clock,' said Cámara. 'Only minutes before Oliva went flying from his balcony window.'

Torres pressed on the accelerator and the car shot out.

20

Torres's car rolled gently along the avenue as he drew over to the slow lane and eased his foot off the accelerator. Impatient drivers blew their horns as they pulled out from behind and raced past. Driving at anything short of full throttle, particularly at this time of day, was regarded as a quasi-criminal act.

'We've got two almost simultaneous incidents,' Cámara said.

Torres nodded.

'At the first we've got unidentified men not in uniform trying to get inside the building of Amy's flat by claiming to be postmen, just moments before she's murdered. And in the second . . . '

'And in the second,' Torres said, 'we've got a witness hearing the same word being used on the intercom with the street outside Oliva's block of flats. Seconds before Oliva takes a dive out the window.'

He paused and the car rolled on. The traffic lights ahead of them were on green, but had changed to red by the time they reached them. Torres braked and they came to a halt.

'Coincidence,' he said at last. 'How many times a day does that happen? I have people coming round all the time ringing the bell. People with leaflets, delivery men, the gas men. And nine times out of ten, just like everyone else,

I simply buzz the door and let them in.'

'Exactly,' Cámara said. 'We all do, everyone does. But the point is that your witness didn't hear someone claim to be delivering a package or bottles of *butano*. He said *cartero*. The same word used at Amy's place.'

'What if it *was* the postman?'

'Have you checked? What time does he normally come round to Oliva's?'

The traffic light changed and they set off again. Torres was silent.

'This has to be looked into,' said Cámara.

'It's the slimmest of slim leads. Don't tell me, you've got a *feeling* about it.'

A gentle mocking of each other was a part of their relationship, and they both enjoyed it: it was something they shared, something that told them — and others — that their partnership was different. But it was always in jest, never meant. This time, however, the tone was changing. Was it the uniform? Could the simple act of putting on his official police costume have effected such a change in Torres?

'The only person who can tell us one way or another is Oliva,' Cámara said. 'Which is why we need to talk to his doctors.'

'And you think they're going to pull him out of a coma like magic just because you turn up and snap your fingers?'

The car turned into the final straight before the hospital turn-off. Cámara said nothing.

★ ★ ★

Intensive care was far enough away from the emergency ward for him. He had not expected to be back here so soon, but he could trick his mind enough to convince himself that this had nothing to do with the events of three nights before.

Nothing at all.

Intensive care was supposed to have some degree of control over people coming and going, but it looked as though a steady traffic of non-medical personnel was passing in and out of the swing doors at the end of the unit. In front of the entrance there was a small waiting area, with hard chairs for the anxious to sit on during their lengthy vigils.

Cámara could see half a dozen people scattered around, some dozing, others pacing up and down, a couple chatting nervously.

'That's Oliva's ex-wife, Sonia Busquets,' Torres said. Cámara saw a woman approaching forty with oily skin and dark bleached hair tied back in a ponytail. Her eyebrows were finely tweezered, but she had not put on any make-up that morning. She had probably been there all day.

'I'm not sure if it's a good idea for her to see us,' Torres said. 'If she and the family members start seeing police here they might wonder what's going on. She's going through hell as it is.'

Cámara walked on down the corridor, away from the waiting area. A man in a white coat appeared from the far end walking quickly. Cámara flicked his police badge in his face and caught his attention.

175

'We need to talk to someone about a patient in intensive care. It's urgent.'

The doctor scuttled off, promising to fetch someone for them.

'Subtle,' Torres said. 'Why not announce on the tannoy that we've arrived?'

Cámara ignored him. A few moments later another doctor introduced himself.

'What's this about?'

He was young — perhaps in his early thirties, and looked as if he had not shaved for four days. The rings under his eyes screamed out for sleep. He was coming to the end of his shift, Cámara was certain.

'Inspector Torres,' he said, motioning towards his uniformed colleague. 'And I'm Chief Inspector Cámara. We're from the murder squad.'

At the word 'murder' the doctor gave an almost imperceptible jolt. Cámara had his full attention.

'We need your help,' Cámara said. 'It's a very delicate situation. I hope I can take you into my confidence.'

The doctor listened to Oliva's story, nodding as Cámara explained.

'We were told it was a suicide attempt,' he said, his eyes widening.

'It's very important,' Cámara said. 'We're hitting a brick wall with the case, and the only person who can take us forward is Oliva himself.'

The doctor bowed his head and stared at the ground.

'Whoever did this to him,' Cámara continued,

176

'and I'm convinced he was pushed — needs to be caught. Quickly.'

The doctor was shaking his head.

'His head injuries are quite severe,' he said. 'We don't know yet how much of it is permanent. There's injury to the brain tissue, haemorrhaging, swelling.'

'Is there any way that you can help us?'

Cámara was aware of Torres rolling his eyes.

'Anything at all.'

'Well, we can't just bring him back,' the doctor said. 'There's no button to press. If there was we could do it with everyone in a coma.'

Torres was already shifting his weight on to his other foot, as though to start walking away. They were wasting their time.

'Anything.'

The doctor sighed, his head still bowed.

'What about zolpidem?' Cámara said.

The doctor looked up, surprised.

'Zolpidem?'

'What's that?' Torres asked.

'It's a sleeping drug,' Cámara said. 'They've used it on coma patients. It can wake them up.'

'Look,' the doctor shrugged his shoulders. 'That kind of thing makes for a good news story, but it's not that simple.'

'A sleeping drug that wakes people up?' Torres was mumbling into his beard. 'Pah!'

'But you could try it,' Cámara said.

'We've used it in the past, but the success rates are almost negligible.'

'But not entirely.'

The doctor was still with them; he had not

177

walked away. There was still a reason to insist.

'Very occasionally you may see a slight improvement. But it's not always permanent. And it can only stimulate parts of the brain that haven't been damaged. Even if you saw more brain activity, he might not be able to respond in any meaningful way.'

'But it's worth a try.'

The doctor dropped his head again, his shoulders hunched. He was tired and was losing the energy to resist.

'Do you have any in stock?' Cámara asked.

'Not much,' said the doctor. 'We're running out of a lot of drugs at the moment.'

'But you've got some zolpidem.'

The doctor sighed.

'Come on,' he said.

They entered the ward from the far end so as not to be seen by Oliva's ex-wife and family. Cámara and Torres were given flimsy throwaway green robes to place over their clothes, with caps from the same material for their heads and slip-on covers over their shoes.

'Even if he can't speak, he might be able to respond in some way by a squeeze of the hand,' the doctor said. 'Here, take these.' And he passed a box of latex gloves over.

They waited as he administered the drug.

'It will take a while.'

Cámara took a chair and sat by Oliva's bed. The man's neck was in a brace and breathing apparatus stuck out from his mouth, obscuring much of his face. His eyes were closed and heavy bruising stained much of the visible skin. A membrane had been placed over his skull. Tiny whiskers seemed to glisten over his cheek, reflecting the overhead lights.

'How old is he?' Cámara asked.

'Thirty-eight,' Torres said.

'That helps,' the doctor said. 'A bit. The younger you are the greater the chances of coming through something like this.'

'There's no danger, doing this, is there?' Torres said.

'I wouldn't be doing it if there were,' the doctor said. 'No. He'll either respond or he won't. If he doesn't there are no ill side effects from this.'

They sat in silence for a few moments. Cámara tried to get a sense of Oliva, of the kind of person he was. It was almost impossible, though. He lay inert, the only signs of life coming from the machines attached to his body and the unnatural sound of the breathing machine.

Cámara reached out and held his hand. It felt warm and limp.

'Is there anything we should be looking out for?'

'It might be a twitch, or some kind of response. Maybe in his eyes, or his hand. Keep holding it. We'll need a few more minutes.'

The steady electronic beat of Oliva's heart marked the seconds. Cámara imagined the drug moving through his body, willing it to have the desired effect. Then almost without realising it, he started talking to him.

'Diego,' he said, squeezing his hand. 'Diego,

179

we've come to speak to you. We're from the
. . . We're friends, Diego. We need to talk to you.
Can you hear me? Can you hear me?'

Oliva was motionless. Cámara kept his gaze on
his face. If there was any sign, he thought, it
would be there. Perhaps just a twitch in his
eyelids. Anything. Perhaps even a smile.

'Diego, Diego . . . '

Time was passing. Torres was sitting on the
other side of the room. He crossed his arms and
legs. Cámara kept talking, gently massaging
Oliva's hand in his as he spoke. There had to be
something, some reaction from him.

'We need to talk to you about what happened,
about your fall. Can you tell us . . . '

The minutes ticked by.

Torres was the first to make a move.

'It should've happened by now, right?' he said,
standing up. The doctor looked at Cámara, then
at Torres.

'If we were going to see a response I would
have expected something by now, yes.'

Cámara did not move, still holding Oliva's
hand.

'Diego . . . Can you hear me?'

'Perhaps we should leave it.'

Torres was clearing his throat, signalling as
loudly as he could that he thought they should
be on their way.

'As I say,' the doctor began, 'enough time has
passed. Any response . . . '

But Cámara tuned out, not hearing him.
Oliva's body lay as still and leaden as when they
had come in. A last attempt? Five more minutes?

No. Understanding came and with a sudden clarity he saw that this was as much about Hilario as it was about Oliva. Yes, he wanted to talk to the man, but he was conning himself if he thought he could bring people back from the dead — or the near-dead in Oliva's case. The loss of his grandfather, the strange hours, not sleeping properly — carry on like this and he would lose his mind. Coming here and trying this — it was almost the stuff of witchcraft.

He got up and took a last look at the inanimate form lying on the bed, the battered face and broken head. And the burning promise flared in his mind.

I'll get them.

★ ★ ★

Torres had gone on ahead while Cámara exchanged some final words with the doctor.

'Thanks very much.'

'I'm sorry we couldn't help.'

Cámara gave his and Torres's numbers on a card.

'Get in touch if anything changes.'

'We will.'

When he'd finished he stepped outside into the dying light of the day. It was almost dark.

He wended his way through the car park. They had been lucky earlier and had found a space near the entrance. The street lamps overhead were flickering on, casting a pink hue. He stepped from behind a van to the place where he knew Torres had parked. But there was nothing but an empty space.

He heard an engine pulling away and looked up.

In the distance, the Seat reached the end of the car park and pulled out with an angry growl, merging with the traffic on the main road and disappearing into the city.

21

'You've got to see this.'

Alicia was in the sitting room watching a twenty-four-hour news channel on television. Cámara shuffled over towards her, his limbs still heavy from the long walk from the hospital.

'What's going on?'

He sat on the arm of the sofa. On the screen he saw a familiar face.

'Emilia?'

'This happened earlier this afternoon,' said Alicia. 'They've been repeating it on a virtual loop ever since. Watch.'

The Mayoress of Valencia appeared to be holding a press conference in the centre of the city. Just behind he could make out the rose window of the cathedral and people making their way around the Plaza de la Virgen. Emilia Delgado was wearing a bright yellow dress with a red carnation buttoned to her collar. A former cabaret performer, she never did understatement when it came to make-up, and her eyelids sparkled with some golden glitter added to her thick dark blue mascara. The crow's feet around her eyes and mouth were only partially disguised, however: she appeared to have aged since last he'd seen her. He was surprised she had not resorted to Botox injections or plastic surgery.

There was history between Cámara and

Valencia's longest-serving chief executive. Years back Emilia had tried to interfere in Cámara's investigation of the murder of bullfighter Jorge Blanco. Cámara had done his best to sidestep her blocking tactics — there had been local elections at the time, which she went on to win for a record fifth time — but her sidekick Javier Flores came close to scuppering everything. Ambitious, unscrupulous and allegedly Emilia's lover, Flores was now hovering in the background as Emilia spoke to the cameras. Wearing a peppermint green jacket with an orange-and-pink checked shirt and brown leather tie, he was hard not to notice.

Aunque la mona se viste de seda, Cámara thought to himself, *mona se queda*. Even when she wears silk, a monkey is still a monkey.

After the bullfighter case, Flores had played a part in a subsequent investigation: the kidnapping of Sofía Bodí, leading Cámara to the guilty party, but again, only for his own benefit. He was the worst kind of politician: self-obsessed, manipulative and drawn inexorably to power like a fly to shit. They said Emilia only allowed him into her bed on occasion, playing her councillors off one against another through sexual favours. Deep down, Flores probably hated her. Now he stood at her side as she spoke and displayed a grave, concerned face.

' . . . *which is why we must condemn these acts in the strongest possible terms.*'

'What's she saying?' Cámara asked.

'It's about the riots again,' Alicia said, not taking her eyes off the screen. 'They're still going on about them. I hadn't realised how bad it got — it all happened while we were busy with Hilario. There were fifty arrests, and fifteen demonstrators and three policemen were wounded. It turned into a pitched battle. Then earlier today Emilia showed up to make a statement where it all took place. Said she had to reclaim the streets for law-abiding citizens.'

'. . . *this cannot be allowed and the perpetrators will be brought to justice.*' Emilia's voice sounded even huskier in real life, like a fully laden cement mixer, supposedly from too much drinking and smoking. A rumour went that she had worked as a prostitute when she had been in cabaret, but if anything the allegations only made her more popular. She was a maverick and knew that many Valencians supported her because she championed the city, wearing her identity as a Valenciana like a badge of honour. No scheme was too grand, no project too costly for Emilia and her home town, not even now, when the coffers were bare and the debts threatening to drown the place for generations to come. For all her faults — her tackiness and authoritarian instincts — the city had become almost her personal fiefdom: her position was never seriously threatened. Other local politicians came and went, some whisked off to Madrid, others shipwrecked by corruption and scandal, but Emilia was always there, as if she had become a permanent fixture. *Valencia, soy yo* went the joke. In the style of Louis XIV, Emilia believed that she was Valencia.

185

Cámara watched as she continued her speech, demonising the protestors, calling for law and order to be restored, and a counter-demonstration to be held to show the city's respect and good wishes for the King. With the people's prayers, she insisted, he would make a full recovery.

'Prayers and a load of public money spent on his private healthcare,' said Alicia.

'So far, so predictable,' Cámara said.

'Wait. Watch this.'

He kept his eyes on the screen. Flores was the first to be hit, with what looked like an egg smashing into the side of his head. His closely cropped head jerked to the side as the projectile impacted. Cámara sat up in his seat.

'Bloody hell!'

'There's more.'

There was something of a scuffle among Emilia's entourage before more missiles came streaming in. The images were blurred as the cameraman had clearly moved and ducked for cover himself. As the image stabilised for a moment on the ground, stones and rocks — broken pieces of masonry or rubble — came into view. The camera then looked back up at Emilia's group. The mayoress was holding the side of her head, doubling up, yet still on her feet. A cracking, thumping sound could be heard as other missiles rained down. More rocks and eggs, pieces of rubbish, what looked like the contents of someone's shopping basket: cartons of fruit juice, half a lettuce and a packet of biscuits.

'Get her out! Get her out!' came a voice. A security man was finally reacting and the images went black just as arms were thrown around Emilia and she was led away from the crowd. The sounds of shouting and whistling carried on for a few seconds, with angry voices calling out against the mayoress.

'Corrupt thieving bastards!' said one, the only discernible voice. Then the recording stopped.

'Wow,' said Cámara, slipping off the arm of the sofa and down next to Alicia.

The footage cut to the news presenter. It was Canal 9, the local channel, sensationalist and heavily controlled by Emilia's party. At the bottom of the screen a red banner appeared with the words: 'Mayoress targeted by terrorists'.

Alicia hit the off button on the remote.

'That's big news,' he said. 'I would never have thought . . . '

'Big news and a big lie to explain it away,' said Alicia. 'Terrorists? Those were ordinary people throwing stuff at her. She can't understand how angry people are.'

'Perhaps Hilario was right.'

Cámara stood up and walked to the kitchen. He was hit by an urge to get out. Suddenly the flat, the city, felt suffocating.

'Do you fancy a picnic?' he asked.

Alicia checked the time on the wall clock: it was almost half-past ten.

'You're not working tonight?'

Cámara shook his head. She got up from the sofa.

'Come on.'

187

A quarter of an hour later they were on the motorbike and heading towards the sea, a rucksack of supplies on Alicia's back. The Avenida del Puerto was empty and the traffic lights were on their side. A few thrilling moments passed and within minutes they reached the Cabanyal beach. They parked on the other side of Las Arenas and crossed the sand, taking off their shoes and feeling tiny soft grains sifting between their toes. It was the first properly warm night of the year.

The waters of the Mediterranean were calm, with small waves barely a few centimetres high gently stroking the shoreline. Cámara stared out at the horizon, the sky just half a shade lighter than the sea. Lights from a handful of scattered ships twinkled from afar. They ate some bread and cold tortilla that had been sitting in the fridge. Alicia opened a bottle of red wine, took a swig, and passed it over.

I love this woman, he thought, a calm certainty appearing within him like a slowly blossoming flower. And I always want to be with her.

The bottle top was wet with her saliva. He placed it against his mouth, lifted the wine and drank deeply.

'I went to the metro earlier,' she said. 'They're carrying on as usual. Daniel said not to worry, that they can manage. Got some new helpers.'

'Good,' he said.

Bereavement moved within him like a storm, sometimes waning, sometimes blowing so hard he thought he would be swept away. With time, he assumed — as everyone always said — it would lose some of its force. Yet now, so fresh, it had an energy that seemed entirely its own, as though he were merely a spectator caught up in its booming and grandiose performance. Mourning for his grandfather might consume him, he thought at times. And yet only now, sitting by the quiet waters of the sea, was he aware of how powerful and embracing his feelings for Alicia had become.

'I should pop over and see them,' he said.

'They're fine without you. You've got enough going on.'

They ate and drank in silence for a few moments, listening.

'I don't know if this is a good time to tell you,' Alicia said. 'But I've got to say it sometime.'

'What's up?' he said, still looking out towards the dark.

'I did some rummaging around about that American girl you mentioned. The one who was murdered.'

He dug his hand into the sand.

'You've found something.'

'Perhaps. I don't know. I was looking at her Twitter account and saw that she had some friends who were also blogging and doing news stuff like she was. There's this English guy who's got a rolling news site on Spain for expats.'

'What did he say?'

'I got in touch. Said I was a friend of Amy's. They've all heard about the murder now and are shocked, of course, and it seems that some are starting to speculate.'

'Go on.'

'The husband was being questioned, so most people are accepting that he did it. None of these people seem to have known Amy personally, just via the Internet.'

'But the English guy?'

'The English guy said something about Amy being on to a big story. He didn't know what it was, but he said she was really excited about it.'

The scoop, Cámara thought.

'Did he know what it was about?'

'No. He just said the last thing she mentioned on Twitter was that she was going to meet some guy who had some info for her.'

'That's it?'

'I checked out her Twitter feed,' Alicia said. 'To have a look, and it was there.'

She pulled out a piece of paper.

'I jotted it down, her last tweet. Here.'

Cámara read.

'*V excited. Off to meet banker with scoop on high-level VLC corruption.*'

He pursed his lips.

'Banker?'

'I copied it exactly.'

He looked back at the sea. The waves had died down completely now and the waters were so flat that the reflection of the night sky barely shimmered.

'Pass me the bottle,' he said.

It was well past midnight before they started heading home.

'I've written an article,' Alicia said as they traipsed back over the sand. 'About — about what happened to Hilario.'

'Oh?'

'I think it says a lot about the way things are going at the moment.'

'Yes. You're probably right.'

'It's being picked up by some of the foreign press,' she said. 'People want to know. A human story that somehow sums up the situation in Spain.'

He pulled on his helmet and climbed on to the bike.

'Good,' he said. 'I'm pleased.'

They took a different route back, wending their way along side streets as they zigzagged towards the flat. Alicia wrapped her arms tightly around his waist: it was one of the most serenely pleasurable experiences for them both. The exhaust hummed deeply, echoing back at them from the buildings lining the traffic-less streets. The mood of the city had been volatile over the past days, veering from riotous to morbidly quiet almost by the hour, but from the looks of things tonight was calm.

Approaching the edge of the centre, they stopped at a red light. Ordinarily he would have jumped it, but he wanted the experience of the ride home to last as long as possible.

As they sat, waiting, something caught his eye.

'What the hell's that?'

Alicia popped her head round from behind him and looked. On the other side of the junction, perhaps a hundred metres away, a van with its engine running was parked at an awkward angle on the pavement. Behind, partially hidden from view, was a branch of Caja Levante. Three men were scuttling around, moving very lightly on their feet.

'I don't believe it,' he said.

There was a small explosion, a cloud of smoke shot into the air and the bank alarm started ringing violently. A second later, two of the men hauled some metal boxes into the back of the van and climbed aboard. Then they set off, screeching down the road before they even closed the doors.

Cámara had not noticed that the lights had turned green. A bank robbery? In Valencia? As though pulling himself out of a dream, he opened out the throttle and made chase.

The van had gone in the direction of the old river bed. Now he was even more aware of Alicia behind him — their combined weight slowed the bike down and where normally he might expect to catch up quickly he struggled to keep the robbers in view. But curiosity more than a will to bring the men to justice was pushing him forwards. Robbing a bank? They should be given a medal.

They sped over a bridge and into the city centre. The streets were not so empty here and a few cars were cruising by. He thought that the van had gone straight over, but he could not be sure.

'There!' Alicia pointed to their right. At the third turning a van — their van? — was disappearing from view. Cámara pulled out, swerving to avoid the traffic, and pushed on.

'It was Daniel,' Alicia called out from behind.

'I could swear it was Daniel.'

Daniel? From the metro? The men had been too far away to see properly. And it was dark.

They reached the corner and turned. The street was empty. Cámara slowed the bike down to glance along each junction as they reached it. If they could catch sight of the tail lights somewhere they might be able to give chase again. At the first crossroads there was no sign of them; at the second, nothing. The third . . . nothing. Cámara sped on to the end of the street and the final junction. Again, no sign of the van.

'*Me cago en la puta.*' Fucking hell.

He turned the bike around and went back to check, heading the wrong way along a one-way street. The van had vanished. In the distance they could hear sirens screeching into action. The police were on their way to the robbed bank.

'Do you want to call it in?' Alicia asked. 'At least we got a sighting of them. Could give a description.'

'Do you think it's Daniel?'

'I, er . . . I don't know,' she said. 'You're right. We can't be sure.'

He sniffed, pulled the helmet strap tighter on his chin, and they shot off.

They had crossed six or seven blocks heading in the direction of the flat before they saw them. They were in one of the less affluent streets in the old part of town. A group of women was gathered at the far end. Some of them were screaming, others crying. As the motorbike

193

rolled ahead, it became clear that tears of joy were rolling down their cheeks.

'Look! Look!' they cried.

Many of them were holding their hands up, bundles of paper clutched between their fingers.

The group was blocking the road, dancing, cheering, shrieking. One of the women approached Cámara and Alicia as they came close, forcing them to stop.

'They told us to wait here,' she cried. Her eyes were like flares. 'They said a miracle would come. I couldn't believe it but now it's happened. Bless them, bless them.'

She waved her hand in front of their faces. A wad of fifty-euro notes was gripped tightly between her fingers.

'We are saved!'

There was a screech of tyres and Cámara looked up. Over the women's heads he could see the van disappearing from view once again as it sped away. The thieves — whoever they were — were not stealing the money for themselves; in Robin Hood fashion they were distributing it among the city's poor.

'You're lucky,' he said, turning back to the woman, a wide grin stretching over his face. 'I'm very happy for you.'

Cámara and Alicia sat on the bike for a few minutes, soaking up the moment. The robber banks had finally been robbed themselves. And just one drop from the ocean of money that had been handed over to prop them up was now returning to the people who had been forced to hand it over in the first place. Justice? This was justice. Let the squad cars giving chase do their best. He would have no part in it.

Perhaps Daniel was involved. If so, he could imagine no one better for such a job.

'It's happening,' Alicia said. 'Whatever it is, it's happening.'

His phone buzzed in his pocket. He reached down and pulled it out to see. The text was from Torres.

Never interfere in my cases again, he read.

He closed his eyes and was about to put the phone away, when it buzzed again and a second message came through.

Oliva is dead.

22

'I know you,'

Cámara raised an eyebrow. The man was of a similar age to him but thinner and younger-looking. His collarbone was visible above the low-cut neck of his T-shirt.

'You're one of the people helping out at the metro refuge.'

Cámara nodded.

'I've been a couple of times. How do you know . . . ?'

'Word's spreading. You can't keep something as cool as that secret for long. Goodness will out.'

'You understand, though,' Cámara said, looking the man in the eye, 'it's important that the . . . ' He paused. 'That the authorities don't get wind of it. They will eventually, but we want to keep it going as long as possible.'

'Oh, that's absolutely clear. You think I'm going to call the police or something?' The man laughed. 'No way. Do I look like a rat?'

Cámara smiled.

'You're right. We just need to be careful.'

'That's cool. I'm Berto, by the way.'

'Max.'

They shook hands.

'I heard there was some really great old guy working down at the metro. Giving them ideas and stuff. An anarchist from the old days. But they say he died just, like, a couple of days ago or something.'

Cámara was silent.

'Did you know him?'

'A bit.'

'I wish I'd met him. Sounds to have been like a saint. People speak so highly of him.'

Cámara cleared his throat. An 'anarchist saint'. Hilario would have loved the contradiction.

'He was a good man.'

'So what do you think?' Berto said, glancing around them.

They were standing in a large empty room on the ground floor of an old building. Perhaps not long before it had been a shop or a workshop. A few chairs were scattered around and small groups of people were sitting and standing, discussing points from the lecture that had just finished.

'I was passing by,' Cámara said. 'The notice outside looked interesting, so I thought I'd pop in.'

'It's just a beginning, of course,' said Berto. There was an enthusiasm and optimism about him that Cámara warmed to. 'But I think there's going to be more and more stuff like this going on. Lots of groups springing up spontaneously.'

'But you think you can do it? Really step outside the system, set up an independent local economy?'

Berto tilted his head to the side.

'The question is whether the status quo is viable,' he said. 'And if you believe it isn't, then you have to look to alternatives. It may be a case of trial and error, but we have to try. Otherwise we're all going down, even the politicians and the banks and everyone who wants to keep going as if nothing has happened.'

A new local currency, bartering, interest-free credit for small businesses, a food bank, neighbourhood schemes to help the homeless — Cámara had heard all these being mentioned during the tail end of the talk. He had decided to walk to work that night, hoping that stretching his legs would help lift the heaviness that lingered in his body after sleeping through most of the day. And the lights from the meeting and notices outside had drawn him in.

Could something like this really work? And if it got off the ground could it survive? Or would it decay and turn into something lifeless, like so many other 'good' causes? Perhaps Berto was right. Perhaps he was not asking the right questions.

But the word 'banks' produced a spark, a light, and he decided to see if it led anywhere.

'What do you know about Caja Levante?' he asked Berto.

'Caja Levante? What, you looking to buy shares or something?'

Berto smiled.

'Just an interest.' Cámara made a punt. 'All the banks seem crooked, but there's something about Caja Levante that makes me think it's a little bit worse.'

Berto sniggered.

'Yeah, you could say that. They've only been propping up Emilia and her party for the past twenty-five years, spending public money to do so. The whole thing's totally corrupt. Our taxes go straight into their pockets. They can hardly be bothered to hide the fact these days.'

'All the big building projects, you mean. The opera house, Formula One . . . '

'That's just the tip of the iceberg,' said Berto. 'That's just the visible stuff. There's far more under the surface.'

'You know about this, then?'

'I'm an economist by training. Yeah,' he said, 'I know I don't look it. Worked at the university for a while before I jacked it in. You look at the numbers and you realise the whole thing's got to collapse, sooner or later. So I started doing stuff like this, setting up local initiatives. My way of trying to give something back.'

'Let's hope it's a success.'

'It will be. It has to be.'

'But hold on a minute,' said Cámara. 'You were saying about Caja Levante. There's more we don't know?'

Berto waved a hand in the air.

'Much, much more. It will all come out in the end.'

'You don't . . . ' Cámara started, trying to feel his way forward, to see if this could lead somewhere. 'Do you know of someone there called Felicidad Galván?'

Berto squinted at him.

'What's this about?'

'That old guy at the metro refuge, the one you

mentioned,' Cámara said. 'He wanted me to sniff around a bit.'

'OK, cool. I get it.' Berto smiled. 'Well, listen, I used to hear stuff at the faculty. Some of the guys there were from Emilia's lot. They talked, you heard things. How much of it was actually true, I don't know.'

'Do you know Felicidad?'

Berto shrugged. 'Not personally, but everyone knows of her. She's a powerful lady, high up in the Caja Levante, head of the development and investment department. That's just her official post, though. She's probably much higher up in the unofficial bank hierarchy, if you see what I mean.'

His eyes widened and he spread his fingers out, like a magician.

'She's the *éminence grise*.'

'So what does she do?'

'Pff. Pretty much everything, as far as I can gather. Not much happens at Caja Levante without her knowing about it. And she's a party member, so she's well in with Emilia and local government. They use her like their private banker. No checks, balances, anything.'

'What I want to know is how something like that could ever happen?' Cámara asked.

'That's easy,' Berto said. 'They've got a slush fund. Paying everyone off. Not just their own people but opposition politicians, trade union leaders, judges. Whoever they need to keep things sweet. There's this massive web of corruption, and no one's ever going to talk about it because it's not in anyone's interest. There's too much dosh at stake.'

'Where's the money for the fund coming from?'

Berto pursed his lips.

'Political backers? Private companies? I don't know. The truth is that the money is starting to run out for the party these days. Everyone's feeling the pinch, even big companies. So it's a bit of a mystery, but they're obviously getting it from somewhere.'

'And Felicidad is in charge of the fund, right?'

Berto paused.

'Probably. I would think so. But there might be someone behind her. Someone not in the public eye but with connections to the top. That's my guess. It's how these things usually work. It's never quite how it seems. They're like worms, wriggling under the surface, burying themselves deeper and deeper in the shit. And you never know which is the head and which is the tail.'

★ ★ ★

He wrote a note for Laura, deciding against email and opting for pen and paper. Despite the lack of anyone about, an air of suspicion and lack of trust seemed to circulate inside the Jefatura, like mosquitoes looking for fresh blood.

He set out what he had found, giving her the facts as he had come across them, without theorising or conjecture. It was better to let her come to her own conclusions and then compare.

When he had finished, he folded the sheets of

201

paper, sealed them in an envelope and then headed upstairs. Laura's office was locked, as before, and there seemed little chance of getting the spare key again without raising suspicions, so he slipped the envelope under the door, hoping that Laura — and only Laura — would see it in the morning.

It was unorthodox and he was taking a risk by acting like this with someone so keen on doing things by the book, but he felt that he had no other option, given the circumstances.

Back in the murder squad offices, he checked the Webpol intranet service to see if there were any official developments in either the Amy or Oliva cases. He had not expected any notes from Torres after his text message of the night before. Now, it seemed, his colleague was not even writing up anything for viewing on the system.

He rubbed his hands through his hair and was about to turn the computer off, but switched the screen to have a quick look at the news stream coming from the incident room instead. Several flashes glared up, written in capital letters. They were coming directly from the ministry in Madrid. Warnings of serious civil unrest . . . political developments in the capital . . . urgent measures . . . cancelling of all leave . . . economic upheaval . . . protection of bank buildings.

He stared, soaking in the words. No one was spelling it out, but he had a dark certainty about what was happening.

His phone rang. It was Alicia.

'Hello, *cariño*,' he said.

'Max. That article I wrote.'

Her voice was high, her breathing irregular.

'The one that was picked up by the news syndicates.'

'What about it?' he asked.

'Someone doesn't like it.'

The line hissed.

'I've just received a death threat.'

23

The smell of Hilario overwhelmed him as he stepped inside the flat — citrusy and smoky, a blend of the cologne his grandfather used to wear and the joints he rolled. It stopped Cámara in his tracks for a second, the presence — and absence — of the dead man.

After a pause, he managed to close the door behind him, trying to put a brake on his imagination as it ran away with images and scenes from the past, even variations on the present — a present where Hilario was still with him. Perhaps cooking dinner, talking of what had happened that day at the metro, plans for the future, invitations — always — for him to think in new and different ways. His grandfather had annoyed the shit out of him at times, but he never allowed you to sit still and fall into sleepy comfort; he had kept him engaged and challenged. Perhaps that was the greatest gift, the most important lesson, that he had passed on.

The urge to grab the tin of home-grown pulled at his insides, but he pushed it away. There were things to attend to first.

Alicia was asleep: he could hear faint snoring coming from their bedroom. The threat had come in an email — she had printed it out and left it on the table for him to read. It was short and grotesque. Alicia was accused of damaging the reputation of the country abroad through her article, which was condemned as a series of outrageous lies. She was guilty of treason and would be punished. If she stopped writing her lies her life might be saved, but if she continued, her throat would be slit and her body fed to the dogs.

There were threats and threats. An analysis could sometimes determine how dangerous they were by taking into consideration things like the length of the text, the use of specific words and their frequency, or the timing. After the initial surge of anger — and sometimes panic — had died down, Cámara's preferred method was to forget about them. If they then started appearing in his dreams or popping up unexpectedly in his mind later on, he would give them another look and wonder about taking action.

With this one, however, that was going to be more difficult: he was too emotionally engaged.

Down the corridor the snoring had stopped: Alicia had fallen into a deeper sleep. He leaned against the wall; the jar on the shelf grinned at him.

Ten minutes later, as he took a last drag on the joint, heaviness finally seeped into him. He undressed and lay down next to Alicia's motionless body. The sky was already lightening with the first rays of dawn. He did not hear the helicopters as their blades began chopping the air overhead.

★　★　★

Alicia was up and the television was blaring. He lifted himself out of bed and shuffled towards the living room.

'How much cash have you got on you?' Alicia asked as he walked in.

He patted his naked chest, as though searching for a wallet.

'Right now, not very much.'

There was no smile on her face.

'Perhaps fifty or sixty euros,' he said. 'I don't know.'

And then he understood: the messages from the ministry the night before; the expression on her face.

'It's happened.'

He grabbed a blanket from the back of the sofa, covered himself and sat next to her. The news showed aerial shots of thousands of people in the street gathered outside what looked like a bank building. The picture then cut to angry faces, people shouting and holding placards, an old woman beating the television camera with her stick. At the bottom of the screen, in large capital letters, flashed the word *corralito*. It was what everyone had been dreading for months.

'They've closed the banks,' Alicia said flatly. 'Trying to stem a capital flight out of the country. They say billions have gone over the past few days so they have no choice. There's a twenty-four-hour freeze on all non-commercial transactions, then as of tomorrow we can only take out two hundred euros per person per week from our accounts.'

'They've gone bankrupt,' Cámara said softly.

Part of him had known, had seen this coming when the cryptic messages started coming through from Madrid the previous night. The Spanish had taken the word from the Argentinians, whose own financial meltdown years before had been termed the *corralito*. People had been mentioning it as a possibilty in Spain, but he never thought that it would actually happen. Now he realised that he should have gone to the cash machine there and then and taken out as much as he could, should have warned everyone he knew. But the death threat against Alicia had distracted him.

'You'll be lucky if you get paid,' Alicia said. 'They'll have saved all their friends, let them get their fortunes out of the country, and now we've got to pay for their fuck-ups. There'll be worse to come, I'm sure. It's going to be like Argentina. Any money still in the banks will be worthless soon.'

It was only now that he became aware of the sound — perhaps that was what had woken him in the first place. It was just past eleven o'clock in the morning — he had barely slept at all. From the street came a clattering metallic din: it was why Alicia had the volume on the television turned up so high. Still clutching the blanket around him, he stepped over to the window and opened it. Immediately the sound from outside grew louder.

'What the . . . ?'

From almost every flat, every open window, women were leaning out and banging cooking pots as loudly as they could, creating a clashing, thundering racket. Down at street level, people dashed about, some with whistles in their mouths, others climbing into their cars to blow the horn. A general outpouring of rage was exploding into sound all over the city.

'I should go,' Cámara said. He dropped the blanket back on the sofa and walked over to the bedroom. Alicia glanced briefly at him before turning her attention back to the news.

'Have you found your uniform?' she asked.

'No,' he called back.

'I don't suppose anyone's going to care about things like that on a day like this,' she mumbled to herself.

By the time he was dressed, she was sitting at the computer. The printout of the death threat had gone, presumably thrown in the bin.

'Be careful,' Cámara said, leaning down to kiss her. 'I'll call.'

'I'm going to have a very busy day,' she said.

The city appeared to be operating to a different, more frenetic and less predictable rhythm. He took an indirect route to the Jefatura, partly because some of the streets were filled with angry crowds blocking the way as they concentrated around bank entrances, as though hoping that by their sheer weight of numbers they might open them again and reclaim their money. But he was also curious to gauge the mood.

In some areas of the city a degree of normality appeared to be operating: schools and shops were open and people were going about their business, albeit with worried expressions. The helicopters never stopped circling overhead. As he turned a corner he saw smoke billowing from a building and a team of fire engines trying to fight it: the flames were coming from a Catalan-owned supermarket chain. Valencia had always had a complicated relationship with its more affluent neighbour to the north. It looked as though a backlash in the guise of ancient regional rivalries was already under way.

He parked the motorbike at the back of the Jefatura. Two policeman were standing outside the front entrance.

'We need to see your ID,' said one.

'New rules,' said the other. 'It's a high alert.'

Cámara flashed his card at them and was about to step inside, but paused.

'I think I need something to eat first,' he said.

'Pepe's has set up a credit system for police,' the first guard said. 'In case you haven't got any cash on you. You can pay him back later. Half the riot squad's in there now on their break.'

'Thanks.'

Pepe's was the nearest bar to the Jefatura. Cámara usually avoided it, if only because it was always full of other policemen, but today he decided to make an exception. Better to hang on to the little cash he had on him — he did not know when he might be able to get any more.

A crowd of men in dark blue uniform, military-style caps and heavy tie-up leather boots was taking up much of the space inside. Cámara found a free stool at the bar and sat down. After a brief wait, Pepe came over. Cámara reached for his ID card but the bar owner stopped him.

'It's all right. I know who you are.'

Cámara looked surprised.

'Some of the lads have mentioned you. And I've seen you walking past. What can I get you?'

Cámara ordered some snails in tomato sauce, tortilla, sardines and a *café solo*. Pepe jotted down the amount in a red book hanging from a string next to the till.

'I'll keep a record and just pay when you can,' he said. 'We're all in this together.'

'I'll pay now,' Cámara said. His hand was already reaching down into his pocket for the cash. Something about the look in Pepe's eye, about the atmosphere in the bar, disturbed him. This was false generosity, he felt certain. More, much more, would be expected in return.

'You sure?'

Cámara placed a twenty-euro note on the counter. And it was strange how this piece of paper that ordinarily had only a modest importance now seemed to glow with rare value. Pepe snatched it up greedily.

'As you wish,' he said.

Cámara glanced around at the other officers eating and drinking — all of them in the bar owner's debt. Pepe, he noticed, was taking longer than was necessary to bring him his change.

He ate hungrily, mopping up the snail sauce with chunks of bread. There was mint and a hint of rosemary there, but Pepe was no master chef. He had been fooled into coming by the offer of a 'free' meal. Now all he wanted to do was to get out as soon as he could.

It took him a couple of minutes to work out

why he felt so uncomfortable, but as his gaze was arrested by the television in the corner, he began to understand. Every officer there — and they were all police, by the looks of them — was watching it. A press conference was taking place and a man he had seen before — but never in this context — was talking in front of a bunch of microphones. At the bottom of the screen he read the banner: 'Francisco Soler, leader of the LOP'.

He tapped the policeman nearest to him on the shoulder.

'What's the LOP?' he asked.

'The Legionaries of Order and Progress,' came the reply. 'Soler's party.'

Cámara shivered.

Francisco Soler — they all knew him, but Cámara had only come across him as the head of a security firm, not the leader of a political formation. In his early sixties, Soler was a big man with a compact, hard-looking head. His hair was cut almost to his scalp, and his features were round and fatty. His bottom lip was loose and pulled slightly at the corner, while rimless rectangular glasses perched on the bridge of his nose. There was a problem with one of his eyes: the right one was almost veiled from view as he tipped his head to the side — his usual posture. Only when he lifted his face was it visible: a white ball sitting in a smaller socket. As he got carried away by the occasion, his eyebrows rose to make a point, and the strange eye came into view, swivelling and flicking upwards into his skull and then down again.

People in the street called him *el tuerto* — the one-eyed man.

And now he was talking on television, not trying to sell his services as head of a security firm, but making a political speech. Some of the words had already filtered into Cámara's consciousness: 'the unity of Spain'; 'the challenges of immigration'; 'a historic moment'; 'a return to ancient values'.

The name of his party said it all: 'order and progress' had been the watchwords of the Franco regime.

Cámara ate quickly; he had seen enough.

'Spain needs more men like Soler,' Pepe said as he cleared away Cámara's plate. 'Good men, strong men. His time has come.'

A cheer went up from the members of the riot squad. Cámara looked back at the television. Francisco had an angry and determined expression on his face.

'Catalonia and the Basque Country must for ever remain part of Spain,' he said. 'The calls for independence stop here. I call on the armed forces to carry out their constitutional duty and defend the territorial integrity of the country. The soul of Spain is at stake. The separatists should be stopped at once.'

'That's what we need,' said Pepe. 'Stop them in their tracks. They're only using the crisis to their own advantage. But we'll show them. Fucking Catalans.'

The riot policeman standing nearby turned his head.

'Don't worry, Pepe. We've got it covered.'

Cámara walked out. He was still in the street, halfway back to the Jefatura, when his phone buzzed. It was a message from Laura.

The results from the científicos have come in. Need to talk ASAP.

24

'If they'd waited a day longer to do these we might never have got the results.'

Laura asked him up to her office to talk things through.

'Everyone's trying to act like normal, but the place is close to paralysis. This morning I saw policemen supposed to be on patrol driving the squad car to the supermarket to stock up on food. How's that for helping to keep people calm? There'll be nothing left on the shelves by the end of the afternoon.'

Cámara sat in a chair next to her desk and looked around, trying to pretend it was the first time that he had been in there. The smell of air freshener was almost overpowering.

'Nice place.'

'Yes, I feel rather guilty up here on my own. Things can get pretty cramped down in the murder squad offices, right?'

Cámara smiled.

'Sometimes. It's not all bad, though.'

Laura tapped a pen on the surface of the desk.

'The uniform business?'

'I notice you're not wearing one.'

'I don't have to answer to Maldonado.'

Cámara lowered his gaze. The subtext was clear: Laura had as low an opinion of the head of the murder squad as Cámara did. But that on its own was not enough for there to be a connection between them. He still did not know how much he could trust her.

'I got your note,' she said. 'I understand you've been working nights.'

'It seemed appropriate. At least for a while.'

'The, um, the death in the family. Yes, I heard. I'm very sorry for your loss.'

'Thank you.'

'I don't know why they force people to return to work so soon. You should be given more time off.'

'I prefer it this way.'

She paused.

'Yes. Takes your mind off things.'

'I'm a detective. This is what I do.'

She looked at him with a question in her eyes. The dynamic of the conversation was shifting and curious. They were in her office, which gave her a certain authority. And for a brief moment it was as if she were Cámara's superior. Yet at the same time, as she tried to control the conversation, Cámara slipped through her fingers like a live, silvery fish.

She needed him. Her attempts to find Amy Donahue's killer had so far come to nothing.

'The American ex-boyfriend,' she began. 'I don't know if you heard.'

Cámara shrugged.

'He was in Madrid the whole time. Never came to Valencia in the end. I got a report sent over. They interviewed him. Alibis. He wasn't here. It wasn't him.'

'And Ruiz Costa?'

She pursed her lips.

215

'He's free. The tests came back on the rubber marks on Amy's hands. It doesn't match any of Ruiz Costa's shoes. There's not enough on him. Yet.'

'You still think . . . ?'

'We can't rule it out. So he used another pair of shoes, one we haven't found yet.'

'What about the bullets? Did those results come through as well?'

She paused before answering.

'Yes, but they're inconclusive about a silencer being used.'

'Even in as noisy a city as this, I can't imagine five gunshots going off without someone noticing.'

'True. In which case perhaps it was Ruiz Costa who used a silencer.'

He let it go. Statistically, as she had pointed out before, she was right. Besides, she needed to keep face.

There was a box of sweets on the desk. She leanted over, picked it up and offered one to Cámara.

'A present,' she said. 'From a battered wife. We helped sort her husband out for her.'

Cámara grinned and took a sweet.

'Thanks. At times like these you never know when you're going to get your next meal.'

'It's not looking good,' she said. 'Like everyone else, I keep asking myself if there's going to be a proper revolt of some kind in this country. And maybe this will spark it off — first the King falling ill, now closing the banks. But at the same time I think that if it hasn't happened yet it's because it's not going to happen.'

'Is he dead?'

'The King? No, they made a statement this morning. But no pictures, which probably means he's still unconscious. God knows it would be all over the news, covering up the financial mess, if they could just get him to open up one eye at least.'

Cámara sucked noisily on his sweet. It tasted pink, like roses.

'I think we're going to be quite busy for a while,' he said.

'Yes. I just don't know whose side some police officers are on.'

The ambiguity lay between them like a mist. Cámara was silent, happily shrouded. He knew where his own loyalties were. Laura's, however, were still uncertain to him, although he was beginning to have his suspicions.

'But we should get on.'

He was starting to recognise the expression on her face: she was a compartmentaliser. First one thing, then the next; one file, then another. Her brain functioned like her office layout: neat, ordered and with precious little spill-over.

'It was, of course, unorthodox to get a handwritten note like that under my door, but I appreciate your discretion. With hindsight it may seem that I put my neck out over this case. What happened in the interrogation room with Ruiz Costa has done the rounds. I can tell by the way people look at me in the corridors, even ones I've never met.'

'They'll forget it soon enough. They'll have

forgotten it already, what with everything else.'

'Perhaps. But still, communicating directly like that, privately, rather than via email or a report for all to see on Webpol . . . I appreciate it.'

'I'm beginning to think that handwritten notes should be the preferred means of communicating in future,' Cámara said. 'No other method seems secure these days.'

She smiled, as though having picked up some important clue to his character.

'So this link,' she said.

'Perhaps you could tell me,' Cámara said, 'what the results of the tests on Amy's clothes are.'

'Yes, of course.'

She picked up the file sitting squarely in front of her on the desk and handed it over.

'See for yourself. The hairs found on Amy do not belong to Ruiz Costa.'

'Nor are they Amy's,' said Cámara, glancing through the report.

'No match on the DNA database.'

'So I see.'

'They could be anyone's.'

'That's right,' he said. 'But only for the time being.'

He handed her the file. She placed it back on her desk in exactly the same position it had been before.

'I don't have it here,' she said, 'but I did manage to see the results of another test the *científicos* were running at the same time as ours.'

'The Oliva case?'

'Inspector Torres is working on it.'

'What did it say?'

'I don't suppose I'm betraying a confidence here. They gave me the wrong report — Torres's instead of this one. I'd already read it before I realised the mistake and handed it back.'

Cámara smiled.

'They were checking the DNA of material found underneath Oliva's fingernails,' he said.

'You're already aware of it, I see. I understand you and Torres are friends.'

'So what did it say? The report?'

'It's not Oliva's. Organic material — skin — from two other people. Both male, but again, no match from the database.'

Cámara threw his head back.

'So there was a struggle,' he said. 'He was pushed.'

'Inspector Torres wants to turn it into a murder investigation.'

Cámara sat up straight.

'But Maldonado is refusing,' she said.

She looked down at the desk, drumming her fingers on the file. There was a sense of danger: neither wanted to say another word about it.

'But back to our own case,' she said. 'This theory of yours.'

Cámara took a deep breath and crossed his fingers over his chest.

'As far as I can see,' she said, 'we haven't got much else.'

★   ★   ★

Castro was alone in the murder squad offices, her chin resting on her fist as she stared at a computer screen. She looked up as Cámara walked across, a crumpled sheet of printed paper in his hand.

'If you get a moment,' he said, 'perhaps you could take a look at this.'

She took it from him without question and quickly read the violent, threatening text.

'There may be some patterns there — the language used, that kind of thing,' Cámara said. 'There's a database on Webpol somewhere. Not complete, but it might give some indication — in case there's a match.'

Castro looked up at him anxiously and nodded.

'Of course,' she said.

'And then there's the email address it was sent from. Almost certainly masked in some way, and I'm assuming — if they're not total idiots — that a proxy server was used. But you never know.'

'I'll get on to it,' she said. 'Can I ask who . . . ?'

'My friend,' Cámara said. 'My partner. Her name's Alicia Beneyto.'

Castro scribbled it down on the paper.

'OK.'

'Thanks.'

He turned to leave.

'It's probably nothing, but you never know.'

'Absolutely.'

'And if you don't mind, perhaps you could keep this to yourself.'

Castro was silent as he closed the door behind him.

★ ★ ★

Daniel was away.

'He just left,' Dídac said. 'Don't know where he's gone. He'll be back sometime, I suppose.'

Dídac was on dinner shift along with half a dozen others.

'We're getting more food than ever now,' he said. 'Everyone's so sad about Hilario they want to give us more. That, and a feeling that a revolution might be just around the corner.'

Cámara walked across the ticket hall to look for Alicia. The metro station felt subdued that night. It looked as though they had about the same number of people as usual, but the tone had changed subtly. The sense of fun was diminished: there was no music, no sound of children laughing.

'The clown's not coming back,' Alicia told him when he mentioned it. 'Got a chance to do some work in Germany, so he left.'

'Working as a clown?'

'No. I wish. Some cousin in Berlin found him a job at a pizza place, working in the kitchen.'

Cámara nibbled some of the leftovers on the table. They tasted old, on the verge of going rotten.

'I sometimes wonder myself,' he said.

'What? About getting an underpaid job as a pizza chef?'

'About getting out. Out of this country.'

'Aren't we all,' she said. 'But not everyone's got an escape route. Ramón was lucky.'

'Was that his name?'

'He'll miss the paellas. The real ones.'

He reached for her waist, pulled her towards him and kissed her.

'If I did ever go,' he said, 'I'd want you to come with me.'

'I'd kill you if you left without me.'

'Thanks.'

'But it might be me leaving,' she said. 'Then I'd be taking you along with me.'

'I can see this will require some intense negotiation.'

His hand lowered from her waist for a second and he stroked the top of her hip with his fingertips.

'Did you get much done today?' he asked.

'I wrote another article. The syndicate want me to file more pieces on the crisis. It seems that foreign newspapers are picking them up.'

'That's good.'

He paused.

'Any . . . Any more word from . . . ?'

'Oh, that? Nah,' she said. 'I'm not . . . I don't think there's anything to worry about.'

She smiled at him; her eyes were tired.

'There's something I want to show you.'

She took him by the arm and led him across the ticket hall. Groups of people sat at the tables, finishing off their dinner. Many of them looked up and greeted him as he passed; he recognised faces from the funeral. A hand reached out and grabbed his; he looked down and saw a face he recognised but could not place — a woman with Ecuadorean features.

'The chemist's,' she said in answer to the question in his eyes. 'That night when the men came.'

'Yes,' he said. 'I remember now.'

'You saved us,' the woman said. 'My friend and I ran, but we watched from the other street. We saw what you did.'

She still held his hand, squeezing it affectionately, and smiling at him. But there was a doubt there as well.

'You're a policeman,' she said at last.

Cámara nodded.

'That's right.'

'So why are you here? Why are you helping us rather than closing this down?'

Cámara shrugged and smiled.

'He's a good policeman,' Alicia said, leaning in to join the conversation. 'One who knows the true difference between right and wrong.'

'I think perhaps that night you saved my life,' the woman said.

And she stood up and kissed him on the cheek.

'Perhaps we'll see you here tomorrow,' Cámara said.

'Tomorrow I'm flying back to Ecuador. I love Spain, but there's nothing left here for me now. I have no work and I'm frightened. There won't always be someone like you around.'

She squeezed his hand again. Alicia led him away.

'If we carry on like this there'll be no one left at all soon.'

The candles were arranged in a semicircle on the ground. No one had been able to find a photograph, but someone had attempted a drawing instead. It was not a perfect likeness of his grandfather, but he recognised Hilario immediately.

'A shrine?' he said.

'A memorial. Of sorts. The children wanted to do it. I couldn't see any harm.'

He felt the warmth rising up from the candles and bent down to take a closer look. Several dozen notes had been pinned to the cork board next to the drawing. He reached out and touched them.

'We miss you.'

'Hilario, our hero.'

'We love you, Hilario.'

He bent his head, tears welling behind his eyes. Alicia crouched down and put her arms around his shoulders.

'It hurts so much,' he said.

'It hurts so much.'

25

Whoever it was would not be content with leaving a message on voicemail. His phone rang, was cut off, then rang again before being diverted once more. By the third time Cámara decided that it probably needed his attention: the damned thing had woken him already so he might as well climb out of bed.

Alicia was not there — the television and her computer were both switched off and the flat felt silent and empty.

Cámara pressed the answer button just before the call was cut off.

'¿*Sí*?'

'Those night shifts are fucking up your body clock. There's no reason for it, you know? Avoiding Maldo's directives isn't cause enough.'

Cámara looked down at the screen of his phone to check who the caller was.

'Torres?'

'What's the matter? Can't you recognise my voice?'

'I just — '

'Yeah, well. Friends are allowed to have arguments once in a while, aren't they?'

'Sure. Of course.'

Cámara sat down. From an open window he could hear the sound of another demonstration: whistles were being blown to the rhythm of several dozen beating drums. A thousand voices chanted slogans that he could not make out.

The clock on the wall told him it was still only mid-morning. Another day with a minimal amount of sleep. He could feel his head spinning. He needed some coffee — litres of it.

'What's going on?'

'Fancy meeting up?'

Cámara paused for a second. He needed to wash and dress and his instinct was to tell Torres to pop round to his flat. Torres had not seen his new home, and he was the only one who Cámara normally allowed to break the division between police life and 'real' life.

'Let's go to our usual place.'

'La Serenita?'

'Yeah. Give me half an hour.'

Almost an hour later they were sitting outside at their usual table. The sun was warm but tolerable and a cooling breeze blew in from the direction of the sea. Torres was dressed in his uniform.

'My favourite time of year,' he said, putting down his *café con leche*. 'Not too hot, not too cold. Just right.'

Cámara was eating a late breakfast: a sandwich of *jamón serrano* and tomato with three coffees lined up in a row, a full sachet of sugar already poured into each one and stirred.

'I've often wondered how you cope in the summer with that beard of yours. I'd be desperate to shave it off come June every year.'

'It's a cross I'm prepared to bear.'

When Cámara had finished eating they smoked in silence for a few minutes. Another demonstration could be heard some way on the other side of the city centre. Down the street, at the entrance to the square, two riot squad men stood with their arms crossed and legs wide apart, a vanguard for the expected trouble to come.

Torres lifted his hand, cigarette stuck between his fingers, and saluted them.

'*¡Viva la revolución!*' he growled.

Cámara flicked his ash on the floor, waiting.

'Chief,' Torres began. Chief — it was his usual, sarcastic and affectionate manner of addressing Cámara, but it felt like an age since he had last used it. 'Chief, this Oliva case. I've got to tell you the truth. I'm — '

'I picked up some new information recently about Felicidad Galván,' Cámara said.

Over the next few minutes he outlined what he had heard from Berto about Caja Levante and the slush fund that Oliva's former boss was said to run. Cámara did not mention his source; it was irrelevant and might cloud things. The important thing was for Torres to be made aware of what he had discovered.

Torres nodded as Cámara spoke. He had hit a wall with his investigation — first the hint of a connection with the Amy Donahue case and then the death of Oliva. Now he was turning to the only person who could help him — the same person he was also, now, in competition with. The fact hung between them.

'You were right,' Cámara said when he had filled Torres in. 'I shouldn't have got involved in your case. But I thought you might want to know

227

about this. It might be worth talking to Felicidad Galván herself.'

Torres's black eyes sparkled.

'The Caja Levante office isn't far from here,' he said.

Cámara threw his cigarette butt on the floor and ground it out slowly with the ball of his foot. The invitation was clear: a chance to work together as a team again. The special *Homicidios* partnership in operation once more. Fuck Maldonado. This is what they should have been doing from the start.

'I need a piss,' he said.

He stood up, went inside and paid before Torres could say anything.

'Reckon I should be on my guard again?' the bar owner asked as he took the money. Cámara patted his pocket: he would soon be running out of cash.

'The riot police are back. Saw them streaming past an hour ago. Someone mentioned another demo. I tell you, this part of town's in danger of turning into a battle zone. Some of us have to make a living.'

Cámara sniffed the air, as though trying to gauge the level of danger.

'I'd be ready to close up quickly if I were you,' he said. 'It's unpredictable times.'

Outside, Torres was finishing the last of his coffee. He looked up at Cámara, the question still present in his eyes.

'Let's go,' Cámara said. 'But let's take the long way round. Those guys with truncheons up there bring out the worst in me.'

Torres got up and smiled.

'How the fuck you ever became a policeman is a complete mystery to me.'

'I could say the same about you.'

'By the way,' Torres said as they turned and walked in the opposite direction to the square. 'Oliva's death. It had nothing to do with the drug they gave him.'

'The zolpidem.'

'That's right. He got an infection. His body was too weak to fight it off. And he slipped away. Thought you'd want to know.'

'Thanks.'

⋆   ⋆   ⋆

It was clear now what the demonstration was about.

The Caja Levante building took up a whole block in Valencia's small financial district. It was a relatively modern structure — built some time in the 1970s, and although not quite an eyesore it was not exactly attractive either. Cámara had passed it a thousand times, aware of its presence but never taking much notice. Now it was interesting because of the large crowd crammed around the entrance and streaming up the street in both directions, cutting off the traffic. Police on horseback were gathered at one end, near the Plaza del Ayuntamiento, while the heavily armoured vans of the riot squad were parked in a tight line, creating a wall of dark blue steel between the seat of finance and that of local government. So far it looked as though the protesters were being allowed to carry on. Members of the *Policía Local* had been drafted in to divert traffic away.

There was no need to ask why the demonstrators were there. Before the *corralito* there had been a general, background anger at the way bankers appeared to have got away with so much as the country's economy began to suffer. Now, however, ordinary people were being affected in a very direct way: after so many years of theft and corruption at high level they no longer had access to their own money.

Cámara and Torres pushed their way through, making slow progress as they tried to approach the entrance. Torres took off his cap, aware that being dressed in uniform in this environment might cause problems.

'Just tell them you've lost all your savings,' Cámara called back to him. It was hard to make themselves heard against the noise of the demonstration.

'What savings?' Torres said.

The crowds at the front were too tight to get through, and for a moment they wondered about calling off their visit.

'Come back tomorrow?' Torres said.

'The place might not be here tomorrow,' Cámara said. 'This lot look like they might burn it down.'

'Let's try round the side.'

The crowds were almost as large and dense at the side of the building, but at least they could force their way through. Some protestors tried to prevent them when they saw Torres's uniform;

230

others did their best to get out of the way.

The men at the door — armed with pistols and truncheons and dressed in a green uniform — were from a private security firm.

'We're from the Jefatura,' Cámara said, waving his card. 'The board has called us in to coordinate efforts.'

'Thank God for that,' said one of the guards, letting them through.

'Don't know how much longer we can hold out on our own,' said the other. 'Whatever you decide just make it quick, will you?'

Executives in any organisation were always on the higher floors — it was a natural law. Cámara headed straight for the lift and pushed the top button.

'Looks like you already know your way around,' Torres said with a grin. The energy from the demonstration and the thrill of getting inside what effectively had been turned into a fortress was lightening up his usually dour expression.

'You might want to put your cap back on,' said Cámara.

The lift went up smoothly and reached the top floor with a muffled, expensive ping.

'Show time.'

A young woman with heavy make-up and an upstaging cleavage was sitting behind a reception counter. Cámara marched up to her, waving his police ID in front of her face.

'Felicidad Galván,' he said. 'Police emergency.'

The receptionist was clearly startled, her nerves on edge from what was going on outside.

'Yes,' she said. 'I mean, no.'

231

Torres took a step forward and snarled.

'Police?' she said. 'Emergency? It's just that Señorita Galván — '

'Is in a meeting?' Cámara said. 'Point us in the right direction.'

The girl's eyes flickered to her left, down a central corridor.

'They specifically said no interruptions.'

But Cámara and Torres were already on their way.

They passed large pot plants, modern sculptures in bronze and concrete — the work of a celebrated Valencian artist — and large paintings of typical Valencian scenes hanging from the walls. Above them, daylight streamed in through tinted and very thick glass, illuminating the top floor yet keeping the heat out. Cámara felt the sweat on his neck drying in the air-conditioned climate: outside the temperature was close to thirty degrees; here it was in the very low and comfortable twenties.

A trolley laden with bottles of water, fruit, a large chrome coffee pot and several plates of cakes and sandwiches told them where the conference room was. Without a pause they walked over. Torres opened the door and they stormed in.

Out of a dozen or so people sitting around a large oval table — walnut, by the black grain, Cámara suspected — Felicidad Galván was the only woman. She sat near the head, two down from a clean-shaven man in his sixties with near-white hair slicked back over the tops of his ears — presumably the president of the bank.

232

It took a moment for everyone to register the new presence in the room: the discussion was heated, several of the bankers were talking at once. No one looked happy.

The president noticed them. He held up a hand and tapped the tabletop with a pen. Eventually the others saw where he was looking and fell silent.

'This is a private meeting,' the president began. 'You need the head of security. He's one floor — '

'Felicidad Galván,' Torres said, his normally muffled voice calling loudly and capturing everyone's attention. He looked across to the one female presence in the room. 'We need to speak to you.'

'Impossible,' the president said, waving his hand as though to brush them away.

'Is it to do with the riot?'

There was the slightest of tremors in Felicidad Galván's voice, barely audible, but Cámara caught it just at the end of her question. The riot, she said. So far the crowd outside was expressing its anger only through its massive presence and power of voice. He guessed that over ten thousand had gathered, but so far there was no 'riot'. It almost made him laugh. These people had no idea — or had forgotten — what real street violence was like, what a terrifying and unpredictable force it could be. Yet a siege mentality had already set in.

'It's an emergency,' he said. 'You must come with us at once.'

She stood up at the sound of his command,

then looked across at the president. He nodded that she could leave.

'I don't like this at all,' he said.

Felicidad walked away from the table. Torres went to open the door. The others sat in stunned silence. Cámara watched as she walked towards him: of average height, she had a fleshy nose, thin lips and speckled brown eyes. Her dark brown hair had been dyed with purple highlights and her walk was slightly lopsided, the left leg swinging round the right as she moved forward. He sensed doubt, fear and the beginnings of defiance in her. They would have to act quickly while she was still caught off guard.

She stepped past him without a word towards the open door held out by Torres. Cámara caught a whiff of sweet perfume. Her white blouse was closed at the neck by a thin brown tie made of some shiny material, perhaps leather.

'Just a minute,' the president called out as Cámara made to leave. 'What's your name?'

'Chief Inspector Max Cámara of Valencia *Homicidios*.'

'Jot that down,' the president said without a pause.

Torres had led Felicidad along the corridor and found an empty office. Cámara followed, entered and closed the door behind him.

'Make it quick,' Felicidad said.

'Diego Oliva,' Cámara said, sitting on the edge of a desk.

She looked at him, puzzled.

'He used to work for you.'

'Yes, I know who he is,' she said.

'So tell us about him.'

'You pulled me out of an emergency board meeting to chat about one of our ex-employees? We've got thousands of hooligans outside trying to storm in and steal whatever they can. And you want to talk about some guy who used to work for us?'

She made to leave. Torres jumped across and barred her exit. She stared at his chest, willing it to go away.

'You know about Oliva being in hospital, right?' Torres said.

'Are you going to get out of my way?'

'No.'

'Just answer our questions,' Cámara said.

'You haven't asked any yet.'

'Did you know Oliva was in hospital?'

She turned, but did not look at him.

'I heard something. An accident. He fell from his balcony.'

'He fell. That's right.'

'He used to work for you,' Torres said. 'Directly under you.'

Her eyes tightened.

'What's going on?'

'We need to know about his time working here,' Cámara said.

'Why?'

'Talk to us and then you can get back to your meeting. There's a crisis on.'

'You're right,' she said. 'And you're wasting my time.'

Again she tried to make for the door, but Torres leaned back on it, making it impossible for her to leave. From outside, the volume of the demonstration began to increase. She looked towards the window on the other side of the office, then back in Cámara's direction without meeting his gaze.

'He worked in the development and investment department,' she said.

'That's yours, right?' Cámara said.

She nodded.

'Help me. I'm still trying to work out what that bit of the bank actually does.'

'It's a liaison section, ostensibly,' she said, failing to keep the sarcasm out of her voice. 'Dealing with the bank's biggest customers.'

'Local government?'

'The building industry, mostly.'

'That's the same thing, right?' Torres said.

'Can we wrap this up?'

'Why did you fire Oliva?' Cámara asked.

'We didn't. His contract came to an end. Several others left around the same time. It was the beginning of the recession.'

'Natural wastage?'

'That's the phrase that's usually used.'

'We heard there was bad blood.'

'What?'

'Between you and him, specifically.'

'That's not true.'

'Some of your co-workers don't agree.'

'Who? Give me names. It's untrue. Diego worked very well for us. Then he had to leave. We couldn't keep him on. It's as simple as that.'

'But he didn't find a job elsewhere.'

'That's very sad.'

236

'And strange, surely,' Cámara said. 'The recession was beginning to hit hard, OK. But someone with his experience could surely have found something somewhere else.'

Felicidad shook her head.

'As I say, it was a shame.'

'You didn't try and help him, put in a good word?'

'Perhaps you put in a bad word,' Torres said.

'That's a lie. How dare you?'

'Made sure he never worked again. He must have been talented to have got a job in your department in the first place. We can't understand why he was unemployed for so long afterwards.'

'I had nothing to do — '

'What do you think happened?' Cámara interrupted.

'What?'

'His fall. What do you think happened?'

'I don't know. I heard it was a suicide attempt.'

'He couldn't afford his mortgage payments any more,' Torres said. 'A mortgage he got from this bank, the bank he used to work for. Then this happens. Don't you find that ironic?'

'It's tragic,' Felicidad said. 'You might find it funny.'

'It's not funny,' Cámara said. He lifted himself off the edge of the table and stepped towards her.

'Diego Oliva is dead. Died three days ago at the hospital.'

Her expression was stable, unchanging.

'And this is now a murder inquiry.'

Her lips were dry. She parted them slightly to wet them with her tongue.

'I understand,' she said. 'Then Caja Levante must do all it can to assist.'

'We'll be sending some people round,' Torres said. 'I expect them to receive full cooperation.'

'Of course. I shall make certain that everyone knows.'

There was another surge in the noise from outside. Cámara wondered how long the riot police would wait before moving in. Things were still peaceful enough, but there was the potential for a lot of trouble if the wrong decision was made.

'You can go back to your meeting now,' he said. Torres stepped out of the way. She paused, then reached for the handle.

'One other thing,' Cámara said.

She turned.

'What's the connection between Oliva and Amy Donahue?'

'Who?'

'An American girl. She was murdered on the same day that Oliva was pushed from his balcony window.'

She looked blank.

'I'm afraid I can't help you.'

★   ★   ★

There was no way out at either of the exits on the ground floor: the demonstrators were packed too tight around the building.

238

'Try the car park underground,' a guard said. 'Then press the button to open the doors. Comes out round the back.'

They took the lift down, walked past several dozen expensive German cars, then climbed the ramp up towards the street. The automatic doors clanged and creaked as they rolled open.

A smaller group of protestors was in front of them, blowing whistles and banging drums.

'Try getting in down there,' Cámara said, pointing at the car park doors just beginning to close again.

'It's the Achilles heel.'

26

It was late evening by the time he got away. The cemetery was about to close and he had to race north, jumping traffic lights and weaving in and out between the cars in order to get there in time. Pulling away from the main road, he took a short cut down a pedestrian path that crossed the fields. It was unpaved and bumpy, but the new shocks meant that the bike could take it. A few evening joggers were surprised to see him and were forced to jump out of his way. One of them, in a theatrical gesture, put out a hand as though to stop him.

The cemetery guard was tidying his office, carrying out his last tasks before closing for another day. He was disgruntled on hearing a late visitor arriving, just five minutes before he clocked off, but his expression changed when Cámara took off his helmet and showed his face. The guard remembered fondly the torchlit funeral of a few days earlier. There had been real feeling there, and although he had never met Hilario and had no idea who he was, he was convinced that a great man had been buried in his cemetery that day. Some things you just know.

'The mason was here this morning,' he said to Cámara, stepping out of his office to shake his hand. 'Did a good job. I made sure of that. I think you'll be happy with it.'

'Thanks.'

'Nice epitaph.'

'He always lived by it.'

The guard nodded and let go of Cámara's hand.

'Take all the time you need.'

Cámara walked under the colonnade round the edge of the cemetery. His legs felt heavy and his lungs seemed to be pushing up into his throat. Another wave of grief: he should have expected it, coming here again, but he had kidded himself that he was getting over it. Now it caught him unawares. He tried looking at some of the other graves to remind himself that he was not the only person in mourning. For every other corpse in its niche, dozens must have cried and suffered. But the names and photos meant little to him, no matter how he tried.

Hilario's plaque was made from a single piece of limestone and sat neatly over the bricks that sealed his grandfather in his tunnel-like tomb. The flies had gone. He could not have borne seeing them again.

He knelt down and placed his fingertips against the masonry, tracing the words.

'*Hilario Maximiliano Cámara Belmonte*'.

Underneath were carved the dates of his birth and death. No crosses or symbols: Cámara had been insistent. The font was plain and undecorative, yet elegant.

At the bottom, in italics, ran a single sentence. Cámara had wondered about putting something there. It was impossible to sum his grandfather up in a single phrase, and he had been about to

241

scrap the idea. But to leave the plaque with just a name and dates did not seem fitting to Hilario's memory either. In the end, as he had watched over the dead body at the funeral parlour, the right phrase had come to him.

It was the single most important lesson that Hilario had taught him:

'No sientas el tiempo perdido sino el que puedas perder'.

Do not worry about the time you have lost, but about the time you may yet lose.

He stood up, disturbed by the emptiness that had descended upon him.

Wiping his face with his sleeve, he made for the exit. Outside, on the other side of the gate, the single eye of the motorbike stared at him, unblinking.

★   ★   ★

The Barrio Chino prostitutes on his street had organised a barter system to keep going through the crisis. Many were holding pieces of card announcing that they would accept food or 'services' from clients with no cash to pay. He imagined queues of plumbers, electricians and restaurateurs quickly forming once word spread.

He skipped upstairs and found the flat empty, but Alicia had been back while he was out. Her computer screen was on and new notes were scattered on her desk. There was no sign of her, though. He thought of giving her a call, but at that moment a text message arrived.

Interviewing and being interviewed. Will be back late. Kisses.

He checked the fridge: there was half a packet of limp salad leaves, some cherry tomatoes and a stick of chorizo. Nestling in the door were two cans of beer: he would be fine. The crust of a baguette lying on the counter helped fill him up. Swallowing the last of it, he went into the living room, picked some files out of his bag and sat down in a chair near the window. Time to go through things again, from the beginning, taking in every detail that they had amassed during the investigation. It was time to see the murder of Amy Donahue through new eyes.

But the lack of regular sleep over several days and seeing Hilario's grave again dulled him. He read the words but understood none of them. After twenty minutes he gave up, pulled off his clothes and climbed into bed. A last look at the clock before falling asleep told him that it was only half-past nine in the evening.

★ ★ ★

He woke just before dawn, images of metro trains and dank dark tunnels slipping from his mind as he pulled himself up and looked around. Alicia's naked body lay next to his, her ribs rising and falling to the slow, steady rhythm of her breathing. He kissed her shoulder, made sure that the sheets were covering her properly, and got up.

The streets were practically deserted at that hour. A three-wheeled van drove past, bearing lettuces freshly picked from the fields to market. The driver had a cigarette hanging from his mouth and nodded to Cámara from his open window. There was a natural camaraderie among the city's very early risers. Sometimes he had experienced it when returning from being out all night.

Two blocks away there was a baker's oven that served most of the bread shops in the neighbourhood. If you banged loudly enough on the door they usually opened and let people off the street buy a couple of loaves.

'You got cash?' the unshaven man said when he opened. 'We're not giving credit. And we're not interested in any new local currencies or barter systems either.'

Cámara pulled out the last note from his pocket and showed it to him.

'How much do you want?'

Armed with some bread, spinach pasties and two slices of pizza, he strolled back to his street, hopped on the Kawasaki and sped off to the Jefatura.

Azcárraga was at reception on his own.

'You must be about to finish,' Cámara said.

'Another hour to go,' said the sleepy policeman. 'They're changing my shifts again. Don't know if I'm coming or going.'

'Here. You hungry?'

Cámara handed him a slice of pizza.

Azcárraga looked nervously up at the security cameras above the doors.

'Not supposed to eat or drink anything at the desk.'

'Well, look the other way, then.'

Azcárraga smiled.

'*Salud*,' he said, raising the pizza like a drink. Cheers.

'Coffee machine working?' Cámara asked.

Azcárraga leaned down and pulled up a flask.

'Have some of mine,' he said, pouring a cup. 'The piss that machine makes will kill you.'

He almost had to force himself to sit down at his desk. Over the past days he had felt increasingly uneasy in the murder squad offices and now it took all his willpower to enter the room. It was empty — far too early, still, for any of his colleagues to come in — but every piece of chipped furniture, every screwed-up ball of paper in the waste bin and every broken tile on the floor reflected the tensions and low morale in the group. The real poison around here was not manufactured by machines, but by people. By Maldonado.

Azcárraga's coffee was lukewarm, but drinkable. Within a few moments he began to feel its effects. Pulling the files out of his bag and laying them on the desk and on the floor in a rainbow around his chair, he began to concentrate on Amy and the investigation. After a few minutes' warming up, the computer flickered at him as well, and his eyes darted between paper and pixels as he took up the details once again of the American girl's murder and what they had learned so far.

Never forgetting Oliva.

Witness statements, reports, notes from the interviews with Alfredo Ruiz Costa, observations

245

from Albelda, details and facts gathered from social media sites: Lozano and Castro had been looking at everyone who was connected with Amy on the Internet, checking their Facebook and Twitter accounts, blogs and websites. Meanwhile a patrol had been checking up on Ruiz Costa since he had been released from custody: Amy's husband was spending little time at the flat. A relative — an aunt, by all accounts, a sister of his mother — had come round and he had gone to stay with her. They were not keeping formal tabs on him, but a policeman asking neighbours an occasional question could give them enough to go on for the time being.

And for the most part the information tied in with everything they already knew or had surmised. Nothing new or fresh jumped up at him.

Until he went over Albelda's notes for the third time. Which was when he saw something that caught his eye: the gym opposite Amy's flat, and its owner. Albelda had done a thorough job, trawling through the records to find every piece of information that he possibly could about the witnesses he had talked to, the people who had been closest to Amy at the time her life had been extinguished.

And the name he read on the piece of paper lying on the floor at his feet sent a chill up his spine.

27

He only became aware of the footsteps at the last moment, as they approached the office door. He turned as the handle spun and looked up. It was Laura.

'I thought I'd find you here,' she said. 'I needed to catch you before you left.'

They took the lift.

'The first shifts will be coming in soon and we won't be disturbed up here,' she said.

'There's something I want to talk to you about,' Cámara said.

'Good.'

They stepped inside her office and Laura closed the door behind him.

'You go first.'

He had picked up the papers from the floor of the murder squad office and now spread them on Laura's desk.

'The gym opposite Amy's flat,' he said. 'I think we should take a second look at it.'

Laura fell into her chair on the other side of the desk, her mouth open with surprise.

'It's officially owned by a private security company,' Cámara continued. 'Protegival. I've come across them before. They do all sorts — guarding shopping centres, office buildings, patrolling industrial estates. But they're mainly known for operating in the nightclub and prostitution business. Almost every brothel in the local area has Protegival men on the door. You can always spot them — they have dark green, military-looking uniforms with a red, shield-shaped badge on the shoulder.'

Laura nodded as he spoke.

'I know some of this,' she said. 'But go on. I haven't been in the city for long — I'm sure there are gaps in my knowledge.'

'They're something of an institution in Valencia,' Cámara said. 'Because they're everywhere and because they sometimes get into trouble. There have been cases brought against their guards on more than one occasion, usually for excessive violence. Two or three years ago one woman had to have her face rebuilt after falling foul of Protegival men at a disco.'

'What happened?'

'The guard got off. Not guilty.'

'You're kidding.'

'There are reasons to suspect that the company has powerful friends. The head of the organisation is a man called Francisco Soler. Former military commander — he left the army in 1982, after the Socialists got into power for the first time. Which is when he set up the security company.'

'And you're saying the gym opposite Amy's house belongs to him.'

'To Protegival, yes. I was aware that they had one in the city somewhere. I just hadn't clocked that it was that one. Presumably they use it to train and beef up their guards. The thing is, they've been operating in the city for the past thirty years, and they've built up a network of powerful connections.'

'What are you saying?'

'I'm saying that working side by side with various police organisations over that time has created a bond between Protegival and a certain number of our colleagues. Only last year the director general of police here in the city awarded medals to half a dozen of Soler's guards. Meanwhile Protegival has its own training academy where, among other things, they teach recruits how to handle explosives and how to pass the necessary exams to get into both the *Policía Nacional* and *Policía Local*.'

Laura pressed her fingers to her temple, listening.

'Quite a few of the people who work with us here in the Jefatura,' Cámara said, 'were trained by Soler's organisation before joining us.'

'Is there anything wrong with that?'

'Perhaps not on the face of it, I agree. But what I didn't know until a few days ago is that Soler is not only head of the Protegival. He's also the leader of some shadowy political party called the LOP.'

Laura sat up.

'Yes, the Legionaries of Order and Progress,' she said. 'I know about them.'

'Soler was on TV a couple of days ago,' Cámara said. 'The day of the *corralito*. He rarely appears in public. But he was holding a press conference as a political leader. Talking about upholding the unity of Spain, sending troops into Catalonia and the Basque Country.'

There was a moment's silence. They were

straying into politics — not the petty, personal kind that interfered with their work as police officers, but the politics of parties and ideologies that could split the country apart.

'It almost makes you wonder what his guards are really for,' she said, lowering her voice. 'Make the connection between Protegival and the LOP and they almost sound like members of a private army.'

Both of them had lived through the difficult years of the 1970s and the country's transition from dictatorship to democracy after Franco died. Small political groups had been springing up all the time, not all of them peaceful, and various terror organisations had been born — some longer lasting and more effective than others. As the regime crumbled, the forces doggedly resisting change and those demanding it had clashed and brought violence into the ordinary lives of many people. Now that the most notorious and successful of them — ETA — had renounced violence, it was easy to forget that those years had, at times, felt like an echo of the months leading up to the outbreak of the Civil War, when assassinations and bombings had become almost daily events. Now, once again, the country seemed to be caught in a downward spiral — economic collapse, endemic corruption, moves by certain regions to break away and become independent. And this time the central figure around which the country could unite was incapacitated. The King was still lying in a private hospital bed; his son was unproven as a stabilising force.

From his party's name and the language he had used during the press conference, it was clear what Soler's agenda was: the LOP was a Far Right Nationalist organisation yearning for the days of Franco.

'Why do you want to check the gym out?' Laura asked.

What Cámara had detailed so far was interesting, but the connection with Amy's murder was not obvious.

'It doesn't feel right,' he said. 'There may be nothing in it, but I want to take a closer look at them.'

'The funny thing is,' said Laura, 'I think I've already got something.'

Cámara looked surprised.

'This idea of yours that there may be a link between our case and the death that Inspector Torres is investigating,' she said. 'Do you remember the neighbour who talked about hearing someone saying *cartero* over the intercom?'

'Yes. What was his name? Hernández?'

'Manuel Hernández. I went to see him yesterday. Wanted to talk to him myself.'

'Did you mention this to Torres?'

Laura paused.

'I sent him an email,' she said. 'Of course, with all the hundreds arriving in our inboxes every day, it's anyone's guess whether he's read it yet.'

Cámara smiled. Perhaps she was not as straight as he had imagined.

'OK. Go on. What did you find out?'

'Hernández is an old man living on his own.

And he's clearly frightened by what happened to Diego Oliva.'

'But he told you something.'

'Yes. He didn't just hear the supposed postman calling from the street. He saw him as well. Or I should say, them.'

'Them?'

'There was a group of them. Hernández was on his way to the market to do some grocery shopping. He had just stepped outside his own front door and was about to call the lift when he heard *'cartero'* being called out from downstairs. He remembered clearly because it wasn't the time that the postman usually comes.'

'Just like with Amy's place,' said Cámara.

'So he waits for a moment and looks over the banister to see who it might be. He thinks he saw three men.'

'Description?'

'Not much we can go on. They were all wearing baseball caps and he was looking at them from above.'

'Shit.'

'They called the lift from the ground floor before Hernández was able to press the button, so he decided to walk down the stairs. By the time he reached the second floor — Oliva's flat — they had gone.'

'Where?'

'He doesn't know. But he's convinced that not all of them went up in the lift. He heard footsteps on the stairs as he was walking down. But there was no one there by the time he reached the lower floors.'

'Did he hear anything?'

'Nothing. Even assuming that the men were inside Oliva's flat by this time, he might not have heard what was going on inside. That's a solid structure, thick walls. The only reason why he heard the men calling from outside was because there was a missing pane of glass above the door opening out to the street. The stairwell acted like a sound chamber.'

'A missing pane of glass?'

'It's been replaced now. I checked.'

'So we've got three men wearing caps, probably pretending to be postmen or delivery men, entering Oliva's block of flats just before he takes a dive off his balcony,' Cámara said. 'But what's the connection with the LOP?'

'Hernández gave one other detail about the men he saw.'

'From above.'

'That's right. Not the best angle, but every time he mentioned them he seemed to puff himself out, as though trying to make himself bigger. I asked him what he was doing, and he said — he was a bit confused — but he said they were big young men. And he put his hands over his shoulders, as though to bulk them out, or show big muscles.'

'They worked out,' said Cámara.

'Yes, in his own way I think that's what he was trying to say.'

'So the men Hernández saw in Oliva's block of flats were young and beefed up.'

'And were pretending to be postmen.'

'That's it? That's the link with the murder of the American girl?'

'Well, we're looking at links, aren't we? It seemed worth investigating. Then I started digging around and found a connection between the gym opposite Amy's flat and the LOP. Two years ago an anti-fascist group tried to burn the place down, claimed it was a recruiting centre for the Far Right. All they did was leave some scorch marks on the outer shutters. The connection between the LOP and Protegival was unclear, but I started looking into the party to see if Webpol had anything on them.'

'What did you find out?'

'Like you were saying, accusations of violence, but nothing that has ever stuck. Not one single member of the LOP is on the police DNA database. But,' she raised a finger, 'it's interesting that you remember the case involving the woman who had her face destroyed. There's a curious pattern of violence against women in the cases that are brought against them. Beating up girl-friends — or accusations, I should say. But also harassment of women at nightclubs. There was even an incident in which one young man was killed — he had a heart attack while they were beating him up.'

'Protegival guards,' Cámara said.

'The reports didn't say,' said Laura. 'But now you mention it, the pattern fits.'

'You never feel you're getting the full story with these guys, as if someone is always covering up their tracks.'

He paused, his eyes staring into space. Laura coughed.

'So this case,' he said.

'Like with all of them,' Laura said, 'he got off. Insufficient evidence, according to the judge. The boy was shown to have had a heart condition, so they couldn't prove that the arrest had actually caused his death. But it was also reported that the guard had been trying to grope a woman at the disco. The man who was killed was her boyfriend. Again, there's the element of sexual assault. There's a pattern.'

An image of Amy's shattered head flashed through his mind.

'Five shots to the head,' he said. 'We always said there was something wrong about that.'

The next step to take was obvious, but there was the official way of doing it and then there was the Cámara way.

'We'll need permission from the investigating judge,' Laura said as Cámara got up.

'Why don't you ring up the LOP yourself and tell them we're coming round? You might as well with the number of friends they've got. Not just in the police but in the judiciary as well, by the looks of it.'

'Cámara, we can't.'

'You take whatever means of transport you like and I'll meet you there.'

He opened the door and stepped out.

'I'm taking the bike.'

28

Minutes later Cámara was on Amy's street. The shutters in her flat were closed from the inside — firmly, as though making a statement. He wondered if Ruiz Costa was in or had left.

On the other side of the street, the metal shutters of the gym had also been drawn down and firmly bolted to a ring in the pavement. Through the grime and dust that had built up over the years, Cámara could make out the phrase — written with a felt-tip marker long before — 'strength through joy'. An in-joke among the gym's members, presumably, to use one of the catchphrases of Nazi Germany.

It was still early, but already the street was alive to the sounds and movements of a working day. Cámara glanced up and down a few times before kneeling to see if he could pick the lock. But the key was one of the more modern types, less easily fiddled with. He looked around for something heavy: sometimes just giving the things an almighty bash could spring them open. A loose slab of pavement might do the trick. He spotted one nearby and was about to bring it down on the padlock when he heard a shout.

'Stop!'

It was Laura.

'You took your time.'

'Cámara, please. You'll just make it more

difficult to prosecute. The judge will be all over us.'

A new voice spoke.

'Wouldn't do much good.'

Cámara looked up. From the building next door an elderly man with a grey peaked cap and blue overcoat had appeared.

'Those locks are tough as nails,' he said. 'That's why I always use them.'

He sucked on the toothpick jutting from the side of his mouth.

'And I reckon you wouldn't find much even if you did get in.'

Laura stepped over and identified herself.

'I knew you were police,' the man said. 'Some of your lot were here the other day asking questions. It's about the American girl who lived opposite, right?'

'You're Antonio Pascual,' Cámara said.

'That's right. I take care of this place.'

He jerked with his thumb back over his shoulder at the block of flats next door to the gym.

'Sold them that padlock myself,' he said. 'Had a spare and they needed one. Like I say, they're good. Hardest ones to break.'

'You know the people at the gym.'

'Course I do. I'm here every day. You get to know people. Part of my job. I've helped them out a couple of times. Odd jobs, that sort of thing.'

'What time do they open?' asked Laura.

Pascual frowned.

'Don't reckon they'll be opening up at all

today. Or tomorrow.'

'Why? What happened?'

'Can't say for sure. They were here last night, making an awful racket they were. I didn't want to get involved, just watched them from inside my place. Going a right pace, like they were in a rush. Big van parked outside, throwing stuff in. Then they locked up and shot off. Like I say, had something almost terminal about it. That time of night, rushing around. Didn't like the look of it.'

'Did you see who they were?'

'Well, I didn't come out, like I say. But I've known them long enough. There were three of them, I reckon. One of them was Julio, I'm pretty sure. He's got this funny-shaped bald head and a big tattoo on his forearm. Can't say who the other two were.'

'Do you know where they went?' Laura asked.

'Haven't got a clue. Just shot off.'

'What time was this?'

'Oh, I should say some time after eleven. Can't be more exact.'

Laura walked up to the shutters locking her out of the gym and looked as though she was about to kick them with frustration.

Something had stirred inside Cámara.

'This man Julio,' he said to the doorman. 'Why do you say he's got a funny head?'

'Well, it just is. I'm not saying he's abnormal or a weirdo or anything. But . . . ' He raised his hands above his head, placing his fingertips together. 'It's not round like you and me. More like a triangle. If he let his hair grow you

258

probably wouldn't notice, but he insists on shaving it, see?'

Cámara wondered: was he the thug who had shown up that night outside the chemist's?

'Is there any other way of getting into the gym?' he asked.

Pascual shook his head.

'Well, that's your main entrance. And without the key, or some professional to open it, I reckon you're not going to get in.'

'What about round the back? The patio of your building must connect with the one at the back of here, right?'

He pointed at the gym.

'I don't know,' said Pascual. 'There's a wall between them. You could scale it, perhaps.'

Cámara was already on his feet and walking over to Pascual's door.

'Show me.'

'Cámara!' Laura shrieked. But seconds later she was racing after them as the two men headed to the back of the entrance hall and through a little opening.

The back patio of Pascual's building was used as a dump area — old gas bottles were lined up against the side wall, while scraps of rubbish thrown from upper windows were scattered on the ground.

'Don't come out here much,' Pascual said by way of excuse.

Cámara jumped up on to a pair of dusty butane bottles.

'On the other side of this wall is the patio behind the gym, right?'

259

'That'll be it.'

Laura looked on in silence.

'Here,' Cámara said. 'Give me a leg up.'

Pascual sauntered over and put his linked hands out to use as a step. Cámara needed just a small push to get a grip on the top of the wall. He pulled himself up and looked over. The yard at the back of the gym was very different from the one that he was climbing out of. The walls were painted brilliant white and tiles on the floor shone from cleaning and polishing. At the back of the gym, Cámara could see a small clouded window in a door. Not giving it a second thought, he pulled himself over the wall and jumped down. Then wrapping his jacket sleeve over his hand he smashed the glass and opened the door.

'Cámara!'

From the other patio, Laura had heard the sound of breaking glass.

'What are you doing? Wait. I'm coming over as well. Pascual has found a ladder.'

Cámara headed inside regardless. He tapped his pistol to make sure it was there.

Stepping out of a back room, he came into the main area of the gym. Weight machines and benches were arranged neatly in squares, making separate exercise sections. They were just visible in the scant daylight streaming in from the back. He flicked a switch and the lights went on. The place was spotless. Every piece of equipment reflected the lights back at him as though made of the freshest chrome. A large Spanish flag hung from one wall, while the other was taken up

260

entirely by mirrors so that the gym boys could watch themselves as they worked out.

But this was not what he had come to see. There would be an office somewhere: that was what he needed to find.

Behind the last mirror he spotted a small door. He was pulling on the handle when Laura arrived.

'I'm not letting you do this on your own.'

They stepped into the office together. Cámara switched on the lights. Another Spanish flag greeted them, but this time with a black emblem in the centre — a double-headed axe. Whereas the rest of the gym was spotless and ordered, however, here there were signs of chaos. Papers were scattered everywhere — on the single desk at the centre of the room, and across the floor. Laura got down on her hands and knees and started checking through them.

Cámara spotted a bust of Franco that had been knocked over and now sat on its side. He picked it up and held it in his hand. Underneath, still on the desk, was a beer mat emblazoned with the Nazi swastika.

'No doubts about the party's agenda, then,' he said to himself.

Laura was reading one of the documents on the floor.

'Cámara,' she said softly. 'I think you should take a look at this.'

29

Cámara knelt down beside her. The papers looked as though they had fallen out from a file and scattered. Some had footprints on them, others were upside down. He saw lists, numbers, pieces of text; none of which, at first glance, had any order to them.

But a word and a phrase did register as he scanned the documents: 'TARGETS' and 'DIRECT ACTION'.

Laura handed him a sheet.

'Look at this.'

At the top, in red letters, the word 'COPY' had been stamped. Below, lists of names were arranged in columns, three across. The first was labelled 'Separatists', the second 'Known Left Wingers' and the third 'Dangerous Media'.

He did not recognise all the names, but some of them were familiar to him — politicians, a couple of trade union leaders, a political commentator who often appeared on television, even a comedian.

'What do you think it is?' he said.

'Turn over.'

The names continued overleaf. Again Cámara checked them, not sure what he was looking for. Then one, in the third column, leapt out at him.

'You seen it?' Laura asked.

It felt as though a light, cleansing shower had begun to fall on them.

'They were watching her,' he said. 'They had her on this list.'

'And it's dated a month ago,' Laura said. 'She was in their sights for some time.'

He got to his feet, still clutching the sheet of paper, and glanced instinctively in the direction of Amy Donahue's flat, beyond the gym walls on the other side of the street.

'It would have been very easy for them to keep tabs on her,' Laura said. 'Just watching her movements from their own front door.'

She stood up and went to take the document from Cámara.

'They must have dropped it as they were leaving. From the sounds of it they were in a hurry.'

As the significance of the place where they were standing sank in, they began to move around more gingerly.

'We need the *científicos* in here,' Cámara said.

'I'll give them a call.'

'Try to keep Maldonado out of it.'

She raised an eyebrow.

'For as long as possible.'

As she dialled a number, he stepped across the office. A black metal cupboard hung from the back wall. He pulled out a pen from his jacket and swung it open. The brackets for holding five firearms were clearly visible, while an empty brown cardboard box of bullets sat at the bottom.

'They're going to love this,' he said.

He spun on his heel and turned to Laura. She was already on the phone, but saw the expression on his face and paused.

'Try and get Fernández,' Cámara said in a loud whisper. 'He was there at Amy's flat.'

Laura nodded. On the whole the members of the *Científica* were professional and thorough, but getting someone who was already involved in the case was preferable. More importantly, in this case the danger would come from having *científicos* sympathetic to the LOP and its ideas. Cámara did not know what Fernández's politics were, but he had witnessed the bloody scene across the road first hand and had an emotional investment, if nothing else, in solving Amy's murder.

Laura spoke on the phone for a few more moments, then hung up.

'They can't send a team till tomorrow at the earliest,' she said. 'They've run out of money — nothing has come in from Madrid for months, and they can't even afford any latex gloves, let alone more expensive equipment.'

Cámara shook his head.

'The *corralito*,' he said. 'There's no money left.'

'Can you believe it?'

'We'll have to get along without them.'

He pointed to the gun cabinet.

'Take a look at this,' he said. 'It's almost certainly what they were most interested in emptying. We're looking at handguns, judging from the ammunition box they left behind. But also at least one rifle or shotgun. That's a tall cabinet, not just for storing pistols.'

Laura nodded.

'There are no computers in this office,' she said. 'But look at the markings on the desk.'

She pointed down to dents on the surface of the wood.

'This place has been kept very clean and well ordered. But there was almost certainly a computer here.'

'I wouldn't be surprised if they had a considerable amount of cash as well. I can almost smell it.'

Laura smiled.

'The ability to smell money. That's a useful skill.'

Cámara crouched down to look at the papers on the floor again. Laura checked the list of names still in her hand.

'I reckon this is incomplete,' she said. 'The names run on at the end of the page. See if you can find the rest of it down there.'

He carefully slid each page across, looking for a continuation of the list.

'Direct action,' Laura said. 'Nice euphemism.'

'I'm not sure if it's here,' Cámara said. 'But take a look at this.'

She crouched down beside him.

'Look. All these documents refer to something called the 'bunker'. Here,' he pointed to one sheet, 'then here, and here.'

Laura read.

'It's like going back in time,' she said. 'That's what they called the hard-line Francoists in the seventies, the ones who dug in against any change.'

'You think that's what they're referring to here?'

'Probably.'

'I wonder if it's an actual, physical place.'

She thought for a moment.

'This gym belongs to Protegival,' she said.

'Yes.'

'But I'm assuming it's a social club for Protegival guards. They come here to work out.'

'And receive political indoctrination, by the looks of it.'

'Pascual can confirm some of this.'

'Where is he?'

'I left him next door,' said Laura. 'Told him to stay put.

Her knees cracked as she got up from the floor.

'A lot of phone calls need making,' Cámara said.

'Not least to legalise our illegal raid on this place.'

She sighed.

'I've got a feeling that's more my strength than yours.'

'I can give you a lift,' he said. 'Get you back quicker.'

The thin bow of her lips parted to reveal even, pearl-white teeth.

'I'm fine.'

Cámara's phone buzzed. The message was from Alicia.

Think I've got something big for you. Expect a call soon. All well. Kisses.

He made to leave.

'I'll get Pascual to organise some ladders,' he said. 'Make it easier getting in and out till we sort the lock at the front.'

★　★　★

He let the bike find its own way. Riding meant that he had to concentrate on the road, the traffic, and on his balance as he cruised round corners and wove slowly in and out. Which allowed a slower and calmer part of him to think through what they had discovered. He reached the roundabout at the top of the Alameda and shot up past the Estación de Madera. There was little traffic and the avenue seemed to draw him along with a promise of empty, unhurried horizons.

There was no doubt in his mind now that people — men — from the gym were involved in Amy's killing. And that her murder was connected with Oliva's death, possibly that the same group of people were responsible for both. Different individuals, clearly — they could not have been in two places at once. But the link was there.

What was the motive? The list of names had not specified why those particular people were being singled out, but Amy's name had appeared in the 'Dangerous Media' column. If, as he suspected, the young men training at the gym and working as guards for Protegival were also members of the LOP, the suggestion was that they were planning violent acts against people they considered a political threat. Had they seen the current crisis coming? The papers were dated at least a month back, before the King's illness and the sudden worsening in the climate. The background grumbling against the lack of jobs and endemic corruption was now turning into real anger on the streets, yet it looked as though the LOP had been preparing for this moment for some time. Was Amy their first victim? If so, why? What had she done to bring their violence upon herself?

He kept returning to the five shots to the back of her head. Two shots could have been the sign of a professional assassin. But five? It was excessive. Then there was the damage to her vagina and the crushing of her fingers. The thugs he knew from Protegival rarely showed respect for women — the information that Laura had dug up on them confirmed as much. Pumped up with their weight training, their self-importance and — he guessed — some chemical enhancers, he could easily imagine them carrying out Amy's murder. Shot in the back of the head — like a professional would have done, like they probably imagined themselves to be. But then the anger, the lust for violence forced their hand: three more shots than was necessary; a quick fumble between her legs and stomping on her hands as they were leaving.

And why her hands? Of course, because of what she wrote. She was in the media column. It was because of what she was blogging.

Or what she was about to blog.

She had mentioned the scoop herself on her Twitter account. Were the LOP thugs monitoring her? Were they reading her tweets and Facebook messages? What were they trying to stop her from writing? Had Amy written her own death warrant that day when she mentioned on the Internet that she was popping out to meet an important source? She was only an amateur, after all, could never have imagined the danger she was in.

He slowed down and stopped the bike by the side of the road for a moment. It felt as though he had not breathed properly in days, the air stuck in the top of his chest, never flowing freely in and out of his lungs. Not since Hilario had died. Now, taking off his helmet for a second and feeling the breeze blow through his hair, he tried to force his chest, his body, to relax. The tension was becoming such a part of him that he barely even registered its existence any more.

Yet now, as connections began to fall into place, he needed to feel the air coursing through him.

'The importance of breathing well is highly underrated,' Hilario had said to him once. And he heard his voice inside him now almost as though he were standing next to him. 'It can take someone years to learn how to breathe properly.'

Cars, lorries, other motorbikes and pedestrians all streamed past him, and he sat still on the bike, his feet planted on the ground, feeling the vibrations of the engine pulse through him, and he breathed. Did nothing but breathe.

Who was about to give Amy the scoop? Oliva. He was 'the banker' mentioned in her tweet.

What was the scoop about? The Caja Levante.

It must have been something to do with the department where he was working before he lost his job.

Was Felicidad Galván involved in any way? The answer popped into his mind instantly, with an image of her face, the sound of her voice from when he had gone to speak with her at the bank building: yes, certainly.

But how? He could not say.

And how was the LOP involved in this? If Oliva was going to blow the whistle on something at Caja Levante, why was he not going to talk to a journalist from one of the local newspapers? Why Amy?

If the LOP were involved in Oliva's death, did that mean they were spying on him as well? If so, how?

More questions kept coming, but they hung in the air, unanswered, like thunder clouds seeking points on the earth through which to discharge their lightning.

His phone rang and he lifted it out of his pocket. The number on the screen was unknown to him.

'*¿Sí?*'

'Max Cámara?'

It was a woman's voice.

'Yes?'

'My name's Sonia. I'm Diego Oliva's wife.'

Cámara breathed — deeper than he had breathed in what felt like years.

'Can we meet? I think I have something you might want to see.'

30

He had not visited the botanical gardens in years. Earlier, when he first moved to the city and was still working in *UDYCO* — the drug and organised crime squad — he had popped round frequently, pacing up and down the long green avenues, sitting on a bench in the shade, enjoying the solitude. Local people were proud of the place — it had started life as a garden for pharmaceutical herbs five hundred years before, when the city had one of the most advanced medical systems in Europe. Valencia still enjoyed a reputation for having good doctors, but with ever less justification. Now an emblem of a more enlightened time, the gardens were one of the quietest and most beautiful spots in the centre, lying just beyond the Torres de Quart. No one would see or disturb them here.

It was clear from their brief telephone conversation that Sonia was frightened. She wanted to talk to him, but was suspicious. She was only going ahead with this because Alicia — the journalist she had met earlier in the day — swore that Cámara was trustworthy. Sonia had got in touch with Alicia herself after she saw the article that she had written on the decline of the Spanish health system. The two women had got on, and Alicia had conviced Sonia to get in touch. But only with Cámara. She would speak to him alone, in confidence. Nothing could be recorded, nor photographs taken.

Cámara rejected out of hand the idea of meeting at the Jefatura. A bar or restaurant might be possible, but there was always the risk that someone might see them. Who, exactly, he could not say. Nor would she. She had appeared on the point of backing out when the botanical gardens had occurred to him as a venue.

'Yes,' she said after a long pause. 'Yes, that'll do.'

It took him no more than ten minutes to get there. Parking the bike on the pavement outside, he paid the nominal amount to get in and passed through the gate.

It felt like entering a different world: the sounds and strains of the city were muffled by the abundance of greenery, trees arching high over his head, brightly coloured flowers peppering the view wherever he looked.

I'll come here more often, he thought. I've missed it. It's a good place to be.

A central path led him to a square near the greenhouses. There was nobody there. He sat down on the wall of a small fountain, clearly visible and in clear sunlight, and waited.

After less than five minutes he heard the sound of gravel crunching underfoot. A few seconds later the noise stopped and the footsteps tapped more lightly over the terracotta surface of the square. When they were quite close, he turned.

He had seen Sonia briefly at the hospital, waiting outside the intensive care wing for news about Oliva. And although she wore her hair differently today, letting it fall loose rather than tying it behind her head, he recognised her immediately. She was a small woman. Cámara felt he might be able to pick her up with just one hand, as though her bones were those of a bird. In front of her chest she held a dark blue file, squeezing it tightly with both arms.

He stood up.

'I'm Max Cámara.'

She looked at him but said nothing.

'Sonia?'

Her lips were tight and pale. She was trying to hide her trembling. He looked around.

'We could find a more private spot,' he said. 'Would you like to come with me? We can sit under those trees over there.'

He urged her to accompany him.

'Everything's fine. Trust me.'

When she looked into his eyes he felt the fear and grief in her strike him like an arrow. And for a moment he also felt his own mourning stirring inside, woken by the proximity of a kindred spirit. Walking away from the square to the shelter of a palm grove, he did his best to quell the incipient storm: he was here as a policeman; his own feelings and emotions had to be kept in check.

They found a bench in the shade. Cámara sat down and beckoned Sonia to join him.

'I'm very sorry about Diego,' he said, swallowing hard as the words almost caught in his throat.

Sonia looked at him, her eyes reddening.

'Alicia told me you lost someone recently, too,' she said.

Their tears almost mirrored one another. Cámara nodded.

'That's why I came,' she said. 'That's why I'm here with you. I didn't know where to go. And then . . . ' She coughed, trying to loosen her throat so that she could carry on speaking. 'And then I saw Alicia's article and decided to get in touch, she said I should come to you. That you'd understand. That you were the only person there was for me.'

Their hands found each other across the bench and their fingers overlapped. Cámara would have embraced her: something about her frailty made him want to reach out and protect her, to place an arm over her delicate shoulders and shield her.

He straightened his back, wiping his face dry with his free hand.

'I'll help you in any way I can,' he said.

'Thank you.'

She cast her eyes to the ground, her face partially hidden from view as her hair fell across her face.

'Can you tell me something, please?' she said. 'I want to know. Will you be honest with me? Was Diego murdered?'

Tears were falling from the end of her nose and making dark stains on the pavement below.

'Yes,' Cámara said. 'I believe he was.'

Her nails dug into his skin where she held his hand.

'I knew it wasn't a suicide. Diego would never have done that.'

After a moment, the trembling seemed to subside in her. He had the sense that by holding her hand he was earthing something in her.

'You were still friends?' he said.

'Yes. The divorce was . . . probably a mistake. We could have worked things out.'

She sat up, pushing her hair from her face.

'Diego never stopped trying to woo me back. He was a one-woman man, he said.'

Her mouth twitched, as though trying to break into a smile.

'Recently I'd come to think that he was right, that we would be better off together again. I'd told him as much. He was going through such a horrible time, not finding a job, struggling with the mortgage. But somehow it made us closer again. I was trying to help him find work. I was even about to tell him to move in with me — that he could lose his flat, it was OK, that he could come and live with me. That we could start over again.'

She closed her eyes.

'And then this happened.'

The blue file was still clutched tightly to her chest with her other hand. Now she loosened her grip and laid it down on her lap.

'There was a whole load of stuff we didn't sort out after the divorce, loads of bureaucratic things. We had a joint safe at one of these private companies where you can rent one. Each one of us had a key. I'd forgotten all about it. Then yesterday Diego's lawyer sent me a letter. He said that Diego had instructed him to get in touch with me if anything happened to him.'

'If anything happened to him?'

She opened her eyes.

'Is anything wrong?' she asked.

'No,' said Cámara. 'But that kind of language — it's as if he knew he was in danger.'

She nodded.

'What did the lawyer say?'

'He said I should go to the safe,' Sonia said. 'That Diego had told him to tell me that.'

'Nothing else?'

'Nothing.'

'Did he know what was in the safe?'

'I don't think so. The letter seemed to be passing on the message, that's all.'

Cámara looked at the file resting on Sonia's knee.

'So you went,' he said.

'Yes.'

'And found that.'

'Yes.'

She pulled her hand free from Cámara's and placed it on top of the file.

'This is what I think you need to see.'

With one smooth and decisive movement she passed it over to him.

'It's all there. All the documentation, the proof, everything. I've checked.'

Cámara picked the file up and held it without opening it.

'I'm assuming this has something to do with Diego's time at Caja Levante,' he said.

Sonia pushed a hand into a pocket and pulled

out a packet of cigarettes.

'Can you smoke in here?'

'It's only dried leaves,' he said. 'No one will mind.'

He pulled the file open. Sonia lit her cigarette and inhaled.

'Diego wrote a kind of summary of what it's all about,' she said. 'It's at the front. There's a letter. You can read it.'

Cámara pulled out the first sheet and read.

My darling Sonia,

If you're reading this it's either because I'm showing it to you and everything is fine, or it means that something has happened and my lawyer has done what I instructed him and told you to open the safe.

If it's the second scenario, I need to explain. This file contains copies and originals of documents I gathered while I was working in the development and investment department under Felicidad Galván at the Caja Levante. You remember Feli — I think you met her once. And I told you some of the things that I used to do with her, but not everything. The truth about what really goes on in that department and what Feli is responsible for is contained in the papers in this file. You're going to have to decide on your own what to do with them. If something unpleasant has happened to me and that's the reason why you're reading this, then you are probably very frightened right now and just want to burn or throw the documents away. PLEASE DON'T.

Whatever you do, do not destroy what's contained here. Everyone needs to know. If you can't cope with doing something with the papers right now, then put them back in the safe and walk away. There may come another time when you feel strong enough to deal with this. It's a heavy burden, and I don't want to do this to you, but I don't see any other way.

The documents here prove beyond all doubt what the rumours have been saying about Feli and the Caja Levante for years. The development and investment department runs a slush fund for political purposes. I was involved in its running and I am very ashamed of what I did. I only hope that now I can redeem myself by helping to expose what was — and probably still is — going on.

The money was at the disposal of local politicians — specifically members of the Town Hall. Feli controlled everything at the bank. There are lots of things I don't know about the goings-on of the fund. I don't know who Feli was taking her orders from. I don't know exactly where the money went, although I know some of it was channelled to other political parties — not just members of the ruling party. What I do know — and this is the secret that must be made known — is where the money was coming from for the slush fund.

During the years that I worked there, Feli took control of a source of funding that Madrid had won from Brussels when Spain joined the EU. That money was then distributed to regions and cities. It was meant to be spent specifically on healthcare — building new hospitals, developing new medicines, paying staff. Any health costs could be covered using that money. Caja Levante took over the running of it a year before I joined, and was supposed to act as a clearing facility for local government decisions on where to apportion the money. Slowly, however, Feli and Caja Levante started diverting money away from the healthcare it was intended for and into their own slush fund. They got away with it, and when the economy was good, no one realised or even minded — there was so much money around at the time anyway. Only recently, with the crash, have things got worse. I thought that they would start spending the EU money on what it was intended for in the first place. But they got greedy — every year more and more of it was being diverted to the slush fund. It was like a drug. Then when the money was really needed in hospitals and for medicines, they couldn't give it back. They were hooked. It was shortly after that I lost my job.

I copied as many documents as I could and took them with me. One day, I thought, I might need them. I am thinking about taking them to the press but am unsure. I don't know if I can trust local journalists — they're too connected with people in power and I can't be certain they won't give my identity away.

Perhaps one of these new blogger journalists might be a way forward. Someone foreign, even.

I'm marked and dangerous for them — they know that I know the truth. But they don't know that I can prove it. I've placed the documents in the safest place I know. It's possible that if not yet, then at some point they will be keeping tabs on me. I don't like the way the telephone line clicks sometimes when I'm talking.

Perhaps I'm paranoid. I don't know. Otherwise what am I doing writing this letter? I'm sure everything will be fine.

I love you very much. I made some mistakes. I hope you can forgive me. Now I leave this with you, my darling.

The truth must come out. Mothers, fathers, children — all kinds of innocent people are dying in hospitals now because the money that was meant for them, that could save them, is being stolen. Please — your reading this letter means I have failed. Now it is up to you.

With love, for ever,
Diego

Cámara looked up at the sky. The sun shone relentlessly, but it had become dark and lightless for him.

'I'm frightened,' Sonia said. 'I don't know who to trust. These are powerful people. And they've probably already killed Diego.'

'It's all right,' said Cámara.

His vision was black and icy, his path clear, his

next moves clearly laid out before him. They had looked him in the eye and made a terrible mistake, the worst they could possibly have committed.

'Everything's going to be all right.'

He escorted her to the gate of the garden.

'Take that back immediately to the safe and leave it there,' he said, nodding at the file. 'Tell no one about it. Then leave the city for a few days if you can. Stay with friends, family, whatever. Valencia may not be safe for a while.'

She pressed his hands in hers.

'Go,' he said. 'Every moment is precious.'

He watched as she walked down the street, hailed a taxi, and disappeared in the direction of the old river bed.

He picked up his phone and dialled Alicia's number.

There was no answer.

31

Laura, Torres and the others in *Homicidios* needed to know. This was now a double murder case — they would have to coordinate the investigation. If they played it right they might have the first arrests before the end of the day.

The botanical gardens were a short distance from the Jefatura. In little over a minute he was parking the bike and stepping inside the door. Once he had got things off the ground he would try ringing Alicia again.

Azcárraga was at reception.

'No more night shifts, then?' Cámara called out as he rushed past.

The policeman did not reply.

The first face that Cámara saw as he walked into the murder squad offices was Maldonado. He was dressed in his full police uniform, with thick gold braiding on his cap and a row of medals across his chest.

'Chief Inspector,' Maldonado said. He was smiling.

'You look like you've been expecting me,' said Cámara.

'Hah! Of course. Always the game with you, always pretending to be one step ahead. I notice you've deliberately ignored my directive about the wearing of uniforms. Respect for national institutions is important to some of us, but obviously you regard yourself above such things.'

'Look, Maldo — '

'It's Chief Inspector Maldonado. I am the head of this unit and you will respect that.'

Cámara glanced around the office. Albelda, Lozano and Castro were there, dressed in their uniforms. As was Torres, standing behind Maldonado with a troubled look on his face.

'OK,' Cámara said. 'Something's going on here and I don't think it's anything to do with the clothes I'm wearing right now.'

'Chief,' Torres began, trying to take a step forward. But Maldonado put a hand out and stopped him. From somewhere in the corridor two policemen appeared and stood behind Cámara.

'What's up?'

'It's about your lady friend,' Maldonado said. 'Alicia Beneyto. You are intimate, aren't you?'

'Cut the shit, Maldo. What the fuck is going on?'

A cold trembling was moving up his legs and into his guts, as if his body already knew.

'The incident room received a call a few minutes ago,' Maldonado said. The smile had dropped from his face and he had a look of seriousness and concern. 'Alicia's been abducted.'

A wave of nausea, soupy and grey, enveloped him. The threat had been real.

'It was witnessed by some journalist colleagues,' Maldonado explained. 'They'd been talking to her and she was heading off when a car appeared and a group of men bundled her in and drove away.'

The words registered somewhere, but they

were drifting in and out, as though caught on a fierce wind.

'It's your fault,' Maldonado said. 'You've been doing your usual, not following protocol, getting non-professionals involved.'

'How do you know?' The question was unheard, a whisper as his mind raced.

'You asked Alicia to snoop around for you and then she got a death threat.'

Sitting in her usual place, Castro kept her eyes fixed on the computer.

'Which you tried to keep quiet,' Maldonado continued. 'And now you're reaping the reward.'

Cámara stared at the ground, thinking, calculating. His superior's unexpected presence ceased to matter.

'This is for your own good as much as for the benefit of the police.' Maldonado's words had a harsh, metallic quality, as though barked through a loudspeaker, but Cámara's mind was focused on what to do next, where to go, who to find. And fast. If the LOP thugs had their hands on Alicia — and who else would it be? — there was very little time. They were capable of committing horrific acts. He had to move. Now.

He spun on his heels to leave, not bothering to hear the rest of Maldonado's speech, but the two policemen — members of the riot squad? He did not recognise them — stood in his way.

'What?'

'We have to think of our reputation.' Maldonado was still speaking. 'You have done so much to discredit us, and right now — '

'Get out of my way!' shouted Cámara. They

did not move. Then at a signal from Maldonado, they stepped forward. One held Cámara by the shoulders while the other pulled his arms behind his back and clapped a pair of handcuffs on him.

He was too stunned to react.

'Take his phone off him,' Maldonado ordered. 'And take him to the cells.'

Cámara tried to struggle free, but the policemen were too strong for him.

'You can use force if necessary,' Maldonado said from behind, his voice betraying an excitement behind the faux calm.

'Maldonado!' Cámara began to scream.

'We can't have you charging around the city like a vigilante,' Maldonado said. 'The matter is in hand. You would only make things worse. Now please,' he addressed the two policemen, 'take him away. The chief inspector is charged with insubordination and corrupt practice.'

'Torres,' Cámara called out as the policemen began to lead him away. 'Torres, do something.'

'Inspector Torres is leading the investigation into Señora Beneyto's disappearance,' Maldonado added. 'In the professional manner. And he's doing everything he can.'

Cámara glanced back as he was pushed and dragged out of the office. Torres, his police cap planted firmly on his head, had averted his eyes.

32

It had always been the stench of the cells that he hated the most. They were underground, at the far end of the corridor from the murder squad offices. And he avoided them as best he could: just pausing at the top of the stairs, picking up the scent of stale anger and fear, made him want to be sick. Now he was being forced down, not as a jailer but as the jailed. A firm hand was pressed against the back of his head, pushing him into the grimy, subterranean world.

The cell door was opened, the handcuffs unlocked, and he stepped inside. There was no need for force now. He could not break his way out of here: he would need other methods.

The door thudded behind him and he was alone.

Torres. The betrayal had caught him by surprise: Maldonado's game had finally paid off, breaking the partnership that most threatened his control over *Homicidios*. Separated, Cámara and Torres were so much easier to handle; Maldonado would be toasting himself over his great success.

But none of this — not Maldonado, nor Torres, nor even the fact of his imprisonment — weighed heavily on him at that moment. His only priority was getting out as quickly as possible and saving Alicia. He was certain he knew who had taken her, and he had an idea of where they had gone.

But he needed to get a message out to the one person who might be able to help.

He stuck a hand into his back pocket and pulled out a receipt — it was from the ticket he had bought to get into the botanical gardens. The front was printed with numbers, but the back was clean. He only lacked something to write with. He tried scratching it with his nail, but the letters that he marked were indecipherable.

Sitting down on the metal bench at the side of the cell, he started looking around. It was small — about four metres long by two across and about three metres high. The walls and floor were covered in grey, utilitarian tiles. They were cleaned regularly, judging by the scent of chemicals mixing with the more human odours present, but they spoke of nothing but dirt and neglect. Cámara started running his fingers along the wall behind him, finding the groove of the grouting and following its regular grid pattern. It felt smooth to his touch, and nothing caught his skin as he dragged his hands across. Standing up, he followed his course around to the end, before it turned ninety degrees on to the back wall. Here the grouting felt very slightly different — thicker and rougher — an apprentice, not the master, had done this section. He hovered over it for a few seconds, tracing up and down, seeking with his fingertips what his eyes could not see.

Finally he felt something: a tiny loose section of grouting, the broken end of it catching on his nail as he drew it across. Digging in, wriggling it and catching it between three fingernails, he gradually pulled it loose, until a slither of grouting sat, cool and sharp, in the palm of his hand.

It was almost perfect. Crouching by the edge of the bench, he scraped a point and a blade on one edge, disguising the sound from the guards by doing it to a rhythm, as if, bored by his incarceration, he was tapping out a tune.

'You all right in there, Chief Inspector?' one of the guards called out — he had caught a glimpse of the two of them at the desk when he was hauled in and his things confiscated. Chief Inspector, they said. Not Cámara. They knew who he was and were respecting his rank. It was a good sign.

'Hanging in there,' he called out cheerfully.

The guards laughed.

'Hey,' Cámara said. 'Do either of you know Azcárraga?'

'Not sure. Heard of him,' one of the guards said. They were still at their desk. 'Why?'

'Do me a favour, will you?' Cámara said. 'He's on reception. I was supposed to pick his kid up from school, but obviously with the ways things are going . . . '

The guards sniggered.

'Just pop up and tell him I'm sorry but he'll have to make other arrangements, will you?'

He heard the shuffling of feet.

'I'm sorry. He was relying on me. Don't want to let him down.'

'There's supposed to be two of us here at all

288

times,' a guard said.

'Is there anyone else being held down here?'

'No. You're our only guest today.'

'All right. Listen. Nothing's going to happen. I'm clearly not going anywhere soon. It will only take a second to run up and tell him.'

'I'll do it,' said the second guard. 'Just make sure you don't tell our superior.'

'You've got no worries on that score. I'm a delinquent, remember. They wouldn't believe me anyway.'

He heard the guard shuffle off and start up the stairs.

'Azcárraga, right?' he said.

'That's the one.'

When he had gone, Cámara took the sharpened piece of grouting and, making sure not to break it, pushed it into the palm of his hand. Drawing a droplet of blood, he dipped the grouting in it and started to write on the back of the receipt. If he calculated right, he would only have a minute or so to scratch out his message.

The blood dried up quickly and he had to push into his skin again, harder this time, to make it flow. But the grouting broke, leaving just the tiniest slither still embedded in his hand. Carefully, he eased it out, and then holding it with his fingernails, he finished the message. At the top he wrote the name of who it was addressed to, blew on it to dry, and then folded it to make it as small and slim as possible.

Footsteps sounded on the stairs, two pairs this time.

'It's Azcárraga,' the guard called out as he took

the last step. 'Insisted on coming to say hello when I told him.'

Alone in his cell, Cámara closed his eyes and stilled himself.

Footsteps approached his cell door and he stood up.

'What a surprise,' Azcárraga said as he peered in. The door was virtually solid, made of thick square bars, but there were thin gaps between them so that the guards could see inside.

'Thanks for the message. Didn't realise what had happened.'

'And your kid?' Cámara looked him straight in the eye.

'Oh. Yeah. No worries,' Azcárraga said. 'I can — I can make other arrangements. Don't you worry about it.'

'Nice of you to pop down,' Cámara said. He took a step towards the door, the slip of paper held between two fingers. He waved it very briefly in front of Azcárraga, then pushed his hands against the bars. After the tiniest of pauses, Azcárraga mirrored him.

'You left reception unmanned?'

'No,' Azcárraga laughed. 'Someone else can cover for a couple of minutes. Just wanted to make sure you were all right.'

The piece of paper slipped between Cámara's fingers and into Azcárraga's.

'Well, I appreciate it,' Cámara said. 'Nice to know I've still got some friends in the Jefatura.'

The guards could hear everything: there was no need to raise their voices. But so far there was no indication that they had seen anything suspicious.

Azcárraga glanced in their direction, then back at Cámara. The expression of confusion on his face turned into one of concern and determination.

'Don't worry,' he said. 'You've got lots of friends in the Jefatura.'

He stepped away from the door and made to leave.

'Hurry,' Cámara called after him. 'You'd better get back to reception quickly. You never know what might be happening while you're away.'

Azcárraga quickened his step and swept past the guards.

'I'm on it.'

33

Every minute that passed was a minute closer to Alicia being harmed. Or killed.

He sat on the bench and waited, closing his eyes and trying to control the nervous, churning throb in his guts, the stickiness of his hands. The small wound on his palm had stopped bleeding, but was beginning to sting. Everything now depended on Azcárraga.

He had no watch to measure the passing time. And his phone — his usual means of knowing the hour of the day — had been confiscated. Yet he could hear a ticking in his head: every second that he spent motionless in the cell felt like a kick in the ribs.

He tried to force himself into a calm state, listening to his breathing, watching his thoughts racing through his mind. If salvation were to come he would have to be as relaxed as possible in order to react quickly and efficiently. Right now there was nothing he could do.

And so he waited.

He stirred when he heard new footsteps coming down the stairs: a sudden rush of blood, adrenalin flowing. Was this it?

There were voices at the reception desk. Papers were unfolded and handed over. The decision was being made quickly — he could tell. The policemen did not like the situation: it was unorthodox, should never have been like this in the first place.

The jangling of keys and three pairs of feet now walking towards his cell. There was a clang as the key was fitted into the lock. Cámara looked up.

It was Laura.

'I got a direct order from Madrid,' she said. 'It's time to get you out.'

Cámara's legs trembled as he got up. The guards smiled when he walked out and into the corridor.

'We're sorry about all this,' the first one said. 'If it had been my call I would never have allowed it.'

He gave Cámara his phone and keys back.

'It's all right,' Cámara said. 'I understand.'

'Thank you, gentlemen,' Laura said, addressing the two men. 'I appreciate your goodwill, and will remember it. But right now Chief Inspector Cámara and I have some urgent business to attend to.'

They skipped up the stairs and Laura led him to reception.

'Chief Inspector,' Azcárraga said, with a relieved smile on his face. 'Am I glad to see you.'

Cámara spotted his helmet on the desk.

'I picked it up from the murder squad office,' Laura said. 'Thought you'd need it.'

'Thanks.'

He slung the helmet over his arm and made to go.

'Cámara!' Laura called. He stopped.

'What just happened — Maldonado locking

293

you up — that wasn't right. That's why I agreed to get you out. But let me help you now. You can't do this on your own.'

'What do you want me to do? Get the police involved?'

'At least let me do something,' she said.

Cámara grabbed a piece of paper from the desk and wrote a telephone number on it.

'Call this number,' he said. 'Tell them everything.'

He looked around, making sure no one else in reception could hear them.

'Tell them I'm going to the far end. That's where she'll be. The far end.'

Laura looked confused.

'They'll understand,' said Cámara.

'Good luck!' Azcárraga called out.

But Cámara was already out the door.

He slung on his helmet and ran round to the back of the building where he had left his motorbike. He sat down, flicked up the side stand with his heel and pressed the starter button. The engine made a dull whine, and stopped. He pressed the button again. And nothing happened at all.

'Fucking battery.'

He should have changed it months back. Now it had finally given up on him.

Should he take a car? Commandeer something from a passing motorist? The options were rejected in less than a second — they would all take up too much time. He was almost about to get off the bike and start running, when he remembered: the W650 had a kick-starter. He had only used it once, when he first got it, just to try it out. They were rare these days.

He glanced down to his right. The pedal was folded in against the engine. Pushing it out with his fingers, he rested his instep on it, stood up, gently turned the throttle, and pushed down with all his strength. The engine coughed into life, then died. Again he jumped on the kick-starter, careful not to flood the engine, but again it fired up only to switch off again.

With a final effort, he stamped down with his foot, willing the bike into action. It roared, coughed, and settled into a healthy hum.

He released the clutch so hard that he sped down half the street on his back wheel.

It was time to go underground once more.

It was time to save Alicia.

34

Halfway down the Gran Vía, he heard the sirens. Ahead, the street was blocked by a wall of red city buses in what looked like another demonstration.

But there was no time to wonder what it was about; blue lights were flashing in his wing mirrors and he had to hurry.

There was one way in, one place from which he could penetrate the network and start his search. He had to get there fast.

The only way forward was to get off the road and ride down the pavement. The squad cars would not be able to follow him there. He cut right, leaning into the corner, and then dog-legged left into the pedestrian area. People jumped out of his way, terrified of being hit. But the sound of his exhausts — louder and more powerful than the standard ones on the Kawasaki — gave prior warning that he was coming.

He stood up on the footrests to make himself more visible, honking the horn.

'Police!' he shouted. 'Get out the way!'

A woman with twins in a pram stood still in the middle of the pavement, petrified and unable to move at the sight of him speeding towards her. Cámara swerved on the bike. The mother screamed and he barely brushed her shoulder as he passed, throwing the weight of the bike from one side to the other to keep his balance. Straightening himself, he rode on. A quick glance back told him the woman and her children were unhurt.

But to the side, on the road, the squad cars were chasing. Soon they would be held up by the backed-up cars and the buses ahead. But he could see bus drivers already climbing into their vehicles to move them out of the way, alerted by the sirens that an emergency was upon them. It would only take a minute or so for his pursuers to squeeze their way through.

He pressed on, carefully weaving his way around people and obstacles. So far, there were no police motorbikes involved in the chase, otherwise he would lose his advantage.

Beyond the demonstration, where no traffic had been able to flow, his way ahead lay clear. He sneaked around the side of a bus, kicked over a barricade, jumped off the pavement and back on to tarmac, and shot off. This time there was nothing standing in his way. But he had to hurry: before long the police cars would be on his tail again.

The metro station lay half a kilometre down a straight, palm-lined avenue. He knew the area well. This was where the rumblings caused by building the new line in front of his former home had caused his block of flats to come crashing down. Now the station was nothing but an empty hole, a barricaded, abandoned blot on the city landscape.

And this was where he was heading.

The 'bunker'. It was no reference to the last

days of Franco. It was here, down in the forgotten Valencian underworld.

It was here — he knew — that he would find Alicia. Alive or dead.

He pulled up outside. The hole sat in the middle of a wide pavement area in front of a school building. Dusty metal fencing backed with green gauze material circled it, a barrier to getting in. The gauze had been ripped in most places now and hung in rags. The view inside was clear enough: a cement staircase led underground to a central area. Below that would be the tunnel.

Cámara looked back up the avenue. The first cars were beginning to flow, finally being allowed to pass the demonstrating bus drivers. The police would not be far behind.

Leaving the engine running, he got off the bike and quickly scouted around. He would be able to climb the fencing, but once inside would be forced to carry on on foot. And speed was essential.

He wondered about trying to fiddle with the locks, but it would take too long. The police would be on him before he could open them.

A green rubbish container stood nearby. He spied two wooden planks poking out from the top. They looked rough and splintered but had metal rims around the corners: builders must have used them and thrown them away. They would be strong, could take the weight.

He ran over, pulled the container lid open and started hauling the planks out. They were about four metres long. Perfect.

Dragging them back to the hole, he threw first one, then the other over the fencing, pushing them together to make a ramp. The fencing bent just a little with the pressure, leaning in.

From the top of the avenue, he could hear the sirens again. The squad cars had got through and would be with him in less than a minute.

He dashed for the bike and spun it round the hole, heading up a side road, turning round and aligning himself with the planks. He did not want to go too fast; he needed the weight of the bike to push the fencing down that bit more and allow him in. But there would be a jump and a difficult landing on the other side. If he made it through.

The sirens were getting louder. Blue lights were reflecting on the shop windows on the far side of the avenue.

He opened the throttle and gently let out the clutch. He would have only one go at this.

The bike ran forwards, hitting the plank with a thud. The fencing leaned in as Cámara began to shoot up the ramp. As he reached the top, he saw the first squad cars come racing down the avenue.

With a last, tiny squeeze he jumped off the planks. The engine screamed as the tyres spun in mid-air. And he leaned forward as hard as he could, trying to prevent the bike from flipping back on itself. There was a moment of panic, when he barely knew whether he was upside down or the right way up. Would he land straight or had he overshot? Would the bike make it in one piece? Had the policemen seen him as he flew briefly into the air ahead of them before disappearing into the hole?

He gritted his teeth. The bike seemed to pull him down, like a ballast. And with a squeal and crunch, first the back wheel and then the frame of the bike hit the staircase leading underground. He spun to the side for a second, before realising that he was still gripping the throttle. Releasing his hand, he slammed his left foot down and just stopped the bike from crashing to the ground as the front tyre keeled over and started pummelling the stairs, the bike falling and stumbling as it worked its way down into the central station area.

He rode into a shaded, covered section and stopped. His heart beat like artillery, his lungs stretched to the limit. He looked up: the planks of wood had fallen in behind him and lay half smashed on the staircase. The fencing was damaged, but had sprung back, not quite to its original position, but from outside it was not obvious that someone had just ridden a motorbike over it.

He listened. Sirens were still screeching along the street. It was impossible to tell if they were still coming or heading off. He had to move before they found him.

Picking his phone out of his pocket, he checked the time. Alicia had been held for a couple of hours.

A red light shone at him from the screen: there was a message. Hitting the button, he read:

Maldo onto you — order to arrest on sight. Azcárraga.

He turned the bike to head down the next flight into the tunnel itself.

Above he heard the pinging of metal as police officers checked the fencing around the hole.

He made a silent prayer.

And opened the throttle.

35

The motorbike headlight had broken, but enough light ricocheted from the hole above for him to see. He was at the start of the platform, which stretched ahead for another hundred metres or so. Beyond it the tunnel — a black archway set against the shady gloom of the station — beckoned, heading out in the direction of the sea. The tunnel behind him, curling back towards the city centre, barely registered. If his guess was right he needed to carry on straight: that was where he would find them.

He paused for a second. The tunnel would be dark, almost pitch black, and he had no lights. Yet he would have to move fast. The sound of the engine would be heard ahead of him, warning of his approach. His only hope would be that he would arrive so quickly and unexpectedly that his opponents would be caught off guard.

There were no rails laid down yet — the surface was smooth. Yet the jump was going to test the shocks on the Kawasaki to the limit. It had already taken a beating. Now he needed it to perform more wonders.

The engine had slowed to a gentle purr as he geared himself to push on. From above he could make out the sound of voices — policemen in pursuit.

He took a deep breath, clenched his teeth and twisted the throttle hard. The bike sped down the platform, leaving tyre marks on the concrete surface. Halfway down, before he had picked up too much speed, he swerved to the side and leapt down into the well of the train line. Ahead, the black tunnel opened its jaws to receive him.

He lowered his head over the handlebars, supporting his weight on his feet in case he should have to throw himself off. There was an inch of water on the ground and the ripples ahead just caught the last photons of light and reflected back, giving him the barest of indications of where he was going. If he could make it far enough to see the next station without crashing into the side walls it would act as a beacon and help him find his way.

Maps of the new metro line had sprung up around the neighbourhood when it was being built — a few years back, before the money had run out. And he remembered that there was a sharp bend just ahead of where he was now riding. People had commented at the time that it might be a hazard for future trains. No one had imagined motorbikes speeding through the tunnel, but the danger was the same. He slowed down, stretching his left hand out to see if he could feel the walls curling round. It had suddenly become totally dark — a patch with no light. He pulled off his helmet and threw it down — he needed all his senses operating fully to get through this.

A rough stone edge took the skin off the end of his middle finger and he pulled his hand back, leaning to the right as his eyes strained at the ground below. If he swung too far over he was in danger of crashing into the other side. He slowed the bike down even more, inching along. He could hear the tyres slicing through the water. If he could make it around the bend, he seemed to remember that there would be a long straight ahead.

Quien busca, halla, he thought. Hilario's voice seemed to sound in his ears: He who seeks, finds.

The full darkness continued, metre after metre. He had not expected to find anyone at the station he had just left: it was too open, too exposed. A secret underground hideaway — a 'bunker' — would be in a more discreet location. Not too far out — that would make it close to where the line rose overground. But not too central either. There were three stations where he thought he had a chance of finding it. The first was not far away, just around this interminable bend. Yet if they were there, by slowing down so much he had almost certainly lost his advantage: the sound of the motorbike had been echoing for several minutes by this point.

The faintest of glimmers on the water ahead was followed by another and then another. Gently, he turned the throttle and pushed forwards. The final curve of the bend came into sight and ahead lay a bright ribbon of shimmering water pointing straight towards the next station, and the pool of half-light glowing over its platform.

The bike growled as he fired the engine and sped on.

He stood up as he cruised past. There was no

sign of life at the station: no litter, no tread marks in the cement dust, no disturbance in what looked exactly like an abandoned building site. No one was here: he would press on.

Ahead, the light of the next station was the palest of blotches at the end of a long black hole. The path was straight: nothing could slow him down. Tears squeezed at the corners of his eyes as he pushed the bike as fast as it could go.

He saw movement ahead: figures bobbing in the shadows. Up at the next platform he had been heard and people there were looking to see what the noise was, what was approaching them out of the darkness.

His guess was correct — they were down here: he knew it in his blood. But if they had heard him, then so had Alicia — if she was still alive. He hoped that the sound of him coming might give her strength.

The platform sped quickly into view, growing larger by the second, and the tiny shadows became people with arms and legs. Some were starting to run, others stayed where they were, waiting to be sure of what was coming towards them. As he drew closer, most of them pulled away until only one remained. Something about his silhouette, about the shape of his head, was familiar. Pascual had mentioned his bald scalp, the narrowing towards the top. The same man Cámara had seen that night outside the chemist's.

It was Julio.

It was not smooth, nor did it reach the bottom of the tunnel floor, but there was a ramp leading

305

up to the platform. Above it, still trying to make out who or what was coming towards him from the dark, Julio stood, holding on to a metal bar set in the wall and leaning out to get a better look. Cámara sped towards the ramp, then opened out the throttle as far as it would go and threw his weight back, trying to pull up the front wheel. But he was already going too fast. The bike caught on the bottom lip of the ramp and somersaulted over him with the momentum. He let go of the handlebars and as his body was hurled off the machine he curled himself into a ball, pulling his arms over his chest as tightly as he could.

The breath was kicked out of him as he crashed into something. It was hard, but he was lucky: whatever it was bent and crumbled under his weight and velocity, absorbing his fall. He had the impression of blacking out for a second — an empty gap like a missing frame from a film reel. Then he opened his eyes, catching his breath, trying to steady himself as bright star-like flashes clouded his vision. Still lying on the ground, he felt his limbs, bending and stretching them. Miraculously, everything worked.

He lifted his head and remembered what had happened, where he was. The bike had landed on the platform several metres ahead of him, skidding along until it crashed into a wall, where the engine had died.

Lying next to him, however, was the figure of a man lying prostrate, practically unconscious. And he realised what had broken his fall so efficiently: Julio.

He leapt over and crouched over him. Julio was still alive but was badly winded. His eyes bulged as he struggled for breath. Cámara looked across and saw the tattoo on his forearm — a shield in the Spanish colours with a black double-headed axe.

With one hand he gripped Julio's throat, reaching with the other for his pistol and placing it at his temple.

'Where's Alicia?' he asked. 'The journalist. Tell me now.'

Julio's eyes rolled as he coughed back to wakefulness. He stared at Cámara, breathing hard, the veins around his temples bulging.

And he gave nothing away, no quick look to the side, no smile as he realised what was about to happen.

The punch struck Cámara at the back of his head, just behind his ear. He was unconscious before his body fell on top of Julio's.

'Get this cunt off me,' Julio told his rescuers.

'And tie him up. We'll finish him off after we've done with her.'

36

The muffled sound of a generator rumbling from somewhere nearby stirred him. He groaned, rolling his head and forcing his eyes open as he tried to shake himself fully awake. His hands were tied behind his back and the cord was attached to a drainpipe running down the wall. A heavy pulse beat at the backs of his eyes. One. Two. One. Two.

He felt an urge to be sick, and swallowed hard to keep it down, but the convulsions in his stomach were too strong. He jerked to the side and the vomit landed with a thick splatter on the floor beside him. He licked his lips clean and tried to clear the stinging acid from the back of his throat. After a couple of moments he felt lighter, stronger.

It was a small room, some kind of storage area. A pale bulb hung from the ceiling casting a cold blue light. Beside him, just within reach of his feet, was a tower of metal shelving supporting cardboard boxes. Wooden crates were stacked high against a far wall while in the centre of the room stood an island of filing cabinets back to back.

Above his head hung a Spanish flag. He glanced up and saw that it bore the Francoist black eagle at the centre. Over the doorway in the far left corner hung a picture of the *Caudillo* in full military uniform.

The LOP had also discovered the secret underground world of the unused metro line, as he had guessed. This was the 'bunker', but it was no refuge for the homeless and hungry.

It was clean and felt overly regimented. Behind the stench of his vomit there was a heavy odour of bleach — the same smell that had struck him at the gym.

His thoughts were cut short by the sound of groaning from behind the door. Alicia's voice was dulled by pain: with a cold, leaden certainty he knew that she had been suffering for a long time already.

He swallowed again and pulled hard at his bonds. But the cord held tight: the piping was firmly cemented into the wall. Brute force was not going to get him out of there.

He had got Alicia into this; he had asked her to get involved, to see what she could discover about Amy. And he had placed her at risk. It was clear that Julio and his thugs had been keeping tabs on Amy; it was only to be expected that they would latch on to anyone coming after them. And what they had done to their earlier victims, now they were about to do to Alicia, and perhaps others.

Except that he was there. He was securely tied up, but he had to do something — anything — to throw things off their present course. By the faintness of her screams he knew that Alicia had already been suffering for a long time.

And then he realised that whoever was in there in the next room with her was not talking to her; no questions were being asked. This was not torture designed to extract information: the pain being inflicted on her was being done purely for pleasure. Another victim, another woman, on whom to carry out their fantasies.

He bit his tongue hard as he forced himself not to call out. And the taste of blood filled his mouth.

These men would not act alone, needing the sadism of the group to carry them forward. Listening more carefully, struggling to ignore Alicia for a moment, he could make out the sound of footsteps and laughter. There were at least two, possibly three men in there. If he could just take out one of them. But how?

He stretched out: his right foot fitted neatly around the nearest leg of the metal shelves. He pushed hard and they scraped along the floor, making a deafening sound. From the next room came male voices: they had heard.

With another flick, he pushed at the shelves even harder, trying to flip them over. They started to rock. Stretching his leg as far as it would go, he gave it a final shove and it came crashing to the floor.

The response was almost immediate. The handle was pulled from the other side and the door was flung open.

'I told you to tie him up properly,' came a voice. Julio stayed in the next room, but one of his thugs came bursting in. Through the doorway Cámara could see smoke and the lower part of Alicia's legs, tied with black straps to a table. Small red circular marks dotted her skin — and he knew immediately that they had been using her to put out their cigarettes.

The man now walking towards Cámara wore a tight white T-shirt, showing off inflated upper-body muscles. He was perhaps one of the foursome who had been present at the chemist's that night; Cámara could not be certain. But underneath the cladding was a young man with a small frame. And the concentration on building upper-body strength meant that he was top heavy.

Cámara flicked his legs round as the man stepped towards him, and with a similar flipping motion to before, brought his hulking weight down. Surprised and unbalanced, the man fell on top of him. Cámara pulled him closer to his face by hauling him up with his knees and before the man could react he had clenched his jaws over his throat, squeezing hard at his windpipe like a big cat choking the life out of his prey.

'What the fuck?'

Julio came running in, tripping over the scattered boxes. Cámara eyed him, his teeth sinking deeper into the thug's neck. The young man was flailing about, trying to struggle free, but Cámara was ignoring his punches and kicks, refusing to let go.

'I should have shot you straight away,' Julio said.

He pulled out a pistol from the small of his back.

'Wait!'

A deeper voice called from inside the other room.

'Not now, Julio.'

311

The thug trapped by Cámara's mouth was beginning to squeal.

'Free José Antonio and bring them both in here,' the voice said. 'I've got an idea.'

After Julio's third punch against the side of his head, Cámara's jaws loosened their grip and José Antonio pulled away. The young man's neck was bleeding where the skin was broken and he struggled to breathe for a few moments.

'Fucker.' Julio spat at him.

José Antonio launched a frustrated foot at Cámara, connecting hard with his lower ribs.

'Enough,' Julio said. 'Help me untie him. You fucked this up, now sort it out.'

After fumbling behind Cámara's back, José Antonio gave up on the knot and pulled out a knife to cut the cord to the pipe. Cámara's hands were still secured as he was lifted on to his feet and led into the next room.

It was larger than the storeroom. Cámara guessed that they were in the ticket area of the station — a passageway led off in the direction of the main tunnel. The walls and floor were painted in glossy, thick white paint, reflecting the light of half a dozen bulbs suspended from the low ceiling.

In the centre, lying on what looked like an operating table, was Alicia. Except for a pair of knickers and the straps holding down her arms and legs, she was naked. So many tears had dried around her eyes that a salty residue clung around her eyelashes. He dared not count the burn marks on her skin.

'Max?'

She managed to lift her head enough to catch sight of him as they dragged him in and threw him against the opposite wall. His legs gave way and he slumped to the floor, just keeping his back upright.

She called his name again.

'It's all right,' he said. 'It'll be all right.'

He heard sniggering. Julio and José Antonio were standing over him, poised to strike lest he should try something. José Antonio was still clutching at his neck, trying to stem the bleeding. But behind Alicia stood two other men: one, from his appearance, was another of Julio's henchmen, wearing the uniform stretch T-shirt and expression of mindless anger. Next to him, however, was someone who Cámara had seen only two days before on television — at Pepe's bar round the corner from the Jefatura.

'I wanted you to see this,' Francisco Soler said, nodding at Alicia's tortured body in front of him.

'So far the loudest screams come from the ones on her inner thighs, near the top. We're about to open a new packet of cigarettes and work our way to more sensitive areas.'

He coughed to the side, his hand rising to his mouth with a touch of theatricality.

'I hate the smoke, and the ventilation down here isn't what you would want.'

'What do you — ?'

Cámara's attempt to speak was cut short by José Antonio's foot smashing into his face.

'You don't interrupt the leader!' José Antonio screamed.

Two streams of warm blood cascaded from

Cámara's nostrils, over his lips, and dripped on to his chest from the point of his chin.

José Antonio prepared to kick him again.

'That's enough.'

On Soler's command he stopped and lowered his foot.

'The chief inspector's arrival has changed things,' Soler said. 'Oh, yes,' he added, 'we know exactly who you are.'

Alicia had started crying again, tears falling down her temples and into the matting of her hair.

'Spare her the soft words,' said Soler. 'Everything is not all right. Nor will it be.'

He walked round from the other side of the table and peered down at Cámara.

'I shall look away,' he said. 'The sight of death revolts me. But I want to seal this image in my mind for ever, like a photograph.'

He turned to the second thug behind the table.

'Gonzalo. Unstrap her,' he said.

Julio looked at him.

'What?'

'I want you to give her a gun,' Soler told him. 'Give her the one the chief inspector had on him when he arrived.'

A fleeting grin passed over Julio's lips as he reached into a pocket and pulled out Cámara's standard issue Heckler & Koch USP, then he went over to help free up Alicia while José Antonio watched over Cámara.

Alicia could barely sit up straight, her body limp with pain. Her face was grey and her shoulders curled defensively inwards. As she tried to shake some life into her legs, wincing with the pain, she lifted her arms to cover her breasts.

But Julio snatched at her wrists and pulled them away. With one hand he flicked off the safety catch on the pistol and then placed it in Alicia's hand, keeping his grip over it.

'Stand away, José Antonio,' he said. 'Unless you want to get covered in more blood.'

José Antonio took a couple of steps back, then in one quick motion Julio pulled out his other gun — which was fitted with a silencer — and placed it against Alicia's head.

'It's simple,' Soler said from the other side. 'Save us the trouble of killing your lover and your own pain stops now. The burning, I promise, will stop.'

And he turned to face the wall.

'Clean up the mess before I turn around,' he said to Gonzalo.

Julio pushed his pistol harder against Alicia's head.

'Of course, if you don't do what you're told, it will only make things worse. And I mean really a lot worse.'

Alicia held the gun limply in her hand and stared down at Cámara on the floor.

'I'm going to count to three,' Julio said. 'If you haven't shot him by then I'll kill him myself. Then start on you again. Understand?'

Alicia was motionless.

'One!' barked Julio.

She raised her hand, the gun shaking as she

tried to point it at Cámara.

'Two!'

Her finger whitened as it began to press on the trigger.

'Three!'

And she fired.

37

Splinters of concrete spat into his scalp as the bullet smashed into the wall just centimetres above his head.

Alicia let the pistol fall into her lap and closed her eyes, her hair sweeping over her face.

Julio rammed his gun against her head, almost pushing her over, then pulled back and punched her with his left hand. She fell to the floor, curling into a ball, her naked back convulsing with sobs.

'Stupid fucking bitch!'

José Antonio decided to join in, and planted a kick against her lower spine.

'Can't do it, then?' Julio called down. 'Can't shoot your fucking boyfriend? We'll just have to do it for you. And make you fucking watch.'

Cámara felt the beginnings of shock start to worm their way into his blood. He had stared down that gun barrel, and in the doubt of the moment, had thought he was going to die. But he knew now that Alicia had deliberately fired too high, was incapable of murdering him, no matter what they threatened her with. And something in him changed; he felt an immense space — white, pure and unsullied — begin to push against the pain and open up in him: a world of potential.

317

José Antonio walked over to Cámara and pulled out a gun, pointing it at his head.

'Can I do it? Please, Julio. The cunt almost ripped my throat out. Let me do it. I want to do it.'

'Wait,' Julio said. 'We'll have some fun first.'

José Antonio lowered his gun a touch, then took a step forward as though about to shoot. Cámara did not flinch.

'Hah!' José Antonio laughed. 'Just kidding.'

Julio was standing over Alicia and called to the second thug.

'Gonzalo, come here and give me a hand.'

Gonzalo walked over.

'You're all right to turn around,' Julio said to Soler.

The fat, older man spun on his heel. His white eye was twitching nervously behind the protection of his glasses.

'Change of plan?' he said.

'Time for some R and R before we get back to work.'

Cámara registered the pseudo-military style of talking. Julio and Gonzalo picked Alicia up by the arms. Her body was limp in their hands and her feet dragged along the floor.

'Over here,' Julio said. 'On the table. Face down.'

They propped her torso at right angles over the tabletop; her legs drooped over one side and her head hung heavily over the other.

'Gonzalo, you hold that arm. José Antonio, you take the other.'

As the two young men moved into position,

Julio grabbed the top of Alicia's knickers and yanked them down her legs. Alicia began to struggle.

'No,' she screamed, kicking against Julio. 'No!'

'Hold her tight, boys.'

Julio wrapped his arms around her thighs, forcing her still, and continued pulling her knickers down until they hung from only one foot, the black cotton fabric catching just above her ankle.

Alicia continued to scream, but was no longer formulating coherent words. Her head bobbed up and down on the other side of the table as she filled her lungs and wailed as loudly as she could.

Her naked buttocks tensed as she pulled her hips in, trying to curl her body inwards, away from danger. But the table was in the way and restricted her movement. Gonzalo took a step closer and pressed a hand down into the centre of her back, forcing her to keep still.

Julio's trousers now fell down around his knees and he pulled out his cock.

'Are you ready for this?' he asked Cámara. 'Wouldn't want you to miss anything.'

And he shuffled forwards, readying himself to penetrate.

'You ready to get a dose?' Cámara coughed.

Julio stopped.

'What?'

Cámara cleared his throat of blood and mucus.

'You ready to get a dose of the clap? Because that's what you're going to get if you do it.'

Julio paused, his cock pressing against the top of Alicia's thigh.

'Fuck off.'

Cámara saw the doubt in his eye.

'She's a slag,' he said. 'Fucks anything. And then brings it home to me. The itching started yesterday. In a couple of days they turn to sores. And believe me, they hurt like fucking hell.'

Julio took a step away.

'It's not the first time. She's a bloody nympho. Great in bed but you never know where she's been.'

'You're lying,' Julio said. He believed every word of it.

'Take a look if you want.' Cámara nodded down at his crotch. 'It's already red and sore. And the creams never work properly. Takes weeks to get rid of.'

Julio glanced over to Gonzalo and José Antonio.

'Perhaps no R and R after all,' Soler grinned from the other side of the room. 'Come on, let's finish this off. We've wasted too much time as it is.'

Alicia's back rose and fell quickly as she caught her breath. Gonzalo took his hand away and grabbed the back of her hair, lifting her face up to him.

'I reckon we can still have some fun,' he said.

He undid his trousers and reached inside.

'If she's such a goer as he says she is, she'll enjoy this.'

He pushed his cock towards her mouth. José Antonio placed his gun against her head.

'Do it or I blow your brains out,' he said.

Alicia clenched her teeth and began to whimper.

The three thugs were now huddled around her. For a second they had forgotten about Cámara. It was his only chance.

He slipped a foot under his hips and hauled himself up. After only two strides he was next to Julio and with a sharp, jerking motion he cracked the point of his forehead against his skull, just above his ear. Julio fell to the floor with a deep groan.

Jumping over him, Cámara threw his weight against José Antonio, falling down with him as the man lost his grip on his gun and let it clatter across the floor. Gonzalo was unarmed and it was essential that Cámara take out the two men with pistols as quickly as possible.

He heard shouting. José Antonio was wriggling beneath him, but Cámara was searching again with his teeth for something soft and vulnerable. He felt a hard kick crashing against his ribs, then hands reached around his neck, tightening over his trachea.

'Get him off me!' screamed José Antonio.

A shadow fell across them and Gonzalo's grip on his throat loosened.

'That's enough. Get up.'

Soler had picked up José Antonio's gun and was standing over them. He planted the sole of his shoe against Cámara's face and pushed him off.

'Put him and the girl against that wall,' he told Gonzalo calmly. 'And finish them. Do it now.'

José Antonio sprang up and helped Gonzalo drag Cámara over to the other side of the room.

'Let me do it,' said José Antonio. 'Let me shoot him. Please.'

'Shut up,' Soler ordered. 'You've fucked things up enough already. Gonzalo, make yourself decent.'

Gonzalo hitched his trousers up.

'Now take the girl over there as well.'

Julio was lying on the floor, his hands wrapped around his head.

'We'll sort him out in a minute,' said Soler.

Gonzalo pulled Alicia off the table, stuck an arm beneath her waist and carried her over towards Cámara. Her knickers still dragged from one foot and she wrestled to pull them up again.

'Make them kneel, facing the wall,' said Soler.

Gonzalo dumped Alicia on the floor, pushing her lower legs under her with his foot so that she crouched on her haunches. Then he prodded at Cámara to get into the same position.

'Here,' said Soler. 'Come and take this pistol. And make sure you execute Cámara first.'

Gonzalo stepped over to take the gun. Cámara's mind was racing but no solution, no plan came. He wriggled his hands behind his back, trying for a last time to loosen the knot.

A finger pushed into his palm and he stopped. Alicia had shuffled over on her knees to be closer to him and held out a hand to touch his. He looked into her eyes and gripped her finger as tightly as he could.

'I love you.'

Gonzalo was walking back towards them holding the gun.

'Don't fuck it up,' Soler said. 'I'm going to turn away now.'

'She moved!' José Antonio shrieked. 'She fucking moved closer to him.'

'Calm down,' said Gonzalo in a low voice. 'They're not going anywhere now.'

Cámara felt the hairs rise on his spine; it was almost as if he could see the gun pointing at the back of his head.

And suddenly the racing stopped and he stepped once more into the empty white space.

'I love you too,' he said.

38

The bullet passed through Gonzalo's right shoulder, throwing his weight backwards and spinning down to the floor. Before José Antonio could react, Torres had trained his Heckler & Koch at his head and shouted.

'Drop it now! Now!'

José Antonio panicked, his eyes white with fear, his own gun still firmly gripped in his hand. He made to shoot, but a second figure ran towards him, low and fast, and tackled him to the ground. The gun went off and the bullet punched into the ceiling.

Cámara spun on his knees to see Daniel burst in from the direction of the tunnel and throw himself at José Antonio, wrapping his arm around his neck. Dídac had joined him and was prising the gun out of the thug's hand.

'Careful with that.'

Torres walked quickly towards them, his gun still outstretched. Gonzalo lay on the floor, panting and pale. His left hand was pressed against his shoulder, where blood was beginning to seep through his T-shirt and spill on to the floor.

'Fuck . . . ' José Antonio continued struggling against Daniel until Dídac finally loosened the gun from his grip and stood up, pointing the weapon in his face.

'Police!' Torres shouted.

Soler had stood with his face turned away, but now turned hesitantly to see. Things had not gone as expected.

At the sight of Gonzalo's blood staining his white floor red, his knees buckled under him and he fell, clutching at his stomach and retching.

Cámara loosened his grip around Alicia's finger and tried to get to his feet, but his legs refused to obey.

'Torres,' he tried to say, but his voice caught in his throat.

Still standing over Gonzalo, Torres called over to Daniel.

'Throw him face forwards on to the ground.'

When José Antonio was finally prostrate, Torres walked over, pulled out some cuffs and hooked them around his wrists. Then he took out a second pair and handed them to Dídac.

'Slip them on,' he said, and pointed towards Soler, still doubled over in the corner.

'The other one's all right,' Torres said. 'But we'll have to get him some medical attention fast.'

Cámara detected a movement at the side of the group. Julio had lain silent and motionless throughout, but now began to stir. Leaping to his feet, his gun still in his hand, he started running in the direction of the tunnel.

Torres spotted him and spun round to take a shot.

'Stop!' Cámara shouted.

The bullet hit the wall, spattering cement shards behind Julio's back.

And Julio kept running.

Torres aimed for another shot.

'Don't!' Cámara called.

Julio disappeared from view, down into the tunnel and away.

Torres lowered his weapon slowly.

'You want him to get away?'

'Yes. I do.'

'All right,' Torres said. He holstered his pistol. 'It's your call, chief.'

Dídac had taken off his shirt and vest. The first he wrapped around Alicia's waist, like a makeshift skirt. The second he placed over her top. She shivered in his arms, eyes closed, hands pressed against her face.

Torres handed his pistol to Daniel.

'Here,' he said. 'Watch over this lot.' He nodded towards Soler, Gonzalo and José Antonio.

'I need to find a spot with a signal.'

He whipped his phone out of his pocket and walked up the stairs, away from the ticket area and closer to the surface.

Cámara shuffled over towards Alicia. Dídac hopped over towards him and pulled out a knife. A moment later he had freed his hands. Cámara reached out towards Alicia and she collapsed into his arms.

'Laura Martín got in touch,' Dídac whispered as Cámara and Alicia rocked slowly together. 'Like you told her to. But she spoke to Torres as well. He looked for us at the refuge and we came as fast as we could.'

'How did you get here?' Cámara asked.

'Ran down the tunnel,' Dídac said with half a

grin. 'Brought us straight to you.'

Torres returned from making his call.

'My ex-wife,' he said. 'A couple of her friends are nurses. They'll be here soon. I'll have to open up at the top, let them in.'

Cámara sighed with relief: Torres had understood. No police involvement, nothing official. They had to keep this to themselves.

'Call Laura as well,' he said, looking down at Alicia nestling against his chest. 'I think we're going to need her.'

Torres glanced across at the two men in handcuffs.

'And Albelda,' Cámara added. 'But only Albelda. We can trust him.'

Twenty minutes later, the two nurses had arrived with a medical kit and were attending to Gonzalo. Albelda stood watch over the two other prisoners, while Laura, having brought blankets and drinks, was with Alicia.

'We've got to get them both to a hospital immediately,' she insisted.

Cámara mopped himself clean with some of the nurses' bandages. Strength was slowly returning to his body, driven by the next step he knew that he had to take.

'They need specialist care.'

'Take them quickly,' he said. 'But no word to anyone about what's happened here. Not until I say. This stays strictly between us.'

He leaned down and kissed Alicia on the forehead. She reached out to cling to him and he embraced her, holding her gently and firmly in his arms.

'It's all right,' he whispered.

Her tears flowed into his chest, mingling with the blood soaked in his shirt.

'I need to go, my love,' he said. 'I need to finish this.'

Very slowly he pulled himself away. Her body shivered with pain and fright.

'Laura will look after you. She's a friend.'

He kissed her on the cheek.

'I'll be back very soon.'

It was the hardest thing he had ever done, but there was still so much to do, and they needed to move quickly.

He hobbled towards Torres and leaned on his shoulder. Torres placed his arm around his ribs to help support his weight and gave him his pistol.

'There's only one place Julio will have gone,' Cámara said.

Torres nodded.

'I'm going to need your help one more time.'

39

'A wounded bull has its *querencia*, the place in the ring where it feels safest, where it returns to as often as possible. All we have to do now is go to Julio's *querencia*.'

'And arrest him?'

'And wait. He's hurt and frightened and won't want to be alone for long. He'll be looking for guidance, for someone to tell him what to do next.'

'But we've got Soler, his boss.'

'Soler is only a manager. Someone else is directing, someone with an enormous amount of power. It's why we have to move quickly and quietly. It's why it's only you and me.'

'Look, chief. About what happened . . . '

'It's all right. Really.'

'I should never . . . '

'Forget it. It's over. You saved Alicia, you saved me.'

'I almost fucked things up.'

'We've been manipulated from the start. But it's not always clear who's been trying to pull our strings.'

Delayed shock from the events in the bunker vibrated in his blood, like static from an ill-tuned radio. He was forcing himself to carry on, feeding off the nervous tension, converting it into fuel for one more step.

Cold anger acted like a lens in his mind, his

thinking sharp and decisive, a singularity about every movement he made — all geared towards one end.

The details of everything that had happened circled inside him, had become part of his being. He did not need to dwell on them — neither the burn marks puncturing Alicia's flesh, nor Amy's dissected corpse, nor the swollen, broken body of Oliva lying helpless and inert in a hospital bed. His own body shrieked from the pummelling he had received, but he could ignore the worst of it.

Poised like a cat, he was about to pounce, to reach out his claws and catch the person who was really responsible.

The slush fund had bought favours and loyalties, had corrupted a whole stratum of Valencian society. The LOP had received some of the funds — that much was clear. It was why they had gone to such lengths to silence those who were about to reveal the secret. Murdering Amy and Oliva had not been enough, however. The affair was already messy and out of control. The very methods they used to keep tabs on Amy and her articles were also a weakness — the information itself might not have leaked out, but clues as to what she was involved in had reached her online networks. All it had taken was for Alicia to start chatting to the right people and the dots began to be joined up.

First the link between Amy and Oliva's deaths: the murders had been carried out simultaneously by members of the same group — by Julio, Gonzalo, José Antonio and other LOP thugs answering to party leader Francisco Soler. Those who had not been at the bunker would have scattered, but there would be time to find them later. They were not the important ones: they were actors playing parts handed down to them. Others had been in command.

Soler, certainly. And he would have been in contact with Felicidad Galván, who ran the slush fund. But even she was not in complete control. She too, as Oliva said in his letter to Sonia, was under orders from someone else.

Their investigations had been compromised from the beginning: talk of a competition between the two had been a smokescreen. They were never meant to solve the cases properly in the first place.

Yet the slush fund in itself was not the major crime. Political favours had been commodities on an open market since the beginning of time, accepted as part of the political landscape. Voters seldom cared about such things: they expected their rulers to be corrupt — up to a point.

No, the real scandal was where the money had come from. The slush fund was not created from donations by party supporters or big business, but built on cash destined for medical care — hospitals where now, through a lack of drugs and doctors to treat them, people were dying. There was no way to cover over the shortfalls: theft on such a grand scale was having a real and direct effect. They might as well have stormed into clinics and stolen machines and pills directly from the doctors and nurses. The result was the same: dead patients.

Whoever was behind the scheme was a

murderer, with the blood of hundreds, perhaps thousands of people on their hands. The blood of his grandfather. The blood of Hilario.

Forgiveness was not part of his plan.

There were no parking spaces available, so Torres pulled in behind a car at the crossroads just a few doors down.

'It's further away than I would like,' he said, 'but at least I can cover the entrance.'

'Look at the padlock at the bottom of the shutters,' said Cámara. 'It's open. Julio will already be inside.'

'Hasn't turned the lights on. Clever boy.'

'Wait here. I'll switch my phone to silent, but text me when you see something.'

Cámara got out of the car, checked that his pistol was loaded, and walked along the pavement, stepping quickly Through the pools of street lighting to the next. Pascual was inside the entrance hall of his building, sweeping up at the end of another day. Cámara tapped very lightly on the glass and caught his attention. Raising a finger to his lips, he slipped inside and closed the door before Pascual could say anything.

'Come with me,' he said in a low voice, placing a hand on the doorman's elbow.

Pascual saw his bloody face and clothes and heard the urgency in his voice, and responded immediately. They hurried to the back of the building and the doorway that led to the patio. Cámara explained as simply as he could what was going on.

'And you don't want me to do anything?' the old man asked. His blood was up at the thought

332

of something so dramatic happening.

'Just stay here, out of sight,' said Cámara. 'It's crucial that no one sees you from outside.'

'It's quiet at this time,' Pascual said. 'Midweek. Everyone's in bed. We expecting someone, then?'

'Yes.'

Cámara stepped through into the patio. The ladder was still there from the other day, propped up against the side wall. He lowered his voice to a whisper.

'You can't be seen or heard. But I want you to stay close, just in case.'

Pascual gave him a thumbs-up. His pulse had not raced so much in decades.

Cámara gripped the ladder with both hands and started climbing, silently praising Pascual for having a wooden one rather than the cheap and creaky aluminium kind. He reached the top of the wall and paused, listening and watching for any signs of movement inside the gym. The lights were still off, but he was certain that Julio was in there, hiding, frightened and waiting for his saviour to come. Without Soler he was lost and had only one recourse — to go directly to the very top.

Cámara could not stay on the ladder waiting for something to happen. By the time he got over and down it would almost certainly be too late. There was no alternative but to drop into the patio at the back of the gym as quietly as possible.

He pulled himself up on to the wall and then carefully he slipped his legs over and let his weight slide down the other side, hanging on at the top with his fingers. When he had reached full stretch, he let go.

He dropped a metre and a half and as his feet took the impact, he bent his knees to absorb the fall and rolled backwards on to his haunches, doing a full somersault until he was upright again. He whipped out his pistol and listened. His heart pounded and his damaged ribs screamed. Had anyone heard him?

He waited until he was certain that his presence had not been detected and then began to pace slowly towards the gym, treading silently on the sides of his feet and rolling them with each step. When he reached the door he stopped. The glass was still smashed from his last visit and the shards lay on the floor untouched — either no one had been back here in the meantime, or they had not noticed. He should be able to open it easily when the time came.

He crouched down and waited. From inside he could hear footsteps, the sound of a man sighing, and the click and slide of a gun action being tested. A foolish exercise in the dark, but Julio was anxious and needed something to occupy his hands.

Cámara dug his fingers into his pocket and fished out his phone, placing it near his feet to catch any text messages from Torres. So far none had come through. An intense aching was beginning to spread around his back and down into his thighs. It was hard to keep still for so long and the painkilling adrenalin was subsiding. He longed for a cigarette, but the thought brought a flash of the burn marks on Alicia's skin and he closed his eyes, willing the vision away. He did not know if he would ever be able to smoke again.

The phone shuddered gently at his feet and the screen lit up.

He's here.

Cámara picked up his phone, switched on the voice recorder and pocketed it again. Then he pulled out his pistol and waited. From the front of the gym he heard the sound of the shutter being lifted halfway up and then closed down again. Footsteps closed in, bringing the new person towards the back of the gym. Still waiting, Julio coughed.

'Is that you?'

'You made it then.'

'Course I fucking made it. But do you have any idea how dangerous it is for me to come here?'

Julio mumbled something unintelligible.

'I mean, here of all places?'

'I didn't know where else to go,' Julio said apologetically.

'And just what the fuck is going on? Where's Soler?'

'Police.'

'What?'

'That detective you told us about. He found us.'

'How?'

'I don't know, but he just turned up. We had his girlfriend, the journo woman you mentioned.'

'Is she still alive?'

'Yes. I think so.'

'Fuck, fuck, fuck. And Cámara?'

'Yes.'

There was a silence.

'You have got to be kidding me. I gave one simple order and you fucked it all up.'

'There were others. We had it covered but then others showed up.'

'Other what?'

'I don't know. Police, I think.'

'Impossible. I had that sorted.'

'He had help. They came. Took us by surprise. Shot Gonzalo. I think he's dead. And they got Soler and José Antonio.'

'Where are they now?'

'I don't know. I got away. Came here. I don't know anything that's going on.'

'You fucking stupid idiot. You're like a bunch of fucking monkeys. I pay you to work for me, to do a job and you fuck it up completely.'

'But you can fix it, surely. You always have in the past.'

'Fix it?'

There was a pause. Cámara could hear Julio panting.

'Yeah,' came the voice. 'I can probably fix it. There's a lot of shit to sort out first, though.'

More footsteps.

'Where exactly are you? I can hardly see anything in here.'

'I'm here,' said Julio.

'Walk towards me.'

Julio stepped across the gym.

'Right, there you are. That should do.'

'What do we do now?' asked Julio. 'Tell me. I'm freaking out here.'

'You still got a gun?'

'Yeah.'

'With the silencer?'

'Yeah.'

'Give it to me.'

Silence.

'Thanks.'

'What are we going to do?'

'It wasn't your fault, Julio. You were all right. Just out of your depth.'

'What are you going to do? Wait.'

There was a single shot, high-pitched and short, like a muffled firecracker, and then a heavy slumping sound on the ground.

Still holding his pistol Cámara leapt up and threw himself at the door. Glass scattered over the floor as he pushed his way inside.

'Stop!' he cried. 'Stop!

Two more shots were fired. He dived to the ground and lifted his head. The place was still dark, but thanks to his opening the door a glimmer of light was now streaming in from the back patio. He saw a shadow dart across the open space of the gym, making its way towards the front shutters. Leaping to his feet, Cámara reached up to the wall and felt with his fingers till he found a light switch.

After a stutter, the neon strip lights illuminated the entire area.

Julio's body lay by a bench, a single hole in the front of his face and blood pouring from the back of his head.

And standing at the front of the gym, holding a gun with one hand and furiously trying to open the shutters with the other, was Javier Flores.

Cámara fired once and the bullet hit the shutters, just to the left of Flores's head. Flores ducked and reached down with both hands to pull up the shutters and make his escape.

The second bullet hit him in the hip, and he fell to the ground, screaming. Cámara held his pistol in both hands and walked up to him slowly, aiming at Flores's head.

'This,' Cámara said, 'is for everything.'

40

It was late but lights were still lit on the top floor. Cámara identified himself at the main entrance and took the lift up. The place looked clean and undamaged: it seemed that, despite his best efforts, the demonstrators had not found a way into the bankers' castle. A head-on assault by an angry mob was not always the best way to break a corrupt institution, but there were alternatives.

A passing secretary, carrying a tray of coffee cups and clearly disgruntled at having to stay so late, confirmed what he suspected and pointed him in the right direction. The lush and exotic pot plants on either side of the corridor softened the sound of his footsteps.

Felicidad Galván was on her own, sitting at her desk with hundreds of papers in neatly stacked towers in front of her. He walked in and she looked up over small, gold-rimmed reading glasses, her face expressionless, almost as though she had expected him.

'The policeman from the other day. Forgive me if I don't stand up,' she said.

Cámara walked to the other side of the desk and was going to sit down when he changed his mind, picked up the chair and carried it round to Felicidad's side. As he eased himself down she stared at him, confused.

'I'm assuming you're going to explain yourself at some point.'

Cámara glanced at the papers in front of her and saw handwritten documents with lists of names and numbers.

'Javier Flores has confessed,' he said.

Her eyes widened and a tense smile rippled across her thin mouth.

'Javier Flores?'

'He told us everything. About the slush fund, how it operated, where the money came from.'

She blinked.

'How you were running it,' said Cámara.

Her jaws tightened as she tried to conceal her reaction. For a moment Cámara got the impression that she was going to resist.

'I've just come from seeing Flores now,' he said.

Dried blood still clung to his shirt, his face was pale from the pain in his ribs and back. He wanted a shower and to sleep for days. But first he had to do this.

'It looks like you had a rough time of it,' said Felicidad.

'I also came across some members of the LOP,' Cámara said. 'The Legionaries of Order and Progress. I think you know them. The leader, Francisco Soler, has been arrested. He has some interesting things to say as well.'

She took off her glasses and placed them on the desk.

'Is that why you've come? To arrest me?'

'That depends on you.'

She shuffled in her chair and picked up one of the documents, pondering it for a moment.

'Do you know what this is?' she asked. 'It's

340

one of the many thousands of documents I've been keeping over the past ten years.'

She glanced back at him.

'All handwritten, no copies made. No one else knows they even exist. Not even Diego Oliva. And he knew a lot of things. Too many things.'

'Is that why you look at them late at night, all on your own?'

She smiled.

'Yes, probably. All on my own. You make it sound like a death sentence. Is that it? Am I on my own?'

She shook her head, more resigned than defiant.

'Perhaps I can still buy some friends. I've done it before. With a different sort of currency, of course.'

'You mean those documents?'

'Yes, these documents. You've probably guessed what they're about.'

'Is it all there?'

'Everything. Every cent we received, where it came from, and where it went.'

'And who ordered it to be spent where.'

She paused.

'I suppose that's the most important thing, is it? The puppetmaster behind it all. But yes, you're right. That's here as well. JF. I've used his initials throughout, but there's no doubting who it refers to.'

The solitary siren of a police car screamed down the road several storeys below, very slowly diminishing as it sped past and continued its journey across the city.

'It's funny,' she said. 'In the daytime, with all the background noise, it's as though you can't hear anything up here. We're isolated from the rest of the world, lost in our little tower, removed and yet here, in the heart of things, moving our pieces, playing our grand games. And it's just that we're deafened by so much noise. So it's only at night, when everything is silent, that you can really hear. And understand.'

'Did you think the police car was coming for you?'

She frowned.

'Yes. For a moment I did.'

'But to help you or to take you away?'

She squinted at him.

'What do you mean?'

'I know that Chief Inspector Maldonado has been tipping Flores off,' Cámara said. 'We've known for years. He is so transparent, despite his best efforts not to be.'

For a moment, Felicidad was silent, then slowly she began to nod.

'You almost sound fond of him,' she said.

'It's not quite the word I would use.'

'No, perhaps not.'

'How involved was he?'

'Are you asking me questions now?' She raised an eyebrow. 'Why should I answer you? Am I being arrested? But if so, where are the handcuffs, the investigating judge, the other policemen who would surely be here? Not just a single chief inspector acting alone in the middle of the night.'

'I shot Flores,' he said.

She gasped.

'That's why I'm covered in blood. One of the reasons.'

'Is . . . Is he . . . ?'

'Did you know Julio? One of the LOP men.'

'I . . . '

'Flores had just murdered him, put a bullet through his head. From point-blank range. Hard to miss, although admittedly it was in the dark.'

Felicidad could not speak.

'That's when I found him, with the gun in his hand and Julio's shattered skull on the floor. So I shot him.'

'You . . . '

Cámara spotted a glass of water on the desk. He leaned over and passed it to Felicidad.

'So you see, this is no longer a political game. We're not talking about people wriggling away by claiming they can't remember anything, or simply denying taking kickbacks. You know, the usual way these cases end up, taking years in the courts and the guilty always walking free in the end, paying off the right people.'

Felicidad's hand shook as she put the glass back on the table.

'This is now a murder investigation. And real, easily identified murder. I'm not talking about the subtler, quieter murder of thousands by stealing money intended for their medicines, or to pay for their doctors. As far as I'm concerned, Señorita Galván, you are just as guilty as all the others I put away for stabbing their wives, or cutting up a rival drug dealer. You are a murderer and you are going to jail.'

He looked down at the documents on her desk and then back to her.

'For how long depends entirely on you.'

There was a light knocking at the door and the secretary came in.

'I'm going home,' she said sulkily. 'It's almost midnight.'

'Yes, go,' Felicidad said, waving her away. 'I'm so sorry, I . . . I should have said something before. Take . . . Why don't you take tomorrow off. You've been working very hard.'

The secretary's face brightened a little.

'Now go, please. Take a taxi and charge it to me.'

'Thanks.'

The secretary cast a questioning glance at Cámara and then closed the door. After a pause, Cámara spoke.

'We're alone?'

'A guard is on duty through the night. He stays on the ground floor.'

'Lonely work.'

'Someone's got to do it.'

She smiled.

'I've always been a night bird. The problem is that this job demands early starts as well, so I often stay here through till morning, pretending that I've been the first to arrive.'

'Not much life outside work, then.'

'No. Not much.'

'Until Flores came along.'

She jumped in her seat.

'What?'

'You were sleeping with him, weren't you?'

'How did you . . . ? Did he tell you that?'

'He didn't have to. Those . . . ' He gestured around his neck. 'Brown leather ties. I mean, come on.'

Her hand shot up to her throat. The leather thong drooped listlessly down the front of her blouse.

'I still haven't taken it off,' she said in a low voice, her eyes staring at the floor.

'Did he end it?' asked Cámara.

'Last night,' she said. 'Rang me up, said he was sorry, but . . . Just a load of excuses.'

'Were you in love with him?'

She shook her head.

'No. It was a diversion. Fun. A woman can't get to where I have with things like love getting in the way.'

She laughed.

'Besides, he's in love with Emilia, the mayoress. He only screws around when she's no longer letting him into her bed. It happens every now and again. I think she does it with a few of her councillors — keeps them on their toes.'

Her gaze became unfocused as she spoke.

'We used these,' she said, her hand stroking the tie. 'His and hers. Mine to tie up his right hand and his to tie up his left. Then he'd get me to pretend I was Emilia, all dressed up and shouting at him how bad he'd been. He loved it. Although it didn't do much for me, to be honest.'

'Did Emilia know about the slush fund?' Cámara asked.

She looked up, caught off guard.

345

'No. I mean, I don't know. There's nothing about her there, if that's what you mean.'

She nodded at the towers of documents.

'Is that what this is about? Getting Emilia? Smashing the system?'

She grinned.

'Emilia's too smart for that. Not Flores, but then you've already worked that out.'

'And Maldonado?'

She waved a hand.

'Pah! Maldo is just a grubby messenger boy. He gets his little cut, like everyone. He was kept going, passing information about the police. But it's more the thought that he's currying favours, people who will help him up the ladder. He's not really in it for the money. Although I did notice a gold Rolex on his wrist the last time I saw him.'

Cámara smiled.

'Did you really think someone so stupid and ostentatious could be involved at a higher level?'

'If he was involved, why did he get Torres and me to investigate both the killings? He could at least have buried Oliva's death for a while — it looked like a genuine suicide attempt at the beginning.'

'That was a mistake,' she said. 'He'd already assigned the cases before Flores could get to him. Once he got the nod, however, he did what he could to slow everything down.'

'So he tipped off the LOP,' Cámara said. 'When we went to their gym it looked like they'd left in a hurry. He must have told them.'

'No,' said Felicidad. 'That wasn't Maldo. That was me.'

346

'You?'

'You came here, remember? Fished me out of the conference room. You were getting close. I thought precautions should be made.'

Cámara was silent.

'Is that all right?' Felicidad said. 'As a confession? It makes me feel quite good. There's something almost addictive about it.'

'So you'll give us the documents?' Cámara asked. 'As evidence?'

Her mouth tightened and she turned away.

'You can have them,' she said at last. 'You can have the lot.'

'Tell me,' Cámara said. 'Why the LOP? I mean, OK, I understand they're on the Right, like Flores. But they're extremists, violent thugs.'

'I'm not the person to ask.'

'You're a party member. You were running the slush fund.'

'Managing it,' she said. 'Not making decisions about where the money should go.'

'You knew everything that was going on.'

She sighed.

'They were useful,' she said. 'That was how Flores explained it to me. He used them — to keep tabs on other Far Right parties, to float political ideas sometimes. How voters reacted to Soler's comments about Catalan Nationalism or a new wave of immigrants gave them a chance to test the waters. Then he could harden or soften the Town Hall's own line on these matters depending.'

'They did more, though. Much more.'

'That's how it began. Then Flores started

using them for more direct action. They were told to make friends in the police — it wasn't difficult, as far as I hear. Some of your colleagues are already quite politicised in that direction.'

'I've noticed.'

'But you're right, they were doing more. Flores wanted them to keep an eye on certain people — political opponents, a few journalists. And the idea was to frighten them, perhaps.'

'But then Amy Donahue and Diego Oliva got murdered.'

She pressed a hand to her lips, as though suddenly aware that she was talking — talking too much.

'And Diego had worked for you.'

Still no answer.

'Did you tell them about him? Did you mention that he might be a threat? That he knew about the slush fund?'

Her eyes reddened and with the tiniest of motions she began to nod.

'You told Flores, right? Warned him about Diego.'

'I didn't want him to be killed. I didn't know they would do that. That they would follow him and kill him. And then the girl. The American. How was I supposed to know?'

'But you mentioned him. He was off the leash, out of work, pissed off at how he'd been treated here and knew everything.'

She nodded.

'Why didn't you buy him off?'

'I tried. At first I tried to give him some money, sort him out,' she said. 'But too much time had passed. He was proud, said he'd never forgive me. I never really believed he'd spill everything, though. I mean, he still had a chance of getting a job at another bank one day. He wasn't going to be out of work for ever. But if he went public with what he knew he would ruin everything. No one would ever hire him after such a breach of trust.'

Cámara laughed.

'What?'

'You're all as fucking corrupt as each other,' he said. 'A man goes clean and suddenly no other bank would want to touch him. You're despicable.'

Felicidad closed her eyes.

'Yes,' she said. 'Yes, we are.'

Cámara heard a noise outside, like a footstep, and stood up.

Felicidad looked at him with a curious expression.

'That guard,' Cámara said in a low voice. 'Which company did you say he worked for?'

'I didn't,' Felicidad said. 'But now that you ask, I'm assuming the name Protegival means something to you.'

The door was thrust open violently and before he could react Cámara was thrown to the floor. The guard reached for his wrists, trying to pin him to the ground, and smashed downwards with his head. Cámara managed to turn his face at the last minute and the point of the guard's forehead hit his cheekbone.

'Fucking keep still!'

The guard's head went back to take another

strike. His weight was pressed down on Cámara, but only one knee had managed to immobilise Cámara's left leg. With his right, Cámara jerked upwards and connected with the guard's groin.

A low moaning sound shot from the guard's mouth and he rolled on to his side. Cámara went to grapple with him, but the guard had already unholstered his pistol and was waving it in his hand. Cámara crouched and shunted his head against the guard's stomach as the gun went off. From the other side of the room came the sound of shattering glass: the bullet had hit one of the large windows looking out over the street.

With his head still buried in the guard's abdomen, Cámara reached up and put a finger in his attacker's mouth, pulling it hard to the side and almost ripping the skin. The man went down, screaming. In an instant Cámara had pulled out his own weapon and trained it against his head.

'It stops now,' he said, panting. The guard was in agony, one hand pressed between his legs, the other nursing his face. Cámara reached round the back of the guard's belt and unhooked the handcuffs, then flipped the man on to his front and secured his wrists.

He stood up, still trying to catch his breath, and looked around. There was no sign of Felicidad.

He raced to the open door and checked up and down the corridor, but she was nowhere in sight. Had she already made it downstairs?

On the desk, the towers of documents were all there. She had not taken a single one.

From the other side of the room, a cool breeze was beginning to blow in. Cámara looked up: the window had a much larger hole in it, not the neat circle where the bullet had just passed.

He ran over and peered out. But he already knew.

Felicidad's body lay shattered and destroyed on the empty pavement below.

He stepped back, his head reeling.

On the railing, at the side of the window, hung the brown leather tie.

41

Some of the faces were familiar from the metro refuge. He smiled as he walked the length of the room, squeezing between two long trestle tables. The odd hand reached out in greeting, brushing his arms, patting him on the lower back; they had not seen him for days.

'*Hola, Max,*' grinned a three-year-old boy between mouthfuls of tortilla.

'Hi, Ricky.'

The buffet was laid out at the top table, where Berto was helping to pour drinks.

'Hey, you're back,' he said, catching sight of Cámara. 'The policeman.'

'They told you?'

'Well, it's hardly a secret any more,' Berto said, raising his voice above the sound of a dozen echoing conversations. 'Not after what happened.'

He sniggered.

'You had me fooled,' he said. 'I would never have guessed.'

Cámara shrugged.

'There are policemen and policemen,' he said.

He looked across to where Daniel and Dídac were sitting close by, eating their lunch and watching protectively over the day's intake of people.

'Things working out?' he asked.

'Like a dream,' said Berto. 'Thanks again for

putting me in touch with these guys. There's a great feeling here. I think we're going to do amazing things together.'

'I hope you're right.'

He shook Berto's hand and took a couple of paces across the room. Daniel looked up and beckoned him to sit on a spare seat next to him.

'You hungry?' he said.

'I'm OK.'

'You should try some of this paella,' said Dídac. 'It's delicious.'

'Thanks.' Cámara shook his head.

'No appetite?' Daniel said. 'It'll come back. Eventually. Give it time.'

'I'm getting there.'

'We're all really sorry about Alicia,' said Daniel. 'Really sorry.'

Cámara closed his eyes for a moment and nodded gently.

'Thanks for everything you did.'

'This place is good,' Daniel said after a pause. 'A bit small, but it's fine. I've spotted a boarded-up shop a few doors down. If we need to expand we can liberate it from its current state of unemployment.'

Dídac chuckled.

'Direct action,' Daniel said. 'It's what this is all about.'

'Even robbing banks?' Cámara asked. 'And handing the money out to the poor?'

Daniel stared into the distance.

'No idea what you're talking about,' he said.

'I miss the metro,' said Dídac.

'It was big and fun,' Daniel said. 'But nothing

lasts for ever. You have to learn that.'

Cámara smiled to himself. The way Daniel spoke to his son reminded him of how Hilario used to speak to him.

The anarchist refuge in the metro station had to be abandoned after the story of the LOP broke. Until then no one had suspected that the tunnels were being used illegally. Soler's 'bunker' had been shut down, but so had their own very different corner of the underground city as a result. Putting Daniel in touch with Berto had been Cámara's attempt to help keep things going in a new form, however temporarily. And for the time being it appeared to be working: local restaurants were still offering uneaten food for the project, and more homeless and workless people were being fed as a result.

'No empires,' Cámara said.

'No empires,' Daniel smiled. He turned to Dídac. 'Which means no parties.'

Dídac frowned.

'He wants to set up a new political party,' Daniel explained to Cámara. 'To help establish true democracy.'

'Noble sentiment,' Cámara said.

'But it's not what this kind of anarchism is about,' said Daniel. 'At least not my understanding of it. We do what we can, when we can, and then we move on. Traditional politics will always drag you down, no matter how good your intentions at the beginning. I'm sure Hilario would agree with me if he were here.'

Cámara nodded.

'Yes, I think he would.'

'Look at what Max has achieved,' Daniel continued, pointing to Cámara as he spoke to Dídac. 'A Far Right party has been crippled, its leader banged up in jail. His security firm is now passing to new ownership, the corrupt bank which was paying him off is about to be nationalised, and the ruling party in the city is falling apart as we speak — all thanks to his investigation. That's real activism. That's anarchism at work for you. And he's a policeman.'

Cámara laughed.

'OK,' Dídac said. 'I get it. Time for a revolution. I was at the latest demo last night. Felt like the whole of Valencia turned out. Tens of thousands. They closed the place down. Everyone showed up — the anti-repossession activists, teachers, doctors, nurses. Even civil servants working directly for the Town Hall. Most of them haven't been paid in months. And now they know all about the slush fund and the millions that were siphoned off. They're angry. The police went in hard — loads of people were arrested. But there was a real sense of change in the air.'

'But this morning did you see any banks had been burned down?' Daniel asked. 'Or that protestors had taken over government buildings?'

Dídac frowned.

'Letting off steam, getting into fights with the riot police — that's one thing. Demanding real change is another. And things have to get seriously bad — worse than now, even — for enough people to want that. I don't know if it's going to happen yet.'

The three of them looked in silence at the hungry faces — almost a hundred homeless people chatting, eating and enjoying a moment's pause and relief from the business of having to survive.

'I wonder,' said Cámara.

42

Cámara and Torres sat at their usual bar in the Carmen. It was almost the end of the month and the weather was getting hotter. Soon they would no longer be able to sit outside, forced behind air-conditioned walls to escape the worst of the summer heat.

Cámara had arrived on a borrowed motorbike. After pulling it out of the tunnel and back overground, the mechanic had said he thought he could fix the Kawasaki, but it would take a bit of time. Meanwhile, after a promise that the bill would be paid in cash, he was lending Cámara something to get by on — an old Honda. It was parked on the pavement a few metres away.

Torres and Cámara sipped cool glasses of Mahou, silently watching the world go by. Students moved in packs carrying textbooks, grandparents pushed small children along in buggies, tourists — some in groups but most in pairs or on their own — sauntered about, wearing straw hats and sunglasses.

'I remember when you never saw tourists here,' Torres said. 'Or the ones that did come were usually lost, thinking they were in Barcelona.'

Cámara chuckled. It was true. Ten or fifteen years before there were hardly any foreigners in Valencia. Now thousands were coming to visit, and a few had decided to stay.

'It seems so different from a week or so ago,' he said. 'No demonstrations, no riot police.'

'You reckon that's it?'

'I don't know. The King's still hanging on by the looks of it — just. Perhaps if he actually died . . . '

'They've spent so much keeping him alive in that private hospital I bet they're not letting him die. Poor bastard's probably begging them to pull the plug.'

Cámara shrugged.

'The tensions flare up for a bit then calm down again. Perhaps for a long time. Perhaps the demonstrators will be back tomorrow and bring the whole edifice crashing down. It's hard to say. You might as well try to predict the football results.'

They fell silent again. A busker was setting up on the pavement opposite — a smart, elderly-looking man. Cámara had seen him before; he crooned to a backing track, always a tad out of tune.

'Looks like he used to work in a bank — from the way he dresses,' Torres said.

'Perhaps he did.'

'At least they're letting us take out money from cash machines again. No more *corralito*. Couldn't pay for this otherwise.'

'They probably found a few billion spare somewhere. Hidden in a shoebox.'

'Did you see the Prince on TV?' Torres asked.

'No. What did he say?'

'He was all right. Called for calm, predictable stuff. But he came across well. I don't know,

358

perhaps when the time finally comes he'll be able to pull it off. For a moment I thought things were really going to fall apart. Army sent in, that kind of thing.'

'They still may,' Cámara said. 'But you're right. I know what you mean. The sharpness in the air seems to have dulled a bit.'

'Still, nice to see that civil war has finally broken out in Emilia's party,' Torres grinned.

'She'll slip through. She always does. There's no dirt on her.'

'Not directly. But it's a big scandal. And you broke it. There's no way she'll be re-elected next time. Her right-hand man is up for murder, links with neo-Nazi groups, kidnapping, corruption. She must be finished.'

'I wouldn't like to bet. Seriously. She's been in power for over twenty years. And even if she does go, the next one will be just like her.'

'They're all the same,' Torres said, putting on a hackneyed voice.

'All right, you bastard. I'm just being cynical.'

'It's all bollocks anyway. I'm going to take a leaf out of your book and stop following the news so much. Things never really change.'

'Now you're doing it.'

'All right,' Torres sniggered. 'But did you hear the really important news?'

'What's that?'

'Lozano has proposed to Castro.'

Cámara smiled.

'Really? And?'

'We don't know. She said she'll tell him by tomorrow.'

'I knew they were shagging.'

'Well, congratulations, Sherlock. It was a bit bloody obvious.'

Cámara drank some more beer and sighed.

'They found the papers,' he said. 'The ones Oliva passed to Amy — photocopies of the ones his wife showed me.'

'Where were they? I looked everywhere for them.'

'In the gym.'

'Couldn't be. My team turned the place upside down.'

'They were in a secret compartment in the floor. Underneath where they stacked the weights.'

Torres sniffed.

'So you needed half a dozen musclemen to get at them,' he said.

'That must have been the idea. There were some other papers there as well — an operational manual, how to carry out assassinations and that kind of thing. And you know what? It recommended that the best way to get inside people's homes without causing suspicion was to pretend to be a postman.'

'The *cartero* trick.'

'And of course they had to distract Pascual — he might have seen something. So I reckon they came up with the broken pipe for him to fix just to keep him out of the way.'

'Makes sense.'

Cámara looked into space.

'Still wish I hadn't stopped you?' Torres said. 'You were about to kill that bastard. I saw it.'

'Yes,' said Cámara. 'I think I probably was.'

'You don't need Javier Flores on your conscience. Besides, he's better off alive. He knows everything. He'll have to come clean eventually. Much more than the slush fund. Trust me, if you'd killed him there's a whole heap of stuff that would never have come out, would have gone to the grave with him.'

Cámara nodded.

'You're right, you're right.'

'You know I am,' said Torres. 'It was just a spur-of-the-moment thing. I bet you're not even regretting it now. You're not a murderer, chief. No matter what the bastard did. You don't avenge Hilario through stuff like that.'

'*Si piensas en venganza haz dos tumbas que una será tuya*,' Cámara said. If you're thinking about revenge, dig two graves, for one of them shall be yours.

'There, you see. Bet Hilario taught you that himself.'

'Yes,' said Cámara. 'He did.'

'Let Flores suffer. He's banged up in jail, taken a bullet in the hip, hated by his former friends — did you hear they formally revoked his party membership? You've got to laugh. This is agony for him. One of the most powerful men in the city now having to shit in a bucket in the corner of a tiny dirty cell. And it's going to go on for years. This is much better, believe me.'

Cámara chewed the corner of his mouth in silence.

Torres coughed.

'It's a while since we had a proper lunch

361

together,' he said. 'You know, like the old days, a couple of hours over a paella and a bottle or two.'

'On police time.'

'Of course. Makes the rice taste better.'

'You reckon Laura won't mind?'

'She won't have to find out. Pardo never bothered. It was only with Maldo in charge that things got tense.'

'Missing him already?'

'Fuck off. Did you know they stripped him of everything — all his medals, honours, the works.'

'I just wish they could sack him. Properly, I mean. Throw him out of the police altogether.'

'He's too high up. They'll keep him out of the way. Send him off to Extremadura, or somewhere.'

'I tell you one thing, though.'

'What's that?'

'With him gone from *Homicidios* they won't have to look for someone else to get rid of.'

Torres screwed up his nose.

'Yeah.'

'What's the matter?'

'I heard something,' Torres said. 'They're still trying to cut costs. Looks like someone's going to get the chop.'

'You're kidding?'

'Nope.'

Cámara grabbed his helmet and got up to leave.

'Hey,' said Torres. 'Where are you going?'

★ ★ ★

Twenty minutes later Cámara was with Laura Martín. The new head of the murder squad was keeping her old office for the time being.

'I'll move out eventually,' she said. 'They'll probably force me to. As long as they don't put me where Maldonado was. I hate it in there.'

'Feels dirty?' Cámara asked.

'Yes. Something like that. Just don't want to be associated with him. Now,' she added, pointing to the seat, 'I'm glad you're better. You needed a decent amount of time to rest and recover after everything that happened. And I'm assuming you want to go through things.'

Cámara shrugged.

'By the way, no hard feelings, I hope. I know you were an obvious candidate — '

'I didn't want the job,' Cámara interrupted her. 'And I'm very glad they've made you head of *Homicidios*. Really. I can't think of anyone better.'

'Thanks.' She smiled. 'That means a lot to me.'

'Although I'm a little bit surprised,' he said. 'I saw you as something of a crusader in the sexual violence squad. It must be hard, leaving that.'

She raised her eyebrows and looked down at the desk, spreading her fingers out over the surface in a gesture of openness, almost self-exposure.

'I'm ambitious,' she said. 'A dirty word for some, I know, but I couldn't refuse a possibility to run one of the most important murder squads in the country. And for a woman to get the job is a statement of sorts. Besides, the overlap

363

between the two squads is huge. Too often sexual crime results in death, so in some ways I'm carrying on as before.'

Cámara nodded.

'Now,' she said, pulling her hands together and linking them over her stomach, 'about the latest. I have to say I'm very happy that Judge Alonso has taken over the case. I hadn't come across him before, but he seems like one of those liberal types. Just the person to see things through to the end. Political cases like this kick up an enormous amount of dirt, as you know. And I want to keep the police out of it as much as possible. There's been too much mixing in political circles recently for my liking.'

'Good,' said Cámara. 'I'm completely with you.'

'Although I see that some of our number are still intent on it.'

'What do you mean?'

'I sent someone along to Julio's funeral,' said Laura. 'Just to keep an eye on things.'

'A spy?'

'Yes. A spy.'

'Who?'

'Guess.'

'Albelda?'

'Got it in one.'

'We can trust him. And?'

'They gave him quasi-military honours, like a hero. Almost the entire LOP was there. Amazingly, Soler got a temporary pass from custody to be present, although Alonso insisted he couldn't make a speech. But there were Nazi salutes, Francoist flags, everything. And a disturbing number of mourners were members of our own riot squad. Seems they've infiltrated us. They haven't gone away.'

'Yes,' Cámara said. 'I had a feeling. Has Soler given us anything?'

'He's staying tight-lipped. Seems to think it's his best defence. But test results are coming in. The gun that was used to kill Amy Donahue was Julio's. As were the hairs we found on her — the DNA tests gave a clear result. So we can almost say for certain that he murdered her.'

'Who was with him? There was one other. The Dane, Hansen, said he saw two men buzzing the door claiming to be postmen.'

'It wasn't José Antonio, that's for sure.'

'Why's that?'

'Because the DNA found under Diego Oliva's fingernails matches his. He was busy throwing Oliva out the window when Amy was being shot.'

'Two teams,' said Cámara. 'Two for Amy. And the witness Hernández mentioned three men at Oliva's. Five in total.'

'One to take out Amy, led by Julio. The other with José Antonio at Oliva's flat.'

'And Gonzalo — the other guy in the metro?'

'He's in custody, along with José Antonio. The wound is healing well. I think, as soon as he's strong enough, he'll start talking. He's up for kidnapping and attempted murder already — what he did to Alicia — so a plea bargain might help reduce his final sentence if he comes clean about what happened.'

'Well, if he gives us names . . . '

'He'll give us the names of the other two. They're almost certainly LOP members. Then we'll just pick them up and DNA testing will place them at whichever scene they were at. Either Amy's flat or Oliva's.'

It was important for the conclusion of the case. But both knew that the LOP men were mere executioners: their orders had come from Soler and ultimately from Flores.

'Any word about Ruiz Costa?'

Laura held up her hands.

'OK, I admit it. I was wrong about him. And you never thought he did it.'

'I don't mean that,' said Cámara.

'Why was that? How did you know he was innocent?'

'I didn't. But there was something about his socks.'

'His socks?'

'They were pink — the same colour as Amy's. I couldn't imagine a man who wore the same colour socks as his wife could then murder her so cruelly.'

Laura snorted.

'I'm glad you didn't tell me that at the time,' she said.

'So what's happened to him?'

Laura shrugged.

'As far as we know he's gone to live with his aunt. Has barely stepped back in the flat since we released him. I was taking a statement from Pascual yesterday and he mentioned something.'

'Poor bastard.'

'They buried her here. I thought they might fly her body back to the States, but her parents wanted it this way. Something about Amy loving Spain so much.'

Cámara nodded in silence.

'How's Alicia getting on?' asked Laura, changing the subject.

'As well as we could hope,' said Cámara. 'I can't thank you enough for sorting things out at the clinic.'

'It's the least I can do. They know me from past cases. They've dealt with some horrendous stuff, but they're specialists. It's the best place she could have gone.'

'The sores are healing well. But I'm afraid the scars may be there for longer.'

Laura shook her head.

'Yes. I'm very sorry.'

There was an awkward silence for a moment.

'Do you want me to arrange some time off, so you can help her recover?'

'I heard something,' Cámara said. 'Something about a redundancy needed in *Homicidios*.'

Laura sighed.

'It's true,' she said. 'I hate it and there's nothing I can do about it. My hand is being forced. I thought with Maldonado gone . . . But it seems they want a decision by next week.'

'Have you thought about who . . . ?'

'You're safe, obviously. Don't worry. It's the hardest decision to make. We have a very good team, but, yes, there is a name in my mind. He's already an inspector but he's still young. He'll

367

get a good payout and can start something new. I hope.'

'Torres,' Cámara said. 'You mean Torres.'

Laura nodded.

'Yes. I'm sorry. I know you're friends.'

'Fire me,' said Cámara. 'Not Torres. He's got a kid, and his wife left him just a year ago. Really, you can't do this to him. If someone's got to go, fire me. I insist.'

Laura smiled.

'It's very noble of you. But — '

'What do you need? I'm begging you. Fire me instead.'

'I can't,' Laura said. 'It's complicated. You're a chief inspector. It gets harder the higher up someone is.'

'Bollocks. You can fire me now. Just do it. Say the word and I'll go.'

He stood up.

'Cámara. Really, I can't,' she said. 'I'd need a reason. I can't just fire you like that. Besides, you're the best detective in the squad.'

She was getting angry.

'It's my call, my decision. I have to live with it. I appreciate you trying to help, but the answer is no. Absolutely not . . . What are you doing?'

Cámara was undoing his belt, opening the buttons and pushing first his trousers and then his underpants down to his knees. Then his lifted his shirt and very briefly exposed himself.

'What are you doing?' Laura said, horrified.

'I'm giving you a good reason to sack me,'

Cámara said, pulling his trousers back up. 'Gross misconduct.'

Laura slumped in her chair.

'Now get the paperwork started and sack me. I've got somewhere to go.'

43

The clinic was a short way out of the city, a single-storey white building at the edge of the sea surrounded by mature umbrella pines: a refuge for women which, for the time being at least, had survived the spending cuts.

Alicia was sitting in the shade on a wooden bench, reading. The swelling in her face had died down a couple of days before, but dark rings still circled her eyes. She had not recovered her full strength.

'I knew you'd come,' she said, looking up. 'Busy day?'

'Something like that.'

He leaned down and placed his face next to hers.

'Have I told you today that I love you?' he whispered.

'No,' she said. 'You brute.'

She kissed him warmly, breathing in his scent.

She patted the bench beside her, beckoning him to join her.

'There was a letter from Hilario's solicitor this morning,' he said.

He sat down and placed his arm around her shoulders.

'Remember those references to the 'recent work' that he'd done?' he said. 'It was among the papers we found.'

'Yes, I think so.'

'It was his will. He'd sorted everything out, every detail.'

A gentle breeze brushed their skin.

'It's as if . . . '

'Yes. As if he knew. Even now he's dead he still has the power to surprise us.'

'Was there anything more? Any surprises in the will itself?'

He smiled.

'What does that grin mean?' she asked.

'There's not much,' said Cámara. 'Just the flat in Albacete and what was left in his bank account. Some savings.'

'What will you do with it?'

'Nothing,' he said. 'It's all gone to you.'

She coughed.

'What?'

'Yes, to you.' He laughed.

'Oh, my God.'

She pulled away to look at him.

'It can't be. Are you sure?'

'Absolutely. And I know why he did it.'

'I don't understand,' said Alicia. 'Can he do this? It's yours. It should go to you.'

'He loved you very much,' Cámara said. 'As a daughter, I suppose, as a daughter-in-law, of sorts. You see, by doing that he's bringing you into the family, he's making you a Cámara.'

'Turning me into a Cámara?'

'And he's making sure I always stay with you.'

'I still don't get it.'

He pulled her towards him. She rested her head on his shoulder and he felt her hair against his cheek.

'Anarchists don't really believe in marriage,' he said. 'So this is the next best thing. By giving it all to you he's joining us in holy, anarchist, capitalist matrimony.'

Alicia grinned and looked up at him.

'All right. In that case I accept.'

'Is that a commitment?'

'Yes.'

'Me too.'

'You're going to have to explain this to me one day,' she said. 'Hilario's contradictions get the better of me sometimes.'

'I will, one day. When I understand them myself.'

They stared out towards the deep shining blue of the Mediterranean, feeling each other's warmth, breathing the same air.

'How are you feeling today?' Cámara asked at length.

'It doesn't hurt so much,' she said. 'I went for a walk this morning.'

'That's very good news,' he said. 'Because I brought this.'

'More surprises? I'm not sure I can take any more.'

From a bag at his side he pulled out her helmet.

'I thought we might go for a ride,' he said. 'Nice and slow.'

They stood up and she rested her weight on his arm.

'I'd like that,' she said. 'Let's get lost. Just you and me.'

Acknowledgements

My thanks to Esther Maldonado, Sebastián Roa and Rafa Campo of the *Policía Nacional* for all those useful titbits.

To Rob, for being the best sounding board one could wish for. And to Debs Rose, for her advice on medical matters.

To Peter Robinson, Jenny Uglow and Mary Chamberlain, for all their invaluable help.

To Becky Hardie, for her patience.

And to Salud, Arturo and Gabriel, for their understanding.

Also, the following people contributed very generously to the 'Motorbike for Max' fund, which was essential for the research necessary for this book (it also made it a hell of a lot of fun):

Merrylegs, Michael Ivey, Howard Cearns, John Webster, Mary Dowley, S.Ford96, Twigger, Marie Shelton and Loudaisy.

My sincerest thanks to them all. *Vroom, vroom . . .*

We do hope that you have enjoyed reading this large print book.

Did you know that all of our titles are available for purchase?

We publish a wide range of high quality large print books including:
Romances, Mysteries, Classics
General Fiction
Non Fiction and Westerns

Special interest titles available in large print are:
The Little Oxford Dictionary
Music Book
Song Book
Hymn Book
Service Book

Also available from us courtesy of Oxford University Press:
Young Readers' Dictionary
(large print edition)
Young Readers' Thesaurus
(large print edition)

For further information or a free brochure, please contact us at:
Ulverscroft Large Print Books Ltd.,
The Green, Bradgate Road, Anstey,
Leicester, LE7 7FU, England.
Tel: (00 44) 0116 236 4325
Fax: (00 44) 0116 234 0205